PILGRIM GIRL

A Novel by

J. A. Snow

Volume Three in the Series "An American Family"

As one small candle may light a thousand,

So, the light here kindled hath shone to many,

Yes, in some sort, to our whole nation.

William Bradford

Introduction

At the end of Volume Two (Blood and Cobblestones) we left Nick Snow, his younger brother Anthony, and his cousin William standing on the deck of the ship *Anne,* staring down the Thames River, as their ship set sail for their long voyage to America. The Snow family has experienced many changes in recent years, but none has affected the Snow brothers as much as the recent death of their father Nicky. Nicky had been an actor in the Lord Chamberlain's Company for most of his life and had owned a small interest in the Globe Theatre in London. The entire Snow family had worked for the theater in some fashion; growing up Nick and Anthony performed in plays that called for children's parts and later worked on stage and prop building, while their mother Lizzie and little sister Mary sewed the costumes. But as they got older Nick and Anthony did not continue to share their father's passion for the theatre. Now that he is gone, they have begun to think about their own futures, exploring new avenues that interest them. Still *young* men, (Nick is twenty-three and Anthony is twenty-one) they have decided to take their chances in America where opportunities seem to abound. Their cousin Will, reputably the lovable scoundrel in the Snow family, has convinced them to let him tag along on their journey. While their mother Lizzie and their younger sister Mary remain behind in London working at seamstresses for the theatre, it is with their mother's blessing that her sons follow their dreams.

Anthony has become acutely interested in the scriptures, avidly reading every day from the Bible. His desire is to find employment in America, possibly in the ministry, hopefully marry a godly woman and start a family of his own.

Nick just loves the adventure of it all. He has no expectations other than to add more exciting pages to his life story. He has left several young ladies behind in London who would have gladly accepted his proposal of marriage, but he is not ready to settle down with one woman for life just yet. *That woman will have to be very special* he has decided in his mind, and he is determined to take his time in choosing her. Perhaps he will find her in America. Whatever the case he wants to develop a trade, build himself a house and be on a firm financial footing before he even *thinks* about such things as marriage and children!

And Will, their cousin, who has burnt his last bridge in London by reneging on a gambling debt and is being chased out of town in disgrace, is looking forward only to continuing his shiftless life in this new country across the sea. Usually, so long as the beer and the card games hold out, he is content but with the counseling of his two cousins he too is beginning to think about his future as well, whatever that might be.

Many of the passengers on the *Anne* are the Snows' fellow countrymen who had previously fled from England to Holland to escape King James' harsh restrictions on their religious practices. When they arrived there, however, they found themselves in a foreign land where, even though they were allowed freedom to worship as they pleased, they were not treated equally by the Dutch government. Many had difficulty finding jobs because they did not speak the language. Many are following their families who left earlier on the Mayflower, but they all have one thing in common…. the desire to live in a *free society.*

This is where our story begins in 1623.

Part One "Plymouth"

Chapter One "The *Anne*"

The *Anne* was not a young ship, as was her smaller companion, the *Little James*, but she was, nonetheless, a sturdy old dame. Originally, she had been designed for sailing up and down the English and Bristol Channels, carrying cargo no further than the northern coast of France, which she had done all her life. When the captain first announced that they were going to attempt a trans-Atlantic voyage, you could almost feel her black oak timbers shiver with excitement as she sailed into the dry dock in Bristol for her "makeover" that would get her ready for her new challenges on the open sea!

Once *Anne* was out of the water she was *careened*. They removed her ballast heaving it down with cables and pulleys attached between the heads of her lower masts and capstans on the ground. She groaned a bit as they flipped her on her side but soon she was languishing there, starkly naked in the Bristol sunshine, like a pampered queen, as the carpenters replaced all her rotting planks and filled her cracks and weakened seams with wads of sticky oakum, pouring pitch and hot tar on her to waterproof her hull. Then she was laid gently over to her other side for the same luxurious treatment.

Anne was fortunate. Her ten-year-old keel was still in reasonably good shape. Ships in her era seldom lasted longer than fifteen years in the corrosive salt water. Before she was put back in the water, her hull was scraped free of barnacles and repainted with shiny black paint and her ballast of old iron, stones and gravel was again loaded aboard. They stuffed her belly with several months' worth of provisions, that would balance her for a while but eventually, when the casks of ale and water got used up, they would have to be refilled with sea water to maintain her equilibrium. Without an evenly distributed ballast, she would be a dizzy dame indeed, sailing in circles or worse capsizing completely and would have little hope of making it to America all in one piece!

After about three weeks of primping for the long voyage, *Anne* finally shoved off for the port of London with her sails full of wind, puffing out buxomly before her.

"She is a sturdy ship indeed!" said the Lord Commissioner from the Admiralty who climbed aboard and examined every inch of her from bow to stern before he pronounced her sea- worthy. Then, side by side, *Anne* and the *Little James*, who was still fresh from the building yard, sat anchored in the deeper waters of the Thames a short distance from the London docks waiting to welcome their passengers coming across in the longboats. When everyone had finally boarded, *Anne's* flag was hoisted up on the top mast, waving like a red ribbon in her hair, and her anchor was raised as they cast off for America!

Their first day out to sea had *promise*! That was according to Captain William Pierce who commented to Nick Snow about the favorable winds and clear skies he observed from their vantage point on the fo'c'sle. Indeed, that April morning they started out making very good time as the *Anne* sailed out of the mouth of the harbor into the rapid currents in the English Channel being flanked close behind by the *Little James*. They were on their way! *America* waited beyond the horizon on the other side of the ocean with all its mysteries and possibilities! Nick Snow leaned back against the ship's railing and nonchalantly packed a wad of tobacco in his clay pipe, puffing contentedly while he conversed with the captain. He was trying not to look as inexperienced at sailing as he was, but, on the inside, he was giddy with the excitement of a small boy.

Being on board a sailing ship, thought Nick, *is a bit like being blind in a dark room*; for even when he closed his eyes his other senses took him to heights he had never known. He felt acutely alive with everything he encountered from the coolness of the invigorating ocean spray on his face to the snapping sounds in his ears of the wind as it filled *Anne's* sails and the warm smell of damp wood in his nostrils. Looking up, he observed a straight line of gray auks and razorbills perched like sentries on the yards and he asked the captain,

"How long will they stay with the ship before they fly back to England?"

The captain followed Nick's glance and looked up at the birds, shielding his eyes from the bright sun.

"Those are just shorebirds. They will leave us as soon as they begin to lose sight of land," he replied. "They will be back again when we reach the banks."

"The banks?" asked Nick.

"*St. George's banks*, off the coast of Cape Cod," answered the captain. "When you see birds like that again we will be almost to Plymouth Harbor!"

"Can you eat them?" asked another passenger who had climbed up the steps to join them.

"*Those* birds?" replied the captain jokingly. "I don't believe they'd be very tasty unless you're *terribly hungry!* All bones and oily dark meat from what I've heard. Hopefully, our provisions will hold out until we reach Plymouth, so we won't have to test that theory!"

"What *will* we be eating on this trip?" the man asked.

"We have chickens, goats and pigs on board so we will have fresh meat, eggs and milk for a good while," replied the captain. "And we have enough dried beef and beans to get us through before you'll need to start killing sea birds for supper!"

The captain seemed quite amused about the whole thing, the smiling curl of his lips hidden just under his graying mustache.

"By the way my name is Stephen Tracy," said the man.

"Nick Snow," said Nick, shaking the man's hand cordially.

The man was tall with a shock of dark hair and a black beard in stark contrast to Nick's pale blond hair and clean-shaven face.

"Don't you worry, Mister Tracy," said the captain. "I promise you no one will starve on my watch. It may not always be a king's banquet, but our stomachs will be full."

"And how long will it take us to reach Plymouth, Captain?" Tracy asked.

"Two and a half months, give or take, if the winds and weather are with us," replied the captain.

"Then you have been to America before?" asked Nick.

The captain nodded. "My home is in Jamestown where my family is. I've made this trip many times."

"What will the weather be like crossing?" asked Tracy.

"This time of year, we should be fine. It's crossing in the winter that's tricky," he replied. "But the *Anne* is a sturdy ship, and I don't expect any problems," he added as an afterthought, seeing the look of concern still present in Tracy's eyes.

Nick leaned over the railing and watched the side of *Anne*'s hull as she sliced through the deep blue water leaving a bubbling white wake behind her. More birds flew overhead directly crossing the path of the ship; a flock going north for the summer following a route they had taken many times before unlike Nick who had never been outside England.

By the time they had sailed past the chalky cliffs of Dover and reached the jagged rocks of Cornwall, most of the passengers had flocked to the deck and were leaning over the starboard railing to get their last glimpse of England. Soon the Channel merged with the Celtic Sea, and they were surrounded by water; the outline of the English shoreline becoming smaller and smaller behind them. Nick felt the cross currents rock the *Anne* to and fro under his feet and watched the wind in the sails as it shifted from the south to a westerly direction. She leaned gently to one side guided by the wind and currents and straightened her course until nothing but the endless Atlantic now loomed before them.

What will America be like? Nick couldn't help but wonder. The thoughts of discovering a new wilderness with Indians and wild animals and so many other unknowns lifted his spirits. Life for Nick in London had grown stale. He couldn't blame his mother for staying behind; she was no longer a young woman and needed the comfort and familiarity of her roots and his sister would no doubt marry one of the actors in the theatre and then they both would be quite content. But he was, in many ways, still a boy in a man's body who had yet to go out on his own and experience life beyond the boundaries of family and England. This trip made him feel as if he were born anew and starting his life all over again. It was an exhilarating feeling!

Down on the main deck, Will Snow and two young deckhands had pulled up some crates around a hogshead and were playing what appeared to be an innocent game of whist with the dirty dog-eared deck of cards Will always kept in his pocket. Will had learned much to his disappointment that *officially at least* gambling was not allowed on the *Anne.* But Captain Pierce wasn't stupid; he knew men seldom played cards without any stakes up for the taking so he usually overlooked the games as long as they stayed *friendly* and there was no bickering among the crew, especially now that they carried a group of passengers some of whom were very religious and saw gambling as a mortal sin. Captain Pierce decided to let the men enjoy their games for the time being and hoped it would not become a problem before they reached Plymouth.

"Gentlemen, what say we make the game more interesting?" asked Will, lowering his voice. "My cousins and I will be in need of three hammocks on which to sleep tonight."

He shuffled and dealt the cards, smiling at his opponents. "What say ye?"

"Sounds fair to me," said one of the sailors, a young lad with barely a stubble on his chin and the red bumps of adolescence still flaring on his cheeks.

The other sailor, an older man with a pocked nose and years of wear from the ocean winds wrinkling his brow, leaned forward and whispered, "The captain won't care as long as we don't show any silver on the table. Might upset some of our *saintly passengers*, you know."

Will laughed and fanned the cards in his hand. "Humph!" he snorted, taking another drink. "'Twas never raised in the church. Don't know what's wrong with an honest game of cards unless you're playing with the Devil himself!"

Will had a way with cards *and* people. There was no doubt about that. Nick watched his cousin swilling his mug of beer and laughing, his ample belly jiggling up and down under his shirt and his dark hair blowing in the wind. He *was* a scoundrel, but it was hard not to like Will. Like Nick's mother had said, he had a *good heart*. It was just that his *mind* frequently got him into trouble. With no family ties except the two cousins he had recently met for the first time, Will seemed to have few cares in the world. He enjoyed his life to the fullest and did not apologize for it. From the stories he had told them he had always lived a singular life, having been orphaned at an early age and he had survived on the streets of London the only way he knew how: with a deck of cards or a pair of dice in his hands resorting to actual physical labor only as a last recourse. He had rarely gotten emotionally close to anyone in his life until he had met his estranged cousins Nick and Anthony; now they were like his brothers and for the first time in his life Will felt like he was part of a *family*.

Below deck Anthony was sitting on top of their sea bags in the corner of the hold nearest the porthole staking their claim to the only avenue to fresh air in the bowels of the crowded ship. He was trying to read his book of scriptures amidst the chaos around him which he was finding to be an impossible task. The room was packed full of people; mostly women making up beds and stowing their clothing and a group of boisterous children, who were forbidden by their mothers to go on deck and risk possibly falling overboard, running amuck over everyone's belongings on the floor. The room was stiflingly hot, and it felt like July instead of April; already the chamber pots were beginning to stink because the breeze from the tiny round opening above Anthony's head was almost non-existent. The ceilings were so low that only the children could stand up straight without bashing their heads on the cross beams making the space feel ever so much more confined. From another compartment beneath the deck, he could hear the grunting of pigs, the bleating of goats and the cackling of chickens. *How will we ever sleep in such a crowded room?* he wondered. *How will we ever make it to America under these conditions?*

When suppertime came the ship's steward blew a whistle and the passengers lined up as he began to dole out each family their share of food; a small portion of meat, potatoes and bread for each person prepared on an old iron firebox that stood in the middle of the ship's galley. There were only benches at the table to seat about ten, so the families with small children were allowed to eat there and most of the adults took their meals up on deck where they ate sitting on the steps to the quarter deck or just leaning on the ship's railing holding their plates and enjoying their meal in the evening air.

"Well, at least the *food* is tolerable," said Anthony scraping the last morsels from his wooden plate. "But not nearly as good as Mother's."

"I don't remember my mother's cooking," said Will. "But this is much better than the greasy food they served off the wagon behind the theatre!"

"That probably *was* our mother's cooking, Will!" laughed Nick. "Although some of the other wives prepared food when my mother was busy making costumes."

"Well," said Will a bit embarrassed. "I intended no disrespect to your mother. I am sure it was my fault for arriving late for supper and so the food was always cold."

Nick, Anthony and Will relinquished their seats when they were joined by a family from Leiden who spoke Dutch to each other and did not appear to speak any English. They all just smiled and nodded politely at each other. As soon as they sat down the group got very quiet and began to pray over their meal in their foreign tongue. When the prayer had ended the eating commenced.

"God bless us all!" said Nick to break the awkward silence, holding up his mug of beer in a toast.

The older man who had led the group in prayer seemed to understand a few words of English and he smiled and held up his mug also. "God onsallen zegenen!" he said emphatically.

Will raised his mug up smiling. "Good God, good food, and good friends!" he said.

The Dutchman thought for a minute and raised his mug again. "Goed God, goed eten, geode vrienden!"

"I guess *God*," remarked Anthony, "is the same in *any* language!"

By nightfall the winds had died down to barely a spit of a breeze that only rippled *Anne's* sails intermittently and her forward momentum lagged. The Snow men hung their hammocks in the darkness that filled the hold below, dingy pieces of canvas that measured barely three feet by six feet with ropes on either end, looping them over hooks in the corner nearest the porthole. As they prepared for sleep the dark room had become so crowded that once they had hoisted themselves up off the floor cradled in their canvasses other passengers spread out their bedding directly beneath them filling in all the available floor space and making it impossible to step down without stepping *on* someone.

For several hours they just bobbed up and down on the rolling ocean, inducing gentle sleep for those sea-hardy passengers whose stomachs didn't protest at the motion of the ship and the room soon filled with the sound of snoring and mothers singing soft lullabies to their babes. It wasn't very long however until the rolling movement of the ship began to send others with more delicate constitutions to the deck where they stood heaving over the side in the moonlight. Anthony felt it first, jumping out of his hammock and waking several disgruntled people sleeping beneath his feet. He stumbled up the steep hatchway toward the deck and fresh air. After he had lost his supper, he couldn't bear the thought of returning to the crowded, sweltering cabin below and he sunk to the deck where he curled up in a fetal position and closed his eyes.

With the dawn, the winds had begun to blow again, and the *Anne* picked up speed and ceased her stomach-churning up and down motion. Anthony opened his eyes and sat up; he could see he was not alone. A good number of the passengers were curled up with him along the railing in different stages of sleep and shared misery. He sat there hugging his knees tightly to his chest and leaning against the side of the ship while welcoming the ocean air on his face and he closed his eyes again. With his whole body aching from the violent vomiting of the night before his arms were limp and his legs shook not from the cold but vibrating up from somewhere deep within his body along with the bitter taste of his stomach juices that lingered in his mouth.

When Nick and Will finally awoke and came up on deck to find him his stomach had stopped lurching, but he still could not entertain the thought of food.

"Are you sure you don't want *anything* to eat Anthony?" asked his brother offering him a piece of bread.

"No! I don't care if I *ever* eat again," said Anthony weakly. "Honestly I have never been so sick in my life as I was last night."

"I didn't even hear you get up," said Will cheerfully. "You will get used to it Cousin! It will take a few days, but you will soon have your sea legs!"

"I certainly hope so," replied Anthony. "I daresay if I am going to feel like this for the entire voyage you might as well throw me overboard now and be done with it!"

Chapter Two "Patience and Fear"

Anthony finally overcame his sea sickness but only after several long days of intestinal torture and thankfully the necessity of throwing him overboard was negated. Now there was nothing to do but look out over the railings at the endless sea before them. Anthony went back to his reading, finding a much more pleasant spot on the deck, and Will returned to his card games while Nick joined some of the other men who decided to try their hand at fishing to fill the empty daylight hours.

With lines and poles supplied by the crew they baited their hooks with some leftover bits of gristle from the ship's kitchen and they cast their lines out and waited. It didn't take very long until the fish took notice. They soon began pulling in a variety of species, some unknown to the men who were strangers to the ocean; bulgy-eyed fat silver ones and small flat brownish ones and slippery eels. By the end of the day, they had filled their buckets and proudly took their catch down below to the cook.

The amateur anglers soon learned not *all* fish were palatable, however. While eels seemed to be abundant at first and easily caught, they turned out to be most unappetizing and the men ended up cutting them up into pieces to use as bait. It was the flat halibut and the small silver perch that turned out to be most delectable when seasoned and grilled in the firebox. For several weeks the passengers dined on fresh fish and the meals were quite acceptable.

The stench in the sleeping compartment was another matter, however. While most of the women were diligent in the emptying of their family's chamber pots every day, some others were not as concerned, and the stagnant air was becoming most foul. Some even doused their linens with oil of lavender and sweet talcum, but it did little to get rid of the odor. Not only was the air becoming thick with the smell of human excrement and urine, not every family could afford a spare set of bed linens to use while a laundered set dried on the deck railing. Consequently, the sheets and pillowberes in the humid environment were becoming ripe with the onion-like aroma of dried sweat. More than a few passengers feigned sea sickness as an excuse to sleep on the deck and after a few nights so did Nick, Anthony and Will.

Every morning church services were held very early on the deck and those sleeping there were roused to wakefulness with the resounding song of voices in worship. Although none of the Snow men had much experience with church Anthony was most anxious to take part and learn what he could from the Leiden saints. The sermons were delivered in English much to their surprise for unlike the family they had met at supper it seemed most of the passengers who came on board in Leiden were originally from England, having fled to

Holland to escape King James and his unreasonable laws regarding the church.

They found the music to be quite enjoyable especially Nick who loved to sing. Even if he did not know the lyrics he would just hum along with the others. He did not go unnoticed by the young women in the congregation, especially the Brewster sisters, Patience and Fear, who would smile demurely at him from beneath their bonnets. Nick pretended not to notice them and Anthony, who was much too serious and introverted to attract their attention, silently marveled at the charismatic charms of his older brother.

"I swear, Nick," he said later. "Must you *always* have a trail of ladies following you?"

Nick smiled. "Perhaps, dear Brother," he replied. "This voyage may prove to be quite interesting after all!"

It didn't take them long to strike up a conversation after that. The sisters sought him out the very next day while he was again fishing at the railing.

"Good morrow, Ladies," Nick said politely as they passed by him.

The girls could have been twins they were so much alike, from their blond curls spilling out from under their bonnets to the white laced up boots they wore on their tiny feet.

"Good morrow to you, Sir," one of them said.

'Twas the taller one who spoke to me, Nick thought, for he could not tell them apart.

The girls dawdled a bit, peering over the side of the ship, oohing and aahing over the vastness of the ocean. "Pray, pardon me, Sir," said the taller girl. "Are you the one who has been supplying our delicious fish suppers of late?"

Nick smiled. "*Nicholas Snow*, at your service, Ladies," he said, bowing gallantly.

Both girls, the taller and shorter one, giggled in unison. "I am Patience Brewster," said the tall one. "And this is my sister, Fear. We are going to Plymouth to meet our family. Our father is William Brewster, the minister there."

"I am most pleased to meet you both," said Nick.

"Have you caught any fish yet today, Sir?" Patience asked.

Nick shook his head. "Not yet. It seems the fish bite early in the morning and in the evening. I seem to be in between their mealtimes."

The two girls moved along down the deck, but Nick knew they would be back around soon. The *Anne* was, after all, not a very large ship.

Sure enough, just as he was pulling in his first fish they appeared again.

"Oh, *my*!" said Patience, running up to Nick and peering over his shoulder. "That one is *ever* so big! What kind is it?"

"Sea bass, I think," replied Nick. "And I will ask the cook to prepare this one *especially for you*." He removed the hook from the fish's mouth and held it out for the girls to study it before he dropped it into his bucket.

When she realized she was being flirted with, Patience blushed and lowered her head, as well-bred girls were expected to do.

"Thank you, Mister Snow. I shall look forward to tasting your fish tonight!" she said with a smile and the two girls retreated below the decks.

Chapter Three "Eels or Sea Biscuits?"

By the third week of the voyage their attempts at fishing were becoming fruitless.

"Perhaps it's because of the deeper water," remarked Anthony.

"Or perhaps they are tiring of the bits of eel we are offering them," Nick answered as they pulled in their lines for the day. "What else can we use for bait?"

Without fresh fish, the ship's menu soon became slightly monotonous. The captain, who was wise enough to know they could be at sea longer than they expected, explained that he wanted to delay the butchering of one of the pigs below deck to stretch the rations. The fresh fish that had been in abundance was temporarily replaced by dried salted beef, which had to be boiled and rinsed free of the salt before it was palatable. The fresh bread they had enjoyed during the first few weeks was soon in short supply and what was left had taken to molding around the edges in the humid environment below deck. The passengers had their choice of scraping off the green edges or eating a new bread in the form of what the crew called "sea biscuits"; flat tasteless pancakes made of flour and salt and water that swelled in the belly and tasted something like the barrels they were stored in.

"Why don't you try using *these* things as bait?" asked Will, when he tasted his first biscuit.

"I don't think even a *fish* could be so stupid as to eat one of these horrible things!" Anthony said, spitting his overboard in disgust.

For several weeks, the fishing proved to be sporadic at best, and there was some bickering over the meager catch when there was one. The cook tried stretching the fish by cutting it up into small bits and making a sort of fish chowder out of it but it seemed that dried beef and sea biscuits, of which there was a goodly supply, were going to be their regular fare for much of the trip.

Nick had gotten around to meeting most of the passengers by the third week, being the most gregarious of the three Snow men, and he discovered the people on board the Anne were quite a diverse group of characters. There were the Puritans and Separatists from Leiden, of course, but also many like the Snow men themselves, out to find adventure in the new world. Like them, most of the passengers had no idea what conditions they would find in Plymouth but were willing to take their chances.

The Brewster sisters continued to be his favorite companions, if only to boost his male ego, and they had lost their initial shyness, now seeking him out whenever they came on deck. He learned more about their family, the elder of the Plymouth Church, William Brewster and his wife, who had gone on ahead to prepare a home for them. Their chaperone, Mister Robert Long, had accompanied them on their journey and followed them everywhere they went, which Nick found very amusing. Although they were sweet girls, and quite attractive in an immature sort of way, they were a little too empty-headed for his tastes and Nick knew almost immediately neither of them was what he was looking for in a wife.

Besides! I'm not looking for a wife! he reminded himself.

Still, young Patience and Fear Brewster continued to be pleasant company and broke the monotony of the endless days on board the *Anne*.

He also got more acquainted with Stephen Tracy, the man he had originally met the first morning while standing on the foc's'sle with the captain. Stephen was travelling to Plymouth with his wife, Tryphosa, and their little daughter, Sarah. The Tracy family, although originally from England, had come directly from Leiden. Stephen was a very serious fellow, very hesitant about the trip and worried about what conditions they would find in the colony.

"It was my wife's idea," he told Nick one day in a conversation on deck. "I am not usually prone to taking risks like this. First it was Leiden, where we had to learn a foreign language and were treated no better than second class citizens. Now it's Plymouth! Oh, how I miss England!"

Nick tried to reassure him. "It hardly seems likely you will be second class citizens in America since there are hardly enough people to divide *into* classes. But, if you don't like it, I understand the *Anne* will be sailing right back to England as soon as they unload the provisions," he said.

"I have a feeling she will love America and I will be stuck there forever!" said Stephen.

"Well, I intend to at least give it a chance!" replied Nick. "It sounds like an exciting place!"

Tracy shook his head. "Aye, but at *my* age I am not eager for too much excitement!"

He walked away, his shoulders drooping, and his head hung low. *What a poor pathetic man he is*! thought Nick and *so sad that he has no hope for his future*! It made the blood pulse in his chest and left him even more eager to reach Plymouth!

There were many other interesting people on board. There was the Bangs family from Cambridge; Edward Bangs and his wife Rebecca and their two little girls. Edward was a shipwright by trade and Nick was learning a great deal about ships from his discussions with Bangs and Captain Pierce. Nick met Robert Bartlett, a cooper from Devon, Cuthbert Cuthbertson, a hat maker and part time minister from Leiden, and Timothy Hatherly, a felt maker from London. *At least we won't lack for casks and clothes in Plymouth*! Nick thought with a smile.

Anthony had also become friends with Mr. Cuthbertson, as soon as he had let it be known he was an avid student of the scriptures. Morning and evening, Anthony attended the prayer meetings and often sat discussing biblical topics with him afterward. Although the captain did not make it mandatory that all aboard attend the prayer meetings, he insisted that those who did *not* attend pay proper reverence by staying below deck in silence. The overwhelming stench in the hold was undoubtedly at least *part* of the reason so many of the *Anne's* passengers were baptized during the voyage!

Sickness, apart from sea sickness, did not seem to be a problem on the *Anne* until about the fourth week into the trip. Some of the children came down with runny noses, probably from the damp, germ filled cabin where they slept every night. Soon, most of the passengers were coughing and sneezing and the hold was an even more unpleasant place to be. The days were getting hotter and grew longer as summer came upon them. More and more passengers preferred to sleep on deck, and it wasn't long before the crew began to complain to the captain that they could not do their work with so many people sleeping underfoot, so that temporary escape from below was soon thwarted.

The situation in the hold was dire; colds rapidly turned into pneumonia and entire families were bedridden with no one well enough to attend to their personal needs. Soon some of the ladies stepped in to at least empty their chamber pots and change their sheets but there was just no way of airing out the cramped quarters. The sick had to just lie there in the smelly air, sipping beef broth drained off the salted meat.

Six weeks into the voyage there was good news when the captain ordered a pig to be butchered in a celebration; by his calculations they had reached their halfway point to Plymouth! After the evening prayer service, a lively party followed with much dancing and singing on the deck. One of the crew broke out an old accordion and entertained everyone with the only two songs he knew how to play. The cook butchered the animal ceremoniously with a sharp sword and took it immediately below where the aroma of roasting pork was soon drifting up from the galley, a heavenly fragrance to everyone especially the sick people confined to the sleeping quarters. Temporarily forgotten were the suppers of dried beef and sea biscuits when the cook dished out the thick slabs of pork and boiled peas and the sick enjoyed their first broth in weeks made from fresh meat.

"How *ever* can you tell we are halfway, Captain?" asked Patience Brewster over supper that night.

She and her sister were sitting on the steps of the quarter deck, looking like queens on their thrones, surrounded by the crew and most of the unmarried male passengers and being watched closely by their chaperone. Picking at the food on their plates and hiding their mouths behind their handkerchiefs as they chewed, they were quite a pleasant sight for the men.

"We have had good wind for the last week which I believe has made up for the lull we had before," said Captain Pierce. "If the wind keeps up, we might even make it to Plymouth before the end of June!"

It was good news indeed!

Chapter Four "The Storm"

The grey clouds began forming around sunset on their forty-seventh day at sea, hastening the darkness that fell over the *Anne*. It was still warm out; the clouds that were approaching seemed to be coming up from the southern waters, a bad indication to Pierce. He had sailed through gales before but never this far north in the summertime and he continued to watch for lightning and listen for thunder, hoping to sail around the eye of the storm. He looked back toward the *Little James* and saw lanterns glowing brightly from its deck. Although he did not voice his concerns to the passengers, he and his crew knew a big storm might be more than the little ship behind them could take, being of a design that sat lower in the water than the *Anne*. While it only carried a few passengers, its cargo was a valuable one, nonetheless; it brought cannons for the protection of the colony and much needed supplies for the settlers.

Half the passengers were already asleep below decks and the other half were sitting or strolling around on the deck engaged in quiet conversations when the first winds came up and began tossing the *Anne* about. The captain immediately ordered all passengers to go below, and he had his crew climb up the shrouds to tie up the sails and go below to check all the provisions to be sure everything was fastened down securely. Usually candles and lamps were not allowed at night in the sleeping quarters because of the fire danger; this night there was filtered light from the crew's lanterns while they secured the heavy casks and crates in the hold. Some of the younger children started to cry and hid their eyes against their mothers' bosoms as it began to thunder outside. When the wind caused the ship to list to her starboard everyone below braced themselves; some sat back-to-back for support and others caught unprepared were sent sliding across the floor. Nick, William and Anthony clung to each other's hammocks to keep their beds from swinging into the bulkhead. When the crew returned topside taking their lanterns with them the passengers were left sitting wide awake in the total darkness listening to the wind howling outside.

Anne's masts creaked and moaned under the strong wind. The porthole that had once been the only source of fresh air in the sleeping quarters soon had water from the high waves coming in before Nick and Will were able to close it. It made no difference however since the water on deck was soon gushing down like a waterfall over the stairs through the open hatchway and soon the passengers were sitting in several inches of cold sea water. Many of them were already miserable from the lurching of the ship and puking into their chamber pots.

 Captain Pierce was on the quarterdeck, holding tight to the ship's tiller when he looked up and saw one of the topsails suddenly break loose from its bindings and fall, fluttering and snapping wildly in the wind.

"I'll go up and fasten it down," called the boatswain's mate.

The captain shook his head. "No leave it!" he yelled. "The winds are too strong for anyone to go aloft!"

With the next great gust of wind, the sail began to tear and soon it ripped itself free and flew off, disappearing into the darkness and leaving only a ragged piece of canvas still attached to the yard. The captain watched the rolled-up mainsails, hoping he would not lose them as well.

The storm raged for several hours, and no one slept that night. By dawn it had passed, leaving in its wake just one torn sail and several inches of water in the hold. Slowly the passengers began wading through the water to bring their bedding up on deck to dry in the air and the captain sent the crew down with pumps to siphon out the sea water. Nick helped man one of the pumps while Anthony and Will helped the crew secure everything that had broken loose with ropes.

The crew climbed up and brought down the remnants of the sail that had torn loose. With spare canvas they had stored in the hold they spread it out across the deck and altered it to the size needed for the topsail, stitching the edges to keep the canvas from fraying. Several of the women passengers sat down on the deck to help with the sewing.

The animals of the *Anne* did not fare as well as her human passengers, however. When Anthony and Will checked their enclosures, they found the chickens that had survived, standing in their cages, drenched with sea water and shivering under their sopping feathers. The dead birds were taken immediately to the cook and there was chicken in the pot for several days thereafter. The manure from the pigs and goats on the floor had liquefied into a putrid pottage that floated on the surface of the water in the hold and the poor animals were left so traumatized by the whole affair that they stayed huddled in one corner, afraid of anything that moved, for the rest of the voyage. It had lost them a full day's sailing time but that was not what worried Captain Pierce.

When he looked back, the *Little James* was nowhere in sight!

Chapter Five "Plymouth!"

As soon as the newly stitched topsail was aloft, the *Anne* resumed her course. Still there was no sight of the *Little James* behind them but the captain could not go back. There was no telling which direction they had gone, or if they had sunk in the storm. The *Anne* hadn't enough provisions to go on an extended search. He could not lose any more valuable time. He could only keep going west toward Plymouth and hope the little ship would catch up sooner or later.

When they were finally sailing forward again at a good pace, up ahead Captain Pierce could see a fog bank forming all along the western horizon, which often happened after a summer thunderstorm, and it wasn't long before they were surrounded by the thick gray mist. By afternoon, the wind had died down and their visibility was at zero; the ocean around them was as calm as a millpond. Clutching his compass, the captain kept the *Anne* on her course. He could only hope it did not remain foggy all the way to St. George's banks, where there was danger of running aground on the uneven sand shoals.

It was a most miserable week. Without sunshine, the bedding hung over the side of the ship would not dry. The pumps had extricated most of the water but the wood in the hold was now spongy with dampness. The musty odor, combined with the already foul stench below, was almost too much to bear; Nick was the first to tie a handkerchief around his face and soon everyone was wearing makeshift masks over their faces.

For two days the *Anne* limped along blindly, waiting for a wind that would clear the fog away. On the third day the sun finally burnt through the mist, and they could see again. What they saw was a most welcome sight. *Land birds!* They must be near land! The captain felt sure he had not strayed too much off his course; still, there was the possibility they had drifted a little to the north or south. He did not want to worry the passengers with it. He knew the coast like the veins in his arms and he was confident if they didn't come out exactly at Plymouth Harbor, he would be able to find Cape Cod without too much difficulty.

The whispers spread and soon most of the passengers were on deck, straining their eyes ahead in the hopes of seeing Plymouth in the distance. The captain dropped the sounding lines as they entered into the banks, maneuvering south whenever they indicated shallow water. And they watched. They watched all day but still at suppertime they had not seen land. The passengers said their evening prayers and went to bed disappointed and weary, wondering if they would *ever* reach Plymouth.

At dawn, just as they were wiping sleep from their eyes, there was a blast from the boatswain's whistle and a sailor aloft on the yards yelled "Land Ho!" Those who were awakened scurried to the deck in anticipation and, there, out in front of the *Anne,* was the finger of land called Cape Cod. They had made it safely through the banks to the mouth of Plymouth Harbor!

Nick stood near the captain, watching as they rounded the cape, and the little settlement came into view.

"They have made improvements since my last visit," said Pierce. "There are several more houses!"

Nick looked in the direction where the captain was pointing. Several yards from shore there was a row of little houses with thatched roofs against a backdrop of tall trees and spirals of smoke rising from the chimneys. As they got closer, he could see that there was another row of houses hidden directly behind the first. There were people running out to the little wharf that had been built on the bay, waving their arms at the ship. Nick raised his arm and waved back. The passengers on the deck began to cheer and dance around. Husbands kissed their wives openly and the children were jumping up and down in excitement. Will and Anthony joined Nick on the upper deck and slapped each other's shoulders.

"We made it boys!" said Nick happily.

The captain gave the order for the anchor to be dropped and the longboats were loosened from their restraints and lowered down to the water. Frantically, everyone began packing up their belongings and lining up to be the first to go ashore.

On the dock stood a small group of ragged-looking settlers, a very short red-haired soldier in steel armor, one older gentleman dressed in a faded blue suit and one very pious looking man with a long white beard.

Patience Brewster ran up and tugged at Nick's sleeve. *"That's our father!"* she said happily. "I can't wait for you to meet him!"

Chapter Six "Constance"

Constance slipped out of her long skirt and unbuttoned her blouse, feeling the warm shards of sunlight filtering through the pine branches on her bare skin. Testing the water first with her toe, she quickly sat down, only partly submerging her nakedness in the little pool and languished there for several minutes, splashing the water over her legs and under her arms. She had discovered this wonderful oasis hidden among the trees while gathering wild strawberries in the woods earlier in the spring, before the summer drought had all but dried it up and it quickly became her secret place. Now, it was not but six inches deep; still it was better than bathing in the small one room house she shared with her family, where all the family members had to use the same bath water in the big tub in order to conserve the precious liquid. Her younger brothers, Giles and Caleb, were always allowed to go first, leaving her with water that had become tepid, brown and soapy and making it impossible to get her hair clean. Now that Constance was a young woman of seventeen, she desperately needed more privacy than the little house could offer, and she had found it here among the trees. She felt a little guilty, knowing that the colony's crops were dying of thirst in the fields but, she reasoned with herself, the small amount of water in this little pool wouldn't make any difference to the plants; it could only prolong their life another day at most.

She had told her stepmother, Elizabeth, that she was going to go deeper into the woods to gather more berries that day, which allowed her a little extra time to wash her long, red hair in the cool, clear water. There was just something magical about this place; there was an almost spiritual essence to it that took her away from the reality of her daily life. She couldn't explain it to anyone, nor would she; she would never share her secret with anyone!

 She wanted to stay longer, feeling the delightful tingle on her scalp but she dared not. She stood up and walked out onto the shore quickly, pulling her clothes back over her damp body, running her fingers through her hair and shaking off the droplets. With the tiny comb she had brought in her pocket, she pulled out the tangles in her hair. She touched her face softly with her fingers, tracing her cheekbones and touching the tips of her eyelashes as she leaned over and stared down at her reflection in the water. Now that she was of "marrying" age, she felt a constant compulsion to know what she really looked like to the young men of the colony. She had once studied her face in her mother's little hand mirror back home in England, long before her mother died, and her father had remarried. But when they came to America, somehow the little mirror got lost in the shuffling of household goods. Asking her father to buy another was out of the question, for she knew her father's opinion on the subject of *vanity*; she had heard *that* sermon more times than she could count! Still, she couldn't help but wonder what other people saw when they looked at her. Her obscure reflection in the water did not tell her what she wanted to know. *Was she pretty*? *Was her nose too big*? She knew her eyes were blue, as others had told her as much, but *what kind of blue? Were they light, like the sky, or dark, like the ocean? Was her face freckled and brown like her arms were from spending so much time in the garden behind the Hopkins' house or pale and opaque like she remembered her mother's face just before she died*? Oh, how she missed that little mirror!

Marriage had been on her mind quite a bit lately, especially as their little house became more and more crowded. She wanted space of her *own,* even if she had to take a husband in order to get it! It was strange how, following the deaths of her baby brother and sister from the fever, the house had seemed almost *empty*. But, with the arrival of new settlers, her father had seen fit to offer room and board to those who had yet to build their own houses. First, came Stephen Deane and Thomas Prence and then William Hilton, who, thankfully, only stayed a few weeks before his wife and children arrived from England. Now the little house was beginning to feel like it would burst from its seams and spew people out into the street it was so full!

The overcrowded house was not the only reason she was thinking of marriage; in her most private thoughts she was beginning to outgrow her tomboyish ways and being pursued by men, she was learning, could be quite entertaining. Many of the young girls her age had already married, and she was beginning to feel like a bit of a wallflower. She probably had no one else to blame, however, for she was always being told she was far too outspoken. Men seemed to like quiet, submissive women, like her stepmother, and Constance just couldn't force herself to be like that! Although there were a number of eligible young men living in Plymouth, none of them appealed much to her; they were all easily dominated, and Constance saw that as a character flaw. There was the clumsy John Cooke who was the most persistent; following her around, awkwardly trying to hold her hand. Developing romantic feelings for either Edward Doty or Edward Leister, her father's bondsmen, who shared the Hopkins house, sleeping in the loft above her and who stared at her over the supper table as if she had jam on her face, was unfathomable. She no longer considered John Alden, who lived down the street, for he was obviously in love with her friend, Priscilla Mullins. And, of course, there was Stephen Deane, who was very handsome but flirted with *all* the girls, so he couldn't be taken seriously. It didn't really matter though, as *none* of them were what she envisioned her future husband to be like in her dreams. She didn't quite know *exactly* what kind of man she wanted but *she was sure that she would recognize him the instant she saw him!*

There was a flurry of people running around when she rounded the corner near the Brewster house that stood just across the way from theirs and there was obvious excitement in the air.

"What is going on?" she asked Elizabeth, who was just emerging from the Hopkins' doorway, holding five-month- old Caleb on her hip. "Why is everyone running down the street? Is there a fire?"

"No, Child," said Elizabeth. "A ship has arrived from England! We are going down to the dock to meet it! Hurry now!"

A ship? thought Constance. *Wonderful! Just what Plymouth needs are more mouths to feed!* She went into the house remembering the day the ship *Fortune* had arrived, with thirty-five starving people aboard, and how the whole colony had been forced to go on half-rations to accommodate them. *Humph!* thought Constance bitterly. Before the summer drought came upon them, when it finally looked as if they would have a decent harvest after three long years of nearly starving, she was not the least bit overjoyed about sharing their bounty with more outsiders!

She stubbornly refused to follow the others down to the dock, although she knew she would have to explain her absence to her father when he came home. Stephen Hopkins was undoubtedly standing on the dock this very minute, with open arms and words of encouragement for the newcomers!

She sat down in her father's chair and reached into the basket of clothing that needed mending. As she threaded her needle and ran it through her hair, she pulled out a pair of her younger brother, Giles', pants. *How does a boy of sixteen wear the knees out in his trousers*? she wondered as she began to patch and sew them. When he was little, it was from playing with his toys in the dirt, but now it was obviously from helping build the houses of little Plymouth. *Little Plymouth*, Constance thought sourly, *that is getting bigger every minute!*

Chapter Seven "A Gathering of Scarecrows"

By the time Nick, Anthony and Will stepped out of the last longboat coming ashore, the tiny dock was crowded with people greeting each other warmly. Patience Brewster appeared immediately and grabbed Nick's arm, dragging him away to introduce him to her father, the stern looking, William Brewster.

"I am most pleased to meet you," said Elder Brewster, studying Nick up and down in a most critical manner.

Nick smiled and took the old man's hand, which felt as thin and bony as a chicken wing. He was much older than Nick had expected him to be and very sour looking, dressed in a faded black suit with a starched white collar and his white beard was trimmed to a perfect point, giving his face an odd *triangular* appearance. Unlike the other men, who wore wide-brimmed felt cockle hats, the elder wore a flat black skull cap that Nick suspected concealed a bald spot on the crown of his head.

"Thank you, Reverend," he replied. "Your daughters have told me much about you!"

"You have come alone, without your family?" asked Brewster, peering over Nick's shoulder.

"This is my family," said Nick. "My brother, Anthony, and my cousin, Will."

"And, of what *trade* are ye boys?" asked Brewster.

The three Snow men looked at each other, not knowing quite what to say. It didn't seem fitting to tell the man of God that they had been lowly thespians and gamblers!

"We are all quite good at carpentry," said Nick. "We helped to build the Globe Theatre in London."

"I hope to become a minister one day," said Anthony. "I am quite interested in the scriptures."

Immediately, Reverend Brewster's expression changed, and he moved a little closer, putting his arm around Anthony's shoulders. "Well, we will have to put you up in the Common House until you have your houses built," he said. "Come! Follow me into town and I will show you around. You and I, *Anthony,* is it? We shall have to have a good talk of spiritual matters when you are all settled in!"

The three Snow men followed the reverend down the dock and onto the street, through the row of little houses with their thatched roofs and crooked fences. As they walked along, their feet stirred the dust, and the hot July sun turned their foreheads damp with sweat.

"Looks as if you could use some rain!" said Nick wiping his brow.

"Aye, we have been praying for it," replied Brewster. "Our crops are withering in the fields."

Nick could see the rows of drooping corn stalks and several men toting buckets of water from somewhere up the street to give drinks to the thirsty plants. It was not promising, *this first look at Plymouth!*

The Common House was a building with graying clapboard shingles nailed to its walls and a thatched roof made of the same dried water reeds and rushes as the houses around it, but it was much taller because of its second story loft. It served to house the unmarried men, Brewster told them, and stored all the colony's food and ammunition. Once inside, they looked around at the place they would be calling home for a while.

"Well, it's bigger than the hold on the ship!" said Will.

"Aye," agreed Nick. "And it smells much better!"

One side of the huge room had a massive stone fireplace that took up much of an entire wall. In front of it were rows of wooden pallets on the floor, covered by an odd assortment of blankets and pillows on which someone had been sleeping.

Reverend Brewster spied three bare pallets near the far wall and pointed to them. "You may leave your things over there. I will have the mistress fetch you some blankets if you have none. Nights are quite warm now but soon you will need more covering, if you don't have your house built by the time the snows come."

"Thank you," said Nick. "That will suit us most properly. We had hoped to get to work on our house as soon as possible."

That seemed to please the reverend and he smiled, the wrinkles around his eyes turning upward and his teeth appearing yellow against the snow white of his beard. "We rise early here and do not waste the daylight hours in idleness. You will have help with your house, for we work as a community here," he said sternly. "We'll clear the last lot on the street for you, next door to the Eatons. I expect we can have the frame of your house raised by the end of the week."

The reverend turned and started for the door. "I will give you a chance to stow your belongings and freshen up after your long voyage, then we will all meet outside in the square for prayer."

When Elder Brewster was gone, Nick dropped his sea bag on the first pallet and walked over to the window, peering through the wooden shutters at the shoreline and the *Anne* anchored in the harbor. Suddenly, he thought about his mother and sister back in London and felt the pangs of missing them both. *Should they have left them behind*? *Would they be all right, two women alone*? *Yes*, he chastised himself. *The families of the theater will watch over them. They will be fine!*

"Thinking about Mother and Mary?" asked Anthony, putting his hand on his brother's shoulder.

Nick nodded. "Aye. I hope we made the right decision in leaving them."

"We should write to them before the *Anne* sets sail," said Anthony. "I am sure there will be more ships that will carry letters, so that we will know how they are doing."

"Who knows?" said Will. "They may even decide to join us one day!"

"I doubt that will happen," replied Nick. "Mother can be very stubborn. And I am not sure she would be happy here in the wilderness."

"What say, we go check out this place they call Plymouth?" said Will, heading for the door as soon as he had dropped his bag on one of the empty pallets.

"You heard the reverend. After we *pray,* Will," said Anthony. "Just *surviving* our miserable trip aboard that floating chamber pot they call a ship, we *do* have a lot to be thankful for*!*"

"Aye," said Will. "I suppose we do, at that!"

It seemed that the entire town had come out to welcome the new arrivals; mothers carrying infants on their hips, men sweaty from their labors in the fields and children chasing each other around on the dusty street. The Brewster sisters were there, one clinging to each of their father's arms. The young soldier they had seen on the dock, who they later learned was Captain Myles Standish, had removed his cumbersome armor, revealing his everyday clothes, but with his sword still tethered to his belt. The man dressed in blue was William Bradford, the governor of Plymouth, who spoke briefly, welcoming the passengers of the *Anne*.

Most interesting to Nick was a pair of Indians, who stood off to one side of the group, but who were obviously listening to the ceremony. They were half- naked, wearing only leather loin cloths around their middles, showing off their bronze muscular physiques and Nick couldn't help but stare. *What strange beings they are!* he thought, *and, apparently, not wild at all!* for they appeared quite docile and friendly, conversing quietly with each other and smiling with white teeth in sharp contrast to their dark skin.

When it seemed everyone was present, they gathered together, clasping hands, while the reverend said a prayer thanking God for the *Anne's* safe landing, asking for the safe arrival of the missing ship *Little James* and then, went on at length, to beg for rain. Standing in the middle of the *square,* which was nothing more than the intersection of the only two streets in the town, Nick looked around at the people of Plymouth and it suddenly occurred to him how *thin* they all were, not much more than walking scarecrows! All their faces were ruddy from working in the summer sun; even the women could not hide their blistered noses and freckled cheeks under their bonnets. *What had they gotten themselves into*, he wondered? *Had they travelled all the way from England to end up starving to death in this barren place?* He was studying the gaunt faces around him, when they suddenly broke out into joyous singing of hymns, smiling as if they were standing on streets of gold!

What are they all so happy about? Nick wondered.

Finally, the reverend dismissed them, and they all went back to their activities. Nick spied Captain Pierce, lingering on the edge of the crowd, and he approached him. "I want to thank you for getting us here safely, Captain," said Nick.

The men shook hands.

"Will you be sailing again right away?"

The captain nodded. "Yes, as soon as we unload the last of the stores and load up for the return trip. I am going home to Jamestown for the winter. I expect I will be back in the spring."

"I hope you have brought food," said Nick, chuckling. "This bunch looks like they could all use a good meal!"

"It's been a long drought they've been through," replied Pierce. "The rains will come. They always do!"

"I hope so!" said Nick. "I don't fancy introducing my stomach to my backbone just yet!"

Anthony approached them. "We wanted to give you a letter to take to our mother before you go," he said.

"I will let you know when we are ready to shove off," said the captain. "I will be sure your letters arrive safely."

Chapter Eight "Shadow Clouds"

"Constance Hopkins!"

It was her father's voice, booming like the drum the soldiers played when they practiced marching in front of the fort. He burst through the front door of the little house and, in one sudden movement, flipped off his hat and threw it across the room, where it landed precisely on its peg on the wall. His eyes were blazing, and his cheeks were red from more than just the stifling heat outside.

"Where have you been? And *why* did you not come down to the docks to meet our new neighbors?" he bellowed.

Constance looked down at her sewing and took a deep breath, trying to think of a plausible excuse. "I had so much mending to do, Father," she began. "And, it was so *dreadfully* hot outside today, I was feeling a bit faint."

Stephen Hopkins stared at his daughter, and she could see the twitch of a smile in the corners of his mouth. *"You? Faint*?" he asked, shaking his head. "You, the most stubborn and by far the strongest willed young woman in Plymouth? You must think of *another* excuse, Constance, my Dear. That is the *weakest* one you have come up with yet!"

By that time, Elizabeth had come into the house and put Caleb down in his cradle beside the hearth. "I am sure

Elder Brewster noticed your absence, Constance," she said quietly. "It is not a good reputation you are making for yourself. You are old enough now to take part in the affairs of our community."

Constance squirmed a bit in her father's chair. She hated disappointing her parents, but she really didn't understand what good it did to stand out in the sun, praying for rain that never came. Besides, she did enough praying every Sunday when she accompanied Elizabeth and her brothers to church. Why did she have to go sit on those uncomfortable benches and listen to hours of Elder Brewster's boring sermons, while her father stayed home? It wasn't fair! After all, it wasn't *her* idea to come to America! She had been against the idea all along and much preferred to stay in London, where life was *civilized*. And her parents seemed to be changing ever since they had arrived in Plymouth. While Elizabeth had always been quiet and gentle, lately the signs of impatience and frustration were beginning to show in her expressions and in her tone of voice and her father had taken to drinking much more liquor than he ever had back in London!

"I will go and apologize to Elder Brewster," she said, putting her sewing down and retrieving her wide-brimmed beaver skin hat from its peg by the door. She went out into the street, more to escape her parents' chastising words than to beg Elder Brewster's forgiveness, but she decided she would do it, just to keep peace in the family.

As it turned out, Elder Brewster was still out showing the newcomers around and had not yet returned to his home and it was his wife who answered the door.

"Good day, Constance!" said Mistress Brewster. "Do come in! I want you to meet my daughters, Patience and Fear, who have just arrived on the *Anne*!"

Constance suddenly wished she had taken the time to comb her hair, as she stared at the two impeccably dressed girls with identical blond curls and fresh blue dresses. "I am pleased to meet you both," she mumbled, looking down at her faded dress; one of the only two she owned.

"It is so good to meet someone our own age! There were mostly little children and old people on the ship," said Patience or Fear; they both looked so much alike, Constance could not tell them apart!

"There are a few girls our age here in Plymouth. Have you met Priscilla Mullins?" asked Constance. "And Humility Cooper?"

"We have not met anyone yet except those who greeted us on the dock," said one of the identical girls. "Perhaps you can introduce us to the other young women when you have the time?"

Ugh, thought Constance drearily. She hated introductions and all that nonsense! Girls her age could be ever so silly! *Wait until Stephen Deane gets a look at these two*! she thought smugly. *Maybe he will finally leave me alone!* "Of course," she said politely. "I will be most happy to introduce you to everyone on the morrow!"

Excusing herself, she walked off, completely forgetting the reason for her visit! But instead of turning around to go back, she kept walking, down toward the beach where she could slip off her shoes and feel the sand between her toes. It was such a stifling hot day, her morning bath in the woods was now only a pleasant memory. She could feel beads of sweat on her forehead and dampness spreading under her arms as she walked along the shore, carrying her shoes in her hand and letting the water rush around her ankles. She stopped momentarily so as not to frighten a white tail doe and her fawn who had come to the water's edge to lick the salt off the kelp that had washed up onto the shore and looked around her. It was a good day for clamming; she spied dozens of air bubbles in the sand, but she had not brought a basket with her. Besides, she had just laundered her apron and she didn't feel like digging for clams anyway; it took forever to get the smell washed from her hands! She just wanted to feel the breeze off the ocean and be alone.

The *Anne* was out in the harbor, bobbing up and down on the waves that were rolling in from the Atlantic. Suddenly, Constance thought of how wonderful it would be to be going home to London, back to civilization and normal living. Then she remembered the long, uncomfortable journey on the *Mayflower,* with all the sickness and bad weather they had experienced, and she knew she didn't want to take that trip again. No, she would just have to make the best of it here in Plymouth, muddling through with two faded dresses, one pair of worn shoes and a pair of under drawers that had been mended so many times they were beginning to look like a patchwork quilt! Maybe it was a *blessing* they had lost her mother's mirror…. seeing what she looked like would probably make her feel *worse* about living in this dismal place!

She had walked a long way by that time, and she realized the sun was going in and out of the clouds that were moving in over the harbor. *Shadow clouds* she had always called them; little wooly, white puffs that made shady circles on the ground below as they moved quickly across the sky. They were not *serious* clouds, these *shadow clouds.* When they were young children back in London, she and Giles had made a game of chasing them down the street, trying to keep their feet in the shade of their ever-moving shadows.

Constance looked out over the water and noticed a band of grey clouds, rapidly following the shadow clouds ashore, and her heart suddenly raced. A storm was coming! Rain meant there would be water for their crops and ample water to bathe in again! She turned immediately and ran back down the beach toward town and, by the time she reached the little dock, there were already tiny raindrops landing on her cheeks. She stuck her tongue out to taste them and laughed out loud. She was not the only one who had noticed. There were children dancing in the puddles that were quickly forming and half the town was soon standing outside in the rain. Elder Brewster appeared in the square again to lead the entire town in another prayer. Everyone was just smiling at each other; the women all had joyful tears in their eyes and the men took off their hats to welcome the raindrops on their heads. Constance thought to herself how comical they all looked, until she realized *she* was grinning too, standing there with everyone else in Plymouth, looking up at the sky.

Chapter Nine "Love at First Blush"

Nick, Anthony, and Will all agreed; shaking hands to cement the pact before they went to bed that night. They had discussed it at length, for over an hour. While Nick and Anthony were to work on the new house, Will had signed on with a man named Richard Derby to earn wages to help support the Snow household until their house was built. It seemed to be the perfect plan; the brothers who had a bit more experience in construction, having spent years building stages and props for the theater, would work on their house, while their rascal cousin was hired out and was more likely to be on his best behavior being supervised by a stranger. *Two* of their heads rested easy on their pillows that night, as their snores blended in with the others and filled up the darkness in the Common House.

 The next morning Nick and Anthony went out to meet the other men who were to help build their house on the corner lot at the south end of town. The others were already there and were busily laying the lumber for the framework out on the ground; Stephen Hopkins, his son, Giles, his two bondsmen, Ed Leister and Ed Doty, and a red-haired chap named Stephen Deane. Introductions were quick and perfunctory, and they commenced with the work immediately. They split up into two groups; the Hopkins' took axes and went out to cut more lumber from the forest on the western side of the town, while the two "Ed's" remained at the site to plane and shape the rough pieces of wood into more uniform beams and wall supports. Stephen Deane, who had some masonry skills, went out with a three wheeled cart to begin collecting stones to build the hearth.

By afternoon, all the men gathered together to hoist the four wall supports in the air. The welcome rains from the day before had left mud where there had previously been dry dust. Their boots slipped and slid in it as they tried to hold the framework in place so that the nails could be hammered in. With the lower frame now stable, tomorrow they would bring in a ladder and begin positioning the pitched roof supports. It was Stephen Hopkins, who had somehow taken over the supervision of the project, who called it a day and invited everyone to supper at his house.

"Come, Boys," he said. "Elizabeth has a kettle of venison simmering on the hearth and I have a couple of casks of cool beer resting under the floorboards! I can almost taste it from here! Let us stop for today and start again in the morning."

The others had no objections. The dampness from the previous day's rain, combined with blistering white sun, had turned the summer air humid and thick. While the crops in the fields relished it, the effect on the men was quite the opposite, especially those who worked outside in it. Those who had removed their shirts, paid the price with sunburned skin by the end of the day. When they finally all sat down at the long pine table in the Hopkins house, their faces looked a bit like the lobsters caught off the stony Plymouth shore, after Elizabeth had boiled them in the pot.

Stephen Hopkins introduced the rest of his family to the Snow brothers as soon as they entered the door. "This is my wife, *Elizabeth* and my son, *Caleb*. And, that troublesome wench over *there*," he said chuckling and pointing to Constance, whose back was turned toward the hearth where she was stirring the pot, "is my daughter *Constance.*"

Constance whirled around, her blue eyes glaring at her father, who delighted in teasing her, especially in the presence of strangers.

She opened her mouth to say something, but nothing came out. Her eyes passed over the serious looking one named Anthony and locked squarely on the yellow haired one who was grinning brightly. Try as she might she could not think of anything to say, until the silence in the room was broken by her brother, Giles.

"What is the matter with you, Con?" he asked. "You look like you have seen a ghost!"

Constance immediately recoiled and pushed her brother playfully. "I see *you,* dear Brother," she said. "And I could *smell* you from clear across the room!"

The men howled in laughter and Elizabeth shot a disapproving glance at her stepdaughter.

"Constance! Is that any way to greet our guests?"

"It's all right," said Nick. "You are entirely correct, Constance! We could probably *all* use a good bathing! It has been *devilishly* hot out today!"

He smiled directly at Constance.

"I'm sorry," she mumbled, lowering her eyes. "My brother just eggs me on sometimes. I meant no disrespect to you gentlemen."

Elizabeth had indeed been simmering venison all that day and had baked it into round "pastie" pies, with peas and corn and carrots in a thick gravy. She had Constance bring down their best pewter plates from the high shelf, instead of the wooden bowls they usually used. She was wise enough to bake plenty, for each of the men ate two or three in quick succession. By the time the women had finished serving the hungry men and finally sat down to eat themselves, the men had nearly scraped their plates clean and had already emptied the first cask of beer and had started on the second one. The conversation was getting lively, and the laughter seemed to reverberate off the walls in the tiny house.

Constance looked up between small ladylike bites of her supper and her eyes kept coming back to Nick Snow. Nick, by then, had lit a pipe and was leaning forward with his elbows on the table, puffing out little bursts of smoke while he conversed with her father about *something*; she wasn't exactly sure *what.* Ed Doty and Ed Leister were staring at her like idiots from across the table, as was their usual annoying habit, and Stephen Deane glanced at her occasionally, in a provocative sort of way which only *provoked* her.

"What goods has the *Anne* brought to us this time, Father?" she asked, at the precise moment she saw a lull in the conversation. "Have they brought *cloth* to make more clothes?"

Stephen shook his head. "No, Constance, Love; perhaps on the next ship," he said, his words beginning to slur a bit from the beer's effect. "Besides, you would look beautiful to me even if you were wearing a potato sack!"

"Oh, *Father!*" Constance said, rolling her eyes toward the ceiling. "*Be serious!*"

Father always got so silly when he drank too much beer. She looked down with disdain at her faded dress that was beginning to be a bit too tight across the bust. While *that* part pleased her, she was beginning to worry she would split her seams completely before too long! It made her long for London and its amenities even more.

After a while, the conversation at the table seemed to be coming from another room; all burbled and mixed together. The sweltering house, combined with the aroma of the pipe tobacco and the heady smell of the freshly uncorked cask of beer, made her slightly drowsy. She watched him as he leaned back and ran his fingers through his thick head of yellow hair, laughing at something her father had said.

Elizabeth touched her arm gently. "Constance," she said in a low voice. "Come help me with the dishes."

Constance stood up and helped her step- mother clear the table and take all the plates outside, wiping them with dry rags onto the ground for the chickens that were squawking and pecking at their feet. One day's rain did not take away the ordinance that had been adopted by the colony during the drought; using water to wash *anything* was considered wasteful! It was for drinking only!

"Your behavior today has not been very ladylike, Constance," Elizabeth said sternly.

"I'm sorry," Constance replied. "Father and Giles just tease me so!"

"You are of marriageable age, now," her step- mother went on. "Young men do not respect women who blurt out and stare so unabashedly!"

"Stare? Who was I staring at?" asked Constance.

"Young Mister Snow is quite attractive. But…"

"I guess I *was* staring a bit," admitted Constance. "Have you ever seen a man with hair that color?"

"That's still no reason to stare," replied Elizabeth. "It's *impolite.*"

She is right, thought Constance. She was beginning to think she would *never* learn how to act properly, especially around young men. *Why must the world be so silly? Men don't have such rules to abide by! They drink their beer and smoke their pipes and swear. Why do women have to sit around like porcelain dolls with their hands folded in their laps and never say anything?* "I'm sorry, Elizabeth," she said shaking her head. "Sometimes I think I should have been born a man! I have *ever* so much trouble not speaking my mind!"

Elizabeth put her arm around Constance's shoulder affectionately. "I know, Dear. You have inherited your father's spirit," her stepmother replied. "But you must *try* to be a lady. You just have to remember to *think* before you *speak!*"

The women returned to the house just as the men were rising to take their leave. Anthony bowed graciously at the ladies and took Elizabeth's hand. "Thank you for the delicious meal!" he said. "It was the best I have had since I left England."

"You are most welcome, Mister Snow," Elizabeth replied. "You and your brother must come visit often!"

Nick Snow followed his brother, staring at Constance with lips that seemed to want to burst into a toothy grin.

"Yes," he said. "The meal was wonderful, Mistress Hopkins."

It looked as though he was going to say something else, and Constance found herself holding her breath in anticipation. He leaned forward and whispered in her ear, "I promise the next time you see me I will have bathed properly and changed into a clean shirt!"

And then the Snow brothers were gone, and Constance stood there with the blood pulsing in her cheeks.

Chapter Ten "The Land Deals"

Ten days after the *Anne* had arrived, the carcass of the broken and storm-battered *Little James* limped into Plymouth harbor, with her ragged sails waving from her only remaining mast. Elizabeth had literally taken Constance in hand and had run down to the dock to greet the new arrivals and to see the new ship that was to remain in Plymouth to be used as their new fishing vessel.

It was a much smaller group of passengers disembarking from the little ship. In fact, the reception committee far outnumbered the new arrivals. Governor Bradford and Elder Brewster were there, of course, to welcome them; it only took one trip of the longboat to bring them all ashore. Stephen Hopkins and his bondsmen arrived shortly and were engaged in conversation with the ship's captain, who was complaining bitterly about his "greenhorn crew." Constance looked around to see if Nick Snow was with her father but was disappointed. She and Elizabeth stood next to Captain Standish, who had been eagerly watching the people as they stepped down onto the dock, as if he was expecting someone. He was a funny little man, the constable of Plymouth and leader of their guard, very short of stature and his face was ruddy and almost the color of his flaming red beard. Constance liked him though; he had visited the Hopkins house many times and, on one particular occasion, he had helped her and Elizabeth get her father up from his chair and into his bed after a long night of drinking. She watched happily as he finally spied who he had been looking for: a pretty young woman who came running toward him, waving and crying with joy.

"Myles!" she called. "Myles! I am here!"

He took her in his arms and hugged her briefly and Constance could see that there were tears in his eyes also and she was happy for him, remembering when he had lost his wife the first winter to the fever. Rumors had circulated that he had been corresponding with an "old family friend" back in London, for there were no secrets in Plymouth. This was the first time that she could remember seeing the little captain smile.

"Mistress Hopkins! Constance!" he said happily. "This is my fiancé,' Barbara!"

Barbara took their hands in hers warmly. "I am ever so glad to meet you!" she gushed. "I was beginning to think our crippled little ship would never make it!" She looked back at the *Little James* floating pathetically in the harbor. "Still, I must thank God for it," she said, turning back toward the captain. "For it brought me to you!"

Whether Captain Standish was blushing or not it was hard to tell but he immediately whisked her up and hurried her away from the crowd and they got lost in their own private conversation.

"It is a miracle of God that the little ship made it safely," said Elder Brewster. "Let us go and pray in the square."

The group on the dock began to work their way up the street and were joined by many others. Finally, she saw *him*, standing with his brother, leaning against the Brewster's garden fence. When heads began to bow as the elder's voice rose up in prayer, Constance opened one eye to sneak a peek at the strange blond-haired man whom she couldn't seem to get out of her mind. While no one else was looking, she stared at him. As soon as her eyes focused on him, she saw his eyes open slowly, staring back directly at her! His face broke into that toothy grin she remembered, and she closed her eyes quickly, so embarrassed she silently wished she could disappear into a puff of smoke. She hid herself behind her father's shoulder and took a deep breath. *That is him!* she thought incredulously. She, Constance, the stubborn, undisciplined tomboy, who thought she could never be evenly matched with any of the fumbling young men in Plymouth, decided at that moment. *Nick Snow* was the man she was going to marry!

As it turned out, there *were* to be weddings that very month in Plymouth but not for Constance. Governor Bradford had recently proposed to a woman named Alice Southworth who had come from England on the *Anne* and Captain Standish was eager to recite his vows to his sweet Barbara. It was normally the governor who presided over weddings in Plymouth, but Elder Brewster exchanged places with him to say the words, when he was joined with his beloved Alice. Held in the lower room of the town fort, just up the hill from the square, which also served as the town church, they were quick civil affairs; one in the morning and one in the afternoon. Because they were civil and not religious ceremonies, a couple signing a marriage contract in Plymouth had no need of a protracted celebration. There was far too much work to be done and only mischief to be gained from imbibing in strong spirits after such an event. So, as quickly as they were wed, the bridal couples went back to work with everyone else. Still the events were important enough to bring her *father* into the church building, which Constance thought was most comical. Stephen Hopkins had always claimed his relationship with God did not require listening to weekly sermons and taking part in group prayers. It didn't seem fair to Constance that every Sunday, when she, Elizabeth and the children dressed in their best to join the morning march up the hill to the church, her father was at home getting an extra hour of sleep! She swore to herself that someday she would have the satisfaction of seeing Stephen Hopkins sitting on those hard benches, singing hymns with the family. *Indeed, Elizabeth Hopkins shared the same sentiment*.

The last-minute rains had come just in time to save their crops. As the summer was waning and the corn and beans in the field were being plucked from their branches, not everyone was happy about their bountiful harvest, however. Nick and Anthony had finally finished their house and had joined Will and the others in the fields, to get the last of the fruits and vegetables gathered before the snowfall. Some of the men that sat on the council had observed that while the *harvest* was to be stored in the Common House and *equally shared* among the citizens of Plymouth, the share of the *work* had been anything but equal! Across town, lips were beginning to grumble about the matter, and it was beginning to overshadow the spirit of partnership that had once been the model of the colony. With the promise of *equal shares* not everyone was willing to work hard to feed *someone else's* family. There was just no incentive in it!

The council, made up of most of the men who had arrived on the Mayflower, called a meeting and the matter was discussed at length. They all gathered in the room used for their church services, the governor, Captain Standish, Elder Brewster, Stephen Hopkins and a handful of others.

"Something must be done about the men who are not doing their part," Standish said emphatically.

Stephen Hopkins agreed. "It's disgraceful how some of the newcomers are the *last* to arrive to work but they seem to be the *first* in line for food!"

Governor Bradford had been doing a lot of thinking on the subject and he offered his idea to the council.

"Perhaps we need to divide up the land into individual parcels," he suggested. "If the men are working for themselves, they will not be sitting idly by watching others work! They will reap only what they sow!"

The others on the council agreed in theory but differed in their opinions of just how to do it.

"How can the land be divided fairly?" Hopkins asked.

"Who will get the land that has already been cleared and cultivated?" Standish wanted to know.

"I think the only fair way is to base the *size* of the parcel on the *size* of the family, and the newcomers shall have to work with raw land, just as we all did," replied Bradford. "Don't you gentlemen agree?"

"Yes," replied Elder Brewster. "That seems fair."

There was no argument with that. The council ratified the agreement and decided that, as soon as the fall harvest was finished, the news would be broken to the rest of the colony.

To the hardest workers, it was welcome news. To the lazy ones, who worked as little as possible, it was disappointing. Some of them even left Plymouth for other settlements. To the Snow brothers, it meant they would have their own acre parcel of farmland south of town along the Eel River! They didn't care whether it had stones and stumps to deal with. When they returned to their little house at the end of the street that evening, they couldn't stop talking about it. What would they plant? How would they get water? Did they have enough money for tools? They could hardly wait to get out there and start clearing the land!

Starting the next day Nick and Anthony began working from dawn to dusk, while Will worked out his term of indenture with Mister Derby. As it turned out, Constance did not get the chance to see Nick Snow for several weeks. There was just no time for socializing when there was work to be done!

The *Anne* set sail for England as soon as it was loaded full of beaver pelts and lumber. Nick and Anthony saw Captain Pierce off, after they had given him letters to take to their mother and sister in London.

"I will be back in the spring," said the captain. "And don't you worry. I will *personally* deliver your letters to your mother."

Nick reached into his pocket and produced the only two silver coins he had left to his name, and he handed them to the captain. "Can you get me some fabric?" he asked. "Something in light blue…you know *dress* material!"

Anthony cocked his head and glanced sideways. "Are you taking up sewing, Brother?" he asked.

"No," answered Nick and the captain smiled.

"Ah," Pierce said. "I think your brother has his eye on a pretty young wench. And what better way of enticing a lass than with *dry goods*?"

Nick shook his head. "Never you mind what my intentions are, Boys," he said. "Can you get it for this price?"

"Aye," said the captain, winking at Nick as he jumped down into the long boat. "I'll bring it to you when I return in the spring."

Chapter Eleven "Hobbamock"

What was most amusing to all of Plymouth, except for her four doe-eyed, smitten admirers, was the competition for Constance's hand in marriage and it was being whispered about over many supper tables and bed pillows. If bets were to be wagered as to who would eventually win her hand, most would have favored the handsome Stephen Deane, even though he had been seen entertaining several different girls in addition to Constance. Ed Leister and Ed Doty just did not seem to be her type in anyone's imagination and John Cooke, all agreed, was a bit of an oaf and hardly likely to be the "one". Constance herself had not spoken a word; she had not given any hints as to whom she favored. There was a reason for her silence; the object of her affection had hardly spoken to her in weeks and even then it was only a polite tip of his hat and an uttered "Good Morrow, Miss Constance" when he passed her on the street! How was she to know if he favored her at all? She was not about to tell anyone the secret decision she had made that day in the square and make a ninny of herself! No, she had to be patient and wait for *Nick Snow* to come calling on *her.*

By now, Plymouth was in the midst of autumn and while the changing color in the leaves and the crispness in the air was a welcome change from the summer's heat, the ground would soon begin to freeze and harden overnight, making the clearing of the raw land to get it ready for spring planting much more difficult. Nick and Anthony had already broken two spades on the rocks and tree roots; the rocks they piled on one corner of the plot to save for other uses and the tree roots they lugged back to the house for kindling. Day after day they rose early in the morning and with implements in hand trudged down the little dirt road that led out of town toward the river. They spent the daylight hours turning over the hard clumps of earth a little more each day, silently, rarely speaking except when they stopped to go quench their thirst at the river's edge.

On one such day, Nick looked up from the furrow he was digging and spotted the Indian the colonists called Hobbamock sitting on the ground a short distance off, watching them as they labored. When Nick saw him, he gave the Indian a friendly wave and Hobbamock stood up and approached them.

"You have long way to go," said the Indian, pointing his brown finger beyond the furrows that Nick and Anthony had already dug.

"Yes," sighed Nick. "We are trying to get it all turned under before it snows, but the days are getting shorter, and I think we may run out of time."

Hobbamock nodded his head.

"Need more hands," he said and turned around, going back to the spot where he was sitting before. Nick watched as the Indian picked up something from the ground. Then Hobbamock returned with a spade in his hand and started turning over the soil beside them.

"Thank you, Sir," said Anthony. "It is very kind of you to help."

"English are my family now," said the Indian. "I help my new family."

They went back to work and, by sundown, had dug two furrows, each an acre in length. It was good to see the rich brown soil laid back ready to be seeded and nurtured. Nick was feeling a sense of accomplishment when he removed his hat and went to the river's edge to wash the sweat from his head. He returned to his brother and Hobbamock, smiling.

"We haven't any money to pay you, my Friend, but will you come and have supper with us tonight?" he asked.

Hobbamock agreed and the three returned to the Snow house, where they lit a fire, warmed up some of their leftover breakfast and broke open a loaf of bread.

"In the spring," said Hobbamock, "I will show you how to plant your corn."

"You mean there is some special way to put the seed into the ground?" Anthony asked. "We have been city dwellers all our lives and I fear we have a good deal to learn about farming."

Hobbamock's eyes seemed to be smiling but his face did not move.

"We will catch shadd and they must be planted in each hole. Then you will have much corn."

"Shadd?" Nick asked, not at all sure what a "shadd" was.

"A shadd is a little fish," replied Hobbamock. "It is good for feeding your corn."

"Oh, as a *fertilizer* you mean!" Anthony laughed out loud. "I have heard of them using fish meal on rose bushes back in London."

"Fish is good food for people *and* plants," said Hobbamock, "and there must be pockets to hold the water."

"Yes," said Nick. "Since we are so close to the river, I think we can design some way of channeling the water directly into the furrows."

Hobbamock seemed to be a never-ending source of information about planting and crops and they continued their conversation until late into the night.

By the time Will came through the door to the little house, his eyes widened in surprise at seeing an Indian sitting cross-legged in the middle of the floor.

"This is our cousin, Will," Anthony said. "Will, do you know our friend, Hobbamock? He is helping us work our piece of land."

Will nodded. "Glad to meet you," he said.

"I am afraid we finished off the food, Will," said Nick. "Did you eat your supper?"

"Aye," was Will's reply. "Mistress Derby fed me quite properly."

Will sat down at the table and listened to the Indian as he educated his cousins on the subject of farming, studying the strange dark- skinned man in silence.

Hobbamock was tall and muscular and quite handsome in a dark, *savage* sort of way. His hair was like jet, glossy as a raven's feathers and yet thick and coarse like a horse's tail, which even though he tied it up securely at the nape of his neck, was still long enough to brush the bottom of his back. He had learned to speak very good English, being an interpreter between Massasoit, the *sachem* of the Wampanoag tribe and the colony leaders, after the death of Squanto and his expressive eyes beamed with intelligence. He was an interesting character, indeed, with a fondness for Indian philosophy, which many considered mere superstition, but his mind was also a storehouse for a wealth of practical information too.

"Wampanoag once lived here," said Hobbamock. "Right here in what you call *Plymouth*. But there was much sickness from the fever, and many died. Our *sachem* believed the ground was cursed and we moved to another place."

"*Sachem*?" asked Anthony.

"He is a *father* to us, like your *Mister Bradford* is to you," replied the Indian.

"Oh, *sachem* means *chief,*" said Nick.

"I hear the people that arrived on the Mayflower lost many from the fever as well," commented Anthony.

Hobbamock nodded.

"Are there other tribes of Indians that live near here?"

Hobbamock's face took on a serious expression and for a moment Anthony was afraid he had said something to insult him.

"Wampanoag are friendly to the English. We welcome you. But there are other tribes that would do much harm to you."

He paused as if saying the very name of the other tribe was distasteful to him.

"Narragansetts are not your friends," he said quietly. "They would like to decorate their wigwams with the hair on your heads. You must stay away from them!"

Always the worrier, Anthony looked intently at Hobbamock.

"I don't think we have seen any Narragansetts," he said. "How will we know them when we see them?"

"You will *not* see them, for they hide behind the trees," answered Hobbamock. "If you *do* see them, they will not approach you in peace.   They will be screaming with their faces painted red and with murder in their minds."

Anthony looked at Nick and back at Hobbamock.

"But do not worry my friends," said Hobbamock. "*I will watch out for you.*"

Chapter Twelve "The *One*"

Before long, Plymouth was blanketed in a soft cloak of snow. The days became shorter and the nights so cold it seemed as if the very smoke from the town's chimneys would freeze in midair as it spiraled into the winter sky. The sweat on men's beards froze into tiny ice crystals, the women's cheeks became the color of rose and the children frolicked in the snow and seemed to be the only ones who had to be reminded to come inside out of the cold. Finally, working the land became impossible. For the people of Plymouth however there was always a never-ending list of other work to be done.

 Elder Brewster soon took the break from planting and harvesting as an opportunity to take Anthony under his wing and began to impart upon his student his interpretation of the scriptures. Brewster was a rigid taskmaster, often giving reading assignments to Anthony to take home as if he were a schoolboy, and the oil lamp burned well into many nights in the Snow house. His teacher's manner was stern and relentless and if Anthony's hunger for God's word had once been ravenous, it was soon matched by the elder's passion to teach it! He was seldom seen without his mentor at his side. Together, they constructed more pews for the church's meeting room below the fort, so that, at least, the women and children could sit down on the Sabbath. They built a wooden pulpit from which the elder could give his sermons, without the necessity of balancing his

Bible awkwardly in his hands whilst he was trying to preach.

 Nick's friendship with Hobbamock had deepened and soon he was spending as much time at the Wampanoag village as he was with the colonists of Plymouth. Together they trapped and hunted in the snow, ice fished on the river and cut firewood in the nearby woods and Nick learned firsthand the "Indian way" to do things. Hobbamock introduced him to others in the tribe and Nick was especially impressed when he met the *sachem* Massasoit for the first time, finding him quite a likeable fellow. On that particular evening, as the men sat around the fire in the *nush wetu* which was a long bark-covered building with three large fire pits inside, the *sachem* reached out and offered Nick a handful of tobacco. When Nick pulled out his pipe and stuffed the wad of tobacco into it, with the intention of smoking it, all the Indians in the little circle broke into a loud fit of laughter. Nick was confused and couldn't understand what they thought was so funny until Massasoit took another handful of tobacco and dropped it into a pot of boiling water on the fire.

"We do not *smoke* our tobacco," explained Hobbamock. "We *drink* it!"

Nick, always eager for new experiences, tasted the brown brew when the cup was passed to him and grimaced at the bitterness on his tongue. "I think I will stick to *smoking* it for now," he said, lighting his pipe and they all laughed heartily at their new white- skinned friend.

Far from being the savages he had expected them to be back when he left England, he found the Wampanoag to be a warm and compassionate people and, except for the tobacco thing, not much different than Englishmen!

Cousin Will had not fared so well working for Richard Derby; in truth Derby had fired him several weeks earlier for being consistently late to work, although Will hadn't yet explained it to his cousins. He had taken up with a man named John Billington, who had a three acre parcel out on the land near the bay. Billington was a bit of a rogue; he and a couple of other ne'er-do-wells named John Oldham and John Lyford, spent a lot of their time drinking beer and playing cards in the little shack he had built beneath the trees on the edge of his property. Mostly, however, they sat around complaining about the conditions in Plymouth. His land sat mostly uncultivated, and his house was so poorly constructed that the cold winter winds whistled right through gaps in the walls. Most nights, Will came home long after Nick and Anthony had fallen asleep, stumbling in the door in a beer- induced stupor and collapsing in his bed, thinking his cousins were none the wiser about his activities.

It was a *good* winter, for the harvest had been bountiful and the storehouses were packed full of food; a far cry from winters they had experienced in years past. Captain Standish assigned one of his soldiers to stand guard in the Common House to see that no one helped themselves to another family's stores, for even though most of the residents of Plymouth were honest, there were still a few who were not above pilfering from others when the opportunity presented itself. Every new ship brought new people; some that were not very honorable.

Christmas passed quietly; the members of the Church of Plymouth did not believe in the gay celebrations that surrounded the most holy of holidays back in England. The residents of Plymouth were forbidden to consume alcohol and dancing and singing was also prohibited on that day, making it a most solemn occasion. Family members exchanged small gifts with each other without any outward expression of joy. It was one of the things Constance desperately missed about their former life in England, *a festive Christmas!*

 When spring came, Captain Pierce returned on a new ship they called the *Charity,* and all of Plymouth was abuzz with more than its usual excitement. For once, Constance was anxious to accompany her family down to the dock to see *the colony's first cattle arrive!* The captain had maneuvered the ship in as close as he could, without running it aground in the shallow harbor, and they began to get the nervous herd lowered down into the long boat, using slings made of sail canvas tied around their bellies. It was quite a comical sight to see the poor beasts hoisted up, flailing about helplessly in the air and wailing in their most pathetic voices, until their hooves found the security of the floorboards of the boat. When the boat began moving with the currents under them, however, the cows began to thrash around again until they started jumping out of the boat, some with calves at their side, and swimming to shore where the men had to run madly to restrain them. Last to be unloaded was a large red bull, so stout it took four men to hold the ropes to lower him down to the boat where, as soon as he stepped down, put a hoof right through the hull. As he struggled to free himself, the boat capsized. The sailors and the bull all swam to shore together and the whole town followed along, as the herd was led up the street to their enclosure.

Constance returned home feeling very melancholy for she had hoped to see Nick Snow on the docks and the object of her affection continued to be more elusive than ever. Perhaps she *had* been too outspoken when he had visited their home; perhaps she was going to have to give up on him! Had Elizabeth and Caleb not been at her side, she would have burst into tears and thrown herself across the bed. Instead, she headed out to the back yard and knelt down in her little garden, to take out her frustration on the dandelions and goat heads that were sprouting up among her carrots and onions. Ripping the culprits up by the roots, with little regard for the prickly spines it was an exercise which proved to be very therapeutic for the mood she was in. She had been virtually ignoring all her other admirers and still they wooed her doggedly, while the one whose attention she craved wasn't paying the least bit attention to her! Would she be forced to marry a man she had no real feelings for *just for the sake of being married*? She was almost twenty, and, by some, that was thought to be middle aged! While the tomboy in her screamed silently *"Men! Who needs them anyway?"* the woman she was becoming and the feelings that were beginning to stir within her, told her that if she wanted the right man, she had to be patient!

When she had filled up her bucket with weeds, she slapped her hands together to brush off the dirt and wiped the perspiration from her brow. Trudging across the Hopkins' backyard, she pitched the contents of the bucket between the Hopkins' fence and the high palisade that had been built all around the settlement to protect the residents from Indian attack. It all seemed so silly to Constance since none of the Indians she had met so far seemed the *least* bit hostile. She remembered when Samoset, the first Indian who had visited the colony, had spent the night in the Hopkins house; how *furious* she had been with her father for inviting another person to share their already crowded living quarters and *a half-naked savage at that*! She had been afraid of him at first; this peculiar being that looked and smelled unlike anyone she had ever known and was a little confused by his strange customs. But, with time, the friendship between Samoset and the Hopkins family grew, and he still came to visit them when he wasn't out hunting or fishing or doing whatever it was Indians do. And there was poor

Squanto, another of their Indian friends, who had died of the fever in the last winter. She had been fond of him too. And, of course, there was Hobbamock, from the Wampanoag tribe, who now lived among them. No, Indians didn't frighten her anymore. She considered them a welcome break from the monotony that was life in Plymouth.

When she had emptied her bucket, she turned back toward the house and just happened to look up toward the street. There, standing at the fence, was *Nick Snow*! She could not believe her eyes! He had grown a mustache and his hair had gotten longer and he had it tied in a ponytail in the back just like the Indians wore it. He was wearing a fresh white shirt and was holding a wrapped package in his hands. And he was smiling that smile that made her smile right back whether she wanted to or not!

"Hello!" he called and waved to her.

Constance felt herself blushing again and she tried to smooth her hair down around her ears. *Just like a man*! she thought in exasperation. *Always embarrassing you by showing up when you look your worst*! Still, she was drawn to his smile like a magnet, and she walked across the yard trying not to grin like an idiot even though she felt like one. "Good day, Mister Snow," she said, trying hard to act casual and unaffected.

"A little warm today for gardening, isn't it?" he asked, smiling right through his words and reminding her of her outburst on the day they had met.

"Yes, it is, Mister Snow," she replied sheepishly.

"Can we agree to call each other by our *first* names? I feel like you are addressing my father when you call me *Mister Snow,*" said Nick.

"Yes, I suppose we could." Constance didn't know what else to say; her mouth seemed to be momentarily paralyzed.

Nick handed the package he was holding over the fence to her. "I've brought you something," he said. "I hope you like it."

"A gift? For *me*?" Constance wanted to pinch herself to be sure she wasn't dreaming. She took the package and came through the gate.

"Please, won't you come in?" she said leading him into the house. "Elizabeth! Look who came to visit us!"

Nick removed his hat and they all sat down at the table. Constance put the package down.

"May I get you something to drink, *Mister*…. ah …I mean *Nick*?"

"No. Please. Don't trouble yourself. I can't stay but a moment," he replied.

Elizabeth joined them at the table and little Caleb waddled up, reaching out for her to pick him up, while Constance sat staring at the package.

"Well, it won't open itself, Constance," said Nick.

She grasped at the twine and pulled the brown wrapping paper apart. When she unfolded it, there was the loveliest blue linen dress material she had ever seen! She wanted to cry out in joy! She wanted to dance around in a circle! She wanted to kiss him right on his face! "Oh!" was all she said. "It's beautiful, *Nick.*"

"Is it the right color?" he asked. "I thought blue would go perfectly with your blue eyes!"

Elizabeth was sitting there with a knowing smirk on her face and Constance had long stopped worrying that her cheeks were on fire.

"Thank you very much. I don't know quite what to say. It is very kind of you."

"Captain Pierce can get me more, if you tell me the colors you like," said Nick.

"You mustn't spend so much money on me," Constance replied, and she felt her eyelashes flutter involuntarily.

"Well, I am glad you like it. I wish I could stay but I'm in a bit of a hurry."

Constance stood up and held out her hand. "You must come to supper with us soon, then," she said.

He took her hand and Constance felt something like a bolt of lightning between their joined palms; something she had never felt before.

"Tomorrow, then?" Constance asked.

"I am afraid supper will have to wait. Hobbamock and I are going on a fishing and trading expedition on the *Little James*" he said. "I am not sure how long we will be gone."

Seeing the disappointment in Constance's eyes he added, "But, I promise that I will visit as soon as we return!"

And out the door he went, her blond-haired prince, leaving Constance standing there with her knees buckling and her eyes misting.

"Constance?" said Elizabeth.

Constance smiled.

"So, *he* is the one?" asked Elizabeth.

Constance just kept smiling. "Yes, Elizabeth. *He is the one!*"

Chapter Thirteen "A Failed Expedition"

The original crew that had sailed the *Little James* from England under Captain Emanuel Altham had already earned their reputation as troublemakers by the time they had first arrived in Plymouth. A mutinous pair, William Stephens, the gunner's mate, and Thomas Fell, the ship's carpenter, had bullied the rest of the crew into going on strike immediately upon learning they were to be paid in *shares* and not actual *wages,* as was the common practice in the cash- poor colony that was struggling to pay its debt to investors back in England. Even though they had signed on for six years, they claimed they had been duped by the leaders of Plymouth and it wasn't until Governor Bradford promised to *personally* pay their wages from his own pocket, that they settled down and agreed to continue the job of trading and fishing up and down the coast.

The *Little James* had undergone extensive repairs after her disastrous Atlantic voyage; her mainmast had to be replaced and her hull completely refinished. The six small cannons she had been equipped with back in Bristol were all removed and taken to the town's fort and the little ship had been stocked with all the exchangeable goods they could muster that might be attractive to the Indians and the other traders. They had enlisted Hobbamock to come along as an interpreter and Nick, always eager for an adventure, signed up to replace one of several sailors who had simply "run off' soon after their arrival from England. With their little plot of land planted, and Anthony promising to tend their crops until his brother returned, Nick was free to go. Although he didn't give voice to his feelings, Anthony was eager for a respite from the tedious Elder Brewster and Nick's absence was a convenient excuse to get away from his lessons for a while.

The town showed up to see the *Little James* off that April morning, as they hoisted the anchor aboard and sailed out of the harbor, going south around Cape Cod. Captain Altham, who the crew called "Captain Manny", was a likeable fellow but Nick and Hobbamock found the rest of the crew to be a lazy lot, more interested in drinking and sleeping than they were about trading or fishing. Constance was there, waving at the little ship as it disappeared from view. Nick was standing on the bow next to Hobbamock, waving back to her.

"She is to be your wife?" asked his Indian brother.

Nick shrugged. "I have not thought about that yet," he replied, which wasn't entirely true. Actually, he had thought about it a lot!

Hobbamock's eyebrows arched, and his eyes twinkled as he looked back at his friend.

They sailed south along the neck of the cape, through the straits of Nantucket and weaved through some smaller islands Hobbamock called *Noepe* and *Chappaquiddick,* taking their skiff ashore, filled with English goods; pottery, jewelry, and dry goods to trade, After the first attempt, Captain Manny and Hobbamock returned in the little boat empty handed. Apparently, the Dutch traders from the north had already been there and the Indians had no more need of English goods. Not to be discouraged, the captain ordered the men to sail on, dropping anchor at each small settlement along the way, where they got the same answer every time: *they were full up with English goods!* It was a disheartened and downtrodden captain that finally turned the ship around and headed back for Plymouth, the expedition being, so far, a complete failure.

Captain Manny wasn't ready to return to Governor Bradford with empty hands just yet, however. He had the crew drop anchor just outside Plymouth Harbor to chart their next course and refused to let the crew go ashore; he wanted them on board and ready to sail and did not want to have to go looking for them in town.

That night in his cabin, with Nick and Hobbamock at his side, he studied his maps of the fishing grounds to the north; at least they could fill the hold with barrels of salted codfish, even if their trading attempts had been futile. They all went to bed with a new plan of setting sail at first light; Captain Manny in his tiny cabin in the stern of the ship, Nick trying to squeeze his six-foot frame into the narrow wooden bunk below and Hobbamock, as was his custom, stretching out on his blanket on the deck.

When the ship was finally quiet, thoughts of Constance filled Nick's mind; her red hair that sparkled in the sun and the peppering of freckles across her nose. And her eyes! Those brilliant blue windows into her soul, that danced and spoke volumes without her mouth ever uttering a word! What a special young woman she was! Even when he closed his own eyes, he could see her, standing on the dock waving at him, as were all the other settlers beside her, but her uplifted hand was the only one he saw. All his plans of establishing himself before he thought of marriage quickly evaporated with the sight of her and he knew, in his heart, that he had fallen hopelessly in love!

Around midnight Nick awoke, feeling as if his bunk was moving. He sat up abruptly and then he heard it; the shrill whistling of the wind through the hatch and the sound of surf pounding against the ship's outer hull. *Had the captain raised the anchor*? *Why else would the ship be moving?* He jumped up and headed for the deck with the rest of the crew, wiping the sleep from their eyes, to see what had transpired.

A sudden storm had blown in from the Atlantic and was soon tossing the *Little James* around so violently she was soon separated from her anchor. She began spinning around in the swirling water and bouncing up and down with the strong current. The waves were pummeling her so hard they threatened to wash her out to sea, or worse, slam her into the dangerous sand bar known as Brown's Bank, which was dangerously close by. The shiftless crew, more concerned with their own necks than the fate of the ship, spent more time holding on than fastening down the cargo in the hold. The captain steadfastly gripped the tiller in his hands, standing drenched and windblown from the surf crashing over the quarterdeck. Nick and Hobbamock immediately rallied to his side.

"What can we do?" Nick asked, his voice on the edge of panic.

"Go below and get the axe from the hold!" said the captain and Nick ran off without a second thought, slipping down the stairs of the hatch, taking the steps two at a time. When he returned with the axe, the captain ordered him to go and cut down the main mast.

Nick was aghast at the thought. "*What possible good could that do*?" he asked, shocked at the suggestion of such a drastic action.

"The wind is too strong," yelled Captain Manny. "At least, we will not be at the wind's mercy if we have no mast!"

He did not fully understand the captain's logic, but he obeyed his orders, nevertheless, and started chopping away at the mast, while Hobbamock and the crew worked to loosen it from its riggings. When the axe had found the halfway point, Nick heard the wood begin to crack and splinter. He turned toward the captain.

"Give her a push and stand clear!" ordered Captain Manny.

Nick pushed it with his foot and watched as the mast went crashing down over the starboard side, taking a part of the ship's railing with it and toppled over into the water. The ship leaned over precariously, until the bottom of the broken mast slipped off into the ocean. At that point, all the crew could do was hang on and wait until the gale died down and then break out the oars to get back into the harbor.

Governor Bradford and the council were an unhappy lot when the *Little James* finally limped back to Plymouth the next morning, missing her main mast and requiring her deck and railings to be repaired. "All this for a failed trading expedition!" Bradford hollered at Captain Manny. "Is it the *ship* or is it *you* that is cursed, Captain Altham? I cannot understand how *one* vessel can have so many mishaps in such a short period of time!"

They were standing on the dock looking out at the *Little James,* that floated crippled and pathetic in the harbor, while the crew waited in silence to find out what the governor intended to do. He turned to one of the men on the dock. "Have we any replacements ready?" he asked.

The man nodded. "Aye, Governor. We have a pile of finished masts ready to ship back to England. We can have her up and sailing again in no time!"

"*Do* it then!" shouted the governor as he marched off the dock. "And, so help me, Altham, if you destroy the *Little James* again, I will take your command away from you and sue you for damages!"

Chapter Fourteen "Will's Secret"

On the very night that the gale ravaged Plymouth Harbor and destroyed the *Little James* with Nick on board, his cousin Will was sitting at a table in John Billington's shack near the bay, staring at the cards in his hand and listening to the wind blowing outside and the rhythmic dripping of the rain that was leaking through the roof.

 Billington had never hidden his hatred for the leaders of Plymouth Colony, especially his animosity for Captain Standish. Ever since the head of the Plymouth militia had threatened to tie his neck to his heels and leave him in the square for the entire town to laugh at, Billington was just waiting for an opportunity to get even. And, because it was the *court* that had sentenced him for being drunk and disorderly, he now had a deep loathing for the entire town council as well; Brewster, Bradford and the whole lot of them! Now the *pompous little generals*, as he liked to call them, had the nerve to complain about Billington's lack of motivation; they called his house a "hovel" and his plot of weed- choked fields a disgrace. Soon, no one in Plymouth wanted to associate with him. His only friends seemed to be the men sitting around his table; John Lyford, John Oldham and, of course, *Will Snow*.

At that moment, there was a knock on the door. Billington put down his cards and went to open it. Outside, in the blowing rain, stood two Indians. They took a step inside the room and no further, speaking to

Billington in low whispers and Will realized they were not the usual Wampanoags that frequented Plymouth; no, these were two strangers, and their manner was not that of *friendly* Indians.

"Tomorrow then," said Billington.

"Three barrels," replied one of the Indians.

"Aye," answered Billington. "*When the work is done.*"

The Indians left and Billington sat back down in his chair. "Now, let's see…. where *was* I?" he said.

"You were hiring Indians to cultivate your fields," remarked Will.

Billington nodded and played his cards.

"How do you expect to pay them?" asked Will. "You still owe *me* for the last five hands!"

Billington lowered his voice. "In *gun powder*," he said, in a voice barely above a whisper, as if anyone could hear him over the thunder outside.

Will raised his eyebrows but only slightly to disguise his shock. He knew there was a severe penalty for selling guns or ammunition to the Indians. He also knew his companions were known to defy the strict laws set in Plymouth; the limits on the amounts of beer one could make, the law against gambling on the Sabbath, and the like, but he had never known any of them to go this far! "Well, it's *your* neck they'll stretch," he said.

"And, you will keep your mouth shut about it, Snow," Billington said.

Will nodded, unnerved at the threatening tone of Billington's voice.

It bothered him all the way home that night and even after he had climbed into his bed, he tossed back and forth fretfully. When he finally fell asleep, he began to dream. He could see Billington's Indians, running down the street setting fire to all the roofs and raiding the stores in the Common House. Women and children were screaming, and the men of Plymouth were loading their muskets, while tomahawks were flying at them... He bolted upright in his bed, sweating profusely, and shaking as if he were coming down off a three-day drinking binge. Will laid there awake for most of the night, wondering what he should do. How would be ever separate himself from his evil companions now without arousing their suspicions? Should he tell his cousins what was afoot? Without an answer in his head, he finally fell back to sleep.

Anthony had already gone to the fields to work when Will finally climbed out of his bed. He splashed cold water on his face and put on his boots, not feeling very good about himself; he had let his cousins down and yet they never said a harsh word to him. *What would they* think if they knew the wages that had been supporting the Snow household was only money won in a card game? For once in his life, he felt ashamed of who he was. Nick was at sea on the *Little James* and Anthony was out laboring in the fields, both thinking their cousin was doing his share to support their household, when Will knew he had spent his hours gambling and getting drunk. *After all they have done for you!* he thought miserably. Still, he knew he had to break away from Billington and the others *gradually* so that they wouldn't suspect his intentions. He knew far too much about their shady dealings and he was fearful of getting on their bad side. He walked out onto the street, standing there for a moment, not knowing which way to go. He could take the road out to the Billington house, where he knew there were barrels of cool beer in the larder that could ease his pain and blot out his guilty conscience. Or he could march down to the land he owned with his cousins and bare his soul to Anthony, begging his forgiveness? He did not hesitate for long. Suddenly, there was a throng of people rushing past him toward the bay.

"The *Little James*!" someone said to him in passing. "She wrecked on the cape!"

Will started running along with them. *Nick was on the Little James*! He ran faster. *What if his cousin was dead? It couldn't be true!* His head was exploding with remorse and dread by the time he reached the dock and saw the little ship floating in the harbor, her masts gone, her bulwarks smashed. He watched the group of men climbing down from the crippled ship and coming ashore in the long boat anxiously until he spied Nick's yellow hair among the others.

Thank You God! thought Will, surprised at the urgency in his heart, surprised that he had voiced a prayer at *all*. He was *not* a religious man. After living the kind of life he had lived, knowing he had broken most of God and man's laws at one point or another, the mere admission of God's existence and the possibility of going to hell was not something he relished thinking about. Still, seeing his cousin alive and unhurt when he could have been killed suddenly made him want to thank *someone!*

When the news of the disaster that had befallen the *Little James* reached the Hopkins house, Constance immediately ran out into the street and down to the docks, where a crowd had already assembled. The sight of the poor broken ship in the harbor was heartbreaking and she too looked through the crowd for Nick, hoping he had not drowned or been injured in the mishap. She spied him there, talking to the governor and Captain Standish and she just froze in place; taking a rare opportunity to stare at him without his knowledge. *What a handsome man he is!* she thought happily. *My future husband!*

For an instant, she wasn't sure if she had said the words out loud and she suddenly reached up and covered her mouth with her hand. Glancing around, it seemed no one was looking at her, so she was convinced she had said the words only in her head. Then she turned on her heels and ran back to the house where Elizabeth was standing in the doorway.

"What news Constance? Have they all come home safe?" Elizabeth asked.

"Yes," answered Constance. "He is just fine."

Elizabeth cocked her head to one side. "I asked about *all* of the men, Constance. Did you inquire about the welfare of *all* the men on the *Little James*?"

Constance lowered her head. "Oh, Elizabeth, I didn't think," she said. "I was only concerned about Nick Snow."

"Well, you might have asked about the rest of the crew," replied Elizabeth. "Have you invited him to supper tonight?"

Constance shook her head. "I wanted to change into my new dress first," she said.

Elizabeth returned to her sewing and lowered herself clumsily down into the chair, her advanced stage of pregnancy making her feel exhausted from the few steps to the front door. She smiled down at her son who was playing on the floor. "Caleb, I do believe your big sister has fallen in love!"

Chapter Fifteen "New Babies and New Rules"

And what an elusive beau he was turning out to be! Constance bathed as best she could in the small basin they kept in the house, braided her long red hair and had just wiggled into her new blue dress, when her father returned home with the disappointing news; the *Little James* was going back out to sea as soon as the new mast could be installed. Nick had asked her forgiveness, but the crew had been ordered to begin the repairs immediately and it looked as though they would be working into the night.

"He promised to come to supper after they return," said Stephen.

Constance's face took on a dejected expression. "That's what he said the last time," she said flatly.

"Constance, you must be patient," Elizabeth said, trying to soothe her stepdaughter's wounded pride. "Tis a *good* thing he is such a hard worker! You mustn't let him know he has disappointed you!"

Constance knew Elizabeth was right. She shouldn't fault Nick for doing his duty. Still, it all seemed like such a bother, getting all dressed up for nothing! She changed out of her blue dress, smoothing it out and hanging it up in the corner and went to the kitchen to peel potatoes for their supper.

"What's this I hear?" asked Stephen grinning. "Has my daughter got her eye on Nick Snow?"

"And don't you *dare* say a word to him Father!" said Constance.

Stephen chuckled.

"Honestly, Father, if you embarrass me, I'll…." said Constance.

"Oh, I won't say a word," said her father. "My, how you take on, Constance! Poor Nick has no idea what trouble he is in for!"

She wrinkled her nose in his direction and turned back to her potatoes. "You sit down and rest, Elizabeth," she said sweetly. "I'll take care of supper tonight."

Stephen smiled and took his wife by the hand. "You can even have my chair!" he said kissing her sweetly.

The baby was weeks overdue, and they were all doing what they could to help Elizabeth around the house. Giles had tried taking one-year-old Caleb out to the fields, where he would put him on a blanket in the shade but frequently would have to stop working and run to recapture the lively toddler who had crawled off into the dirt. Elizabeth had put a stop to the practice, however, when Giles informed her that he couldn't keep Caleb from eating *bugs*. After that, he helped water the garden in the evenings, while Constance cooked and cleaned and kept the household running. After the recent loss of two babies to the dreaded fever, the Hopkins family was eager to welcome a new little one.

They hadn't long to wait. Somewhere between the changing of the midnight guard at the Plymouth fort and the cackling of the Hopkins' flock of chickens with the morning sun, little Deborah Hopkins was born. Stephen had relinquished his place in the big feather bed with the commencement of his wife's labor and had curled up next to Giles on the floor near the hearth. Constance took over the midwife duties so efficiently Elizabeth was surprised and pleased at how mature her step- daughter had become. When she handed the freshly- scrubbed, swaddled infant to her, Elizabeth reached out and took Constance by the hand. "I could not be prouder of you, had I bore you from my own body," she whispered.

Constance smiled. She had a deep fondness for his father's second wife, and they got along most handsomely. Still, it seemed that the memory of her dead mother always seemed to be a barrier to the true intimacy between a parent and her child and she could just never bring herself to call her anything but *Elizabeth*. Somehow, experiencing the birth of little Deborah gave Constance a new set of feelings for her stepmother.

"You rest now, *Mother,*" she said quietly, as she put out the flame in the oil lamp and soon fell asleep in her father's chair.

With the excitement of having a new baby in the house, Constance temporarily put Nick Snow out of her mind. She was too busy to see them off at the dock when the *Little James* set sail again two days later, with Captain Altham at the tiller and the same sullen, mutinous crew under his command. Having Nick and Hobbamock along was a godsend for him, the captain told them, as they were the only two he truly felt he could trust.

The winds and the currents were favorable and soon they had anchored in the fishing grounds between Damaris Cove and Pemaquid, looking up at the strange face of the rocky Maine shoreline; square, chiseled rocks that were piled like a child's toy blocks precariously one on top of the other, jutting upward as if they were heaved by God himself. Some were carpeted in brilliant orange and yellow lichens, while others were whitewashed with gull droppings and behind them stood a forest of deep green fir trees and fields of wild lupine at their feet, flashing purple in the sunshine. Nick had never seen anything so beautiful.

"I wish I were an artist," he told Hobbamock. "It is a shame to leave this scene to a fading memory."

Hobbamock, who had seen the scenery many times before, no longer looked upon it with awe, but he agreed with Nick that it was, indeed, beautiful. The captain hardly noticed the scenery he was so determined to return to Plymouth with a ship load of fish and furs.

"Let's get the lines in the water," he hollered to the crew. "We have no time to waste!"

Nick and Hobbamock had no sooner retrieved the poles and began baiting the hooks when, suddenly, there was a commotion below decks and the sound of footsteps and angry voices. Stephens and Fell emerged through the hatch and cornered the captain on the quarterdeck.

From the heated conversation that ensued, Nick and Hobbamock learned that Captain Manny had made a few changes since their previous trip, to eliminate more problems and increase the chances of success. Apparently, he had taken on fewer rations of food to make room for more fish that he hoped to catch off the coast of Maine and he had forbidden any alcohol to be brought on board, only barrels of fresh water. The news was not announced to the crew until now, when they were safely under sail. At first, the crew had confronted the cook and when they learned he had only followed the captain's orders, Stephens and Fell had rushed to the deck and were now threatening to blow up the ship with gun powder if Captain Manny didn't turn the ship around and return to Plymouth for more supplies.

"It's bad enough we signed on with a cursed ship!" yelled Stephens. "But you have no right to *starve* us!"

"I am *not* taking the *Little James* all the way back to Plymouth," Captain Manny said adamantly, trying to remain calm. "There are ample stores if we aren't wasteful."

Stephens and Fell were having nothing of it. "*You will turn this ship around or it will be a long swim back for you, Captain*!" he said, standing in front of the crew who remained mute and terrified of what was happening. Captain Manny knew the danger he was in, but he did not back down.

"I can spare *two* men to take the long boat back, if you believe we need more supplies," he said calmly. "But the ship will continue on its course."

Hobbamock and Nick looked at each other nervously. Blowing up the ship was beyond anything they thought even *this* crew capable of. They knew the captain had to stand his ground if he had any hopes of making any profit at all on this trip. They all stood frozen, the crew grumbling and whispering amongst themselves, until finally Stephens broke the silence.

"Fell and I will go," he said, and they went below for their belongings, while the crew lowered the long boat over the side. After they stood there watching the two troublemakers rowing out of the little harbor, Captain Manny turned to Nick and whispered, "*I doubt that they will be back*. In any event, I don't intend to remain here and wait for them."

Nick suspected as much was true; they were well rid of the two troublemakers.

"Hoist the anchor!" yelled the captain. "We're heading for Pemaquid!"

Chapter Sixteen "Caleb and the *Smart* Pills"

There *was* an unexpected arrival in Plymouth harbor the very next day, but it wasn't the longboat from the *Little James.* Instead, it was Captain Pierce returning from England with more supplies and livestock on his new ship, *Charity.* He had waited for the tide to be at its lowest, which facilitated the unloading of the cows and goats very nicely. Instead of chancing damages to his longboats again, Pierce lowered the animals directly into the shallow water and let them swim ashore with several crew members, who swam alongside them to be sure none of them panicked and drowned.

While the cattle were taken to the large holding pen on the outskirts of town, the goats were adopted out to several families to raise in their backyards and the Hopkins family suddenly had two new members: a noisy nanny and her young kid.

"What about my garden, Father?" Constance protested. "You must build a fence to keep them from eating all my vegetables and flowers!"

Stephen agreed and temporarily tied the goats up with ropes, until he could construct a pen for them at the back of the yard. Constance soon learned how to get milk for the household and Giles was assigned the responsibility of cleaning up after them. Little Caleb loved the goats, for since his birth the only animals the Hopkins family owned had been chickens, which did not like to be petted and held in his tiny arms. Every day when either Constance or Giles went outside, their little brother was right behind them, begging to go see the goats.

It was morning and Giles was raking up the goat droppings into a pile, while Constance milked the nanny goat, when little Caleb walked up behind his big brother and pointed to the mound of shiny black pellets beneath the rake.

His little eyes shined as the toddler asked, "Those bugs?"

"No," replied Giles. "Those are *smart* pills."

"*Bugs*!" insisted Caleb stubbornly as he approached the manure pile.

"Go ahead and *eat* one, Caleb," said Giles. "Those pills will make you *smart!*"

Constance stood up from her pail of goat milk when she heard the mischief Giles was up to. "Giles Hopkins!" she yelled. "Don't you *dare* tell him to eat those! *Smart pills indeed!*"

Before Constance could stop him, Caleb picked up one of the little black "pills" and popped it into his mouth. He immediately started coughing and spitting and crying. "*Taste bad!*" he wailed.

Giles fell on the ground, laughing hysterically, when Constance shot him a vengeful look and scooped up the toddler, taking him to the house to wash his mouth out. "Mother will hear about this!" she snapped. "Giles, you are *ever* so mean!"

Elizabeth rarely disciplined Giles or Constance but merely reported any childish transgressions and yielded any punishments to their father. She waited, however, until Stephen had finished his supper and was relaxed after his second mug of beer before she mentioned what had transpired that day.

Stephen sat mute at the table, until Elizabeth had told the whole tale then he turned to his son.

"Is this true, Giles?" he asked. "What on *earth* would make you do such a thing?

Giles squirmed under his father's glare. "I'm sorry. It just seemed funny at the time. Caleb is *always* putting things in his mouth, Father! Bugs, rocks, flowers! I just wanted to teach him a lesson," he replied.

Stephen leaned back and shook his head. "But why *smart pills?*"

"Because," said Giles, "I thought if he ate one it would make him so smart, he'd never put anything in his mouth again!"

Stephen could not help himself. His face turned red, and he let loose with the biggest laugh Constance had ever heard. Elizabeth was mortified but she said nothing.

Constance began to clear the table. She was disgusted with both her father and her little brother. *Men can be so vulgar!* she thought. *Laughing at such a disgusting trick played on poor little Caleb!*

She was beginning to think men were a separate species, one she would *never* understand!

Chapter Seventeen "The Curse of the *Little James*"

Captain Manny was correct in his choice of a fishing spot. Before long, the crew was pulling in cod so fast they had only to drop their lines into the water before they felt the tug of a bite on the hook. Soon the barrels in the hold were filling up with salted fish.

"You see?" the captain said to the men as they sat down to eat their supper that night. "I knew we would be going home soon! We did not need the extra supplies!"

The grumbling died down with regard to the rations, but the complete lack of liquor still did not sit well with the crew.

"Water is for plants and fish!" said one sailor, sitting next to Nick and Hobbamock, looking down with disdain at his cup of cold water.

Nick laughed. "The fish are practically jumping aboard!" he said to the sailor. "At this rate, we'll be back in Plymouth by the end of the week, and you'll have all the beer you want!"

The captain wasn't really concerned about another uprising; without Stephens and Fell to lead them, the rest of the crew were too stupid and cowardly to doing anything on their own. So, after their supper everyone went to bed to get a good night's sleep, the grumbles quickly turning to snores.

It was like a recurring dream; Nick awoke around midnight again, feeling his bunk moving under him. When he first opened his eyes and looked around in the darkness, he was still unsure if he was awake. Realizing the ship *was* actually heaving, he jumped up and climbed up the stairs where he found the crew battening down for a storm. The winds and currents were so strong they were pushing the *Little James* toward the same rocks Nick had thought were so beautiful that very morning; the anchor chain made a strange squeaking sound as it strained to its very limits against the hull. All at once, the ship lurched when the anchor broke loose and capsized, rolling over and finally crashing into the rocks. There had not been enough time to cut down the mast this time and no need; it came crashing down on its own, the splintering main yard falling directly on two of the crewmen, crushing the life out of them instantly. Nick saw the boatswain's mate go over the side, screaming as he tried to hang on to the shrouds that were still attached to the mast. He looked around for Hobbamock and saw him on the quarterdeck with the captain; they, too, were just holding on to anything that would keep them from being washed overboard and onto the rocks.

By the time the storm had passed through, the *Little James* was firmly planted on the rocks, with two gaping holes in her side through which the sea had flooded the hold with sea water. What remained of the crew climbed down onto the rocks, bringing what supplies had not been ruined by the salt water with them. They buried the two crewmen in the sandy earth nearby and searched up and down the shore for the missing boatswain's mate without success.

"Damaris Cove is the closest," announced the captain. "We'll walk that way and surely we can catch a ship going south to Plymouth."

As the soaked and exhausted crew set out, leaving the crippled ship behind them that was impaled on the jagged rocks, Nick couldn't help but think how fortunate he was to be alive when he looked back at the *Little James*! They had lost everything; three men, the salt, the fish and all their trading goods. The captain's log books and all his personal belongings had been washed away out to sea. Hobbamock swore it was the *last* time he was going to go to sea on a ship. Captain Manny remained silent for much of the hike, knowing his sailing days were most likely over.

Fortunately for Captain Manny and his crew, Damaris Cove was a fishing town with a resident shipbuilder and when they reached the town the captain was directed to him. They wasted no time recruiting the man and the captain left in his skiff to see if there was anything they could do to salvage the ship from the rocks while the rest of the crew stayed behind. When they returned the shipbuilder said he thought he could save the *Little James* but demanded payment before he started the job. They elected Hobbamock to go by land back to Plymouth to take the message and the offer to Governor Bradford. When his Indian brother was leaving, he said to Nick, "I am happy to walk home. Never again will I set foot on a white man's ship!"

Nick smiled and gripped Hobbamock's hand. "I will see you soon my friend," he said.

Then all they had to do was wait to hear from the Governor. Hobbamock made good time, even though he only traveled at night and found a safe place to sleep in the daytime. It was not because of the wild animals but rather the *Mohawks*, who were known enemies of the Wampanoag, that he slipped silently under cover of darkness along the coast until he reached Plymouth.

Bradford's face went purple when he heard the news and he ranted for quite a while, while Hobbamock waited for his decision. Finally, the governor had some men pack up all but five hundred beaver skins he had hoped would be a payment to the investors back in England and sent them on a small boat up the coast. Hobbamock refused to go along and returned to tell Anthony and Will the news.

When the furs from Bradford were received, a group of carpenters and coopers from Damaris Cove, accompanied by the crew of the *Little James,* went out to the crash site and spent a day and a night raising her up using water-tight barrels. When the tide came in, the rising water lifted the ship off the rocks and they hauled it back to Damaris Cove, where three weeks later she was ready for sea again and the crew finally returned to Plymouth.

It was all for naught, however. Once Bradford had time to think about the situation, he made a decision; in his opinion, the *Little James* had been so plagued with disaster he had decided to send it back to the owners in England. He wanted no more to do with it! He had her loaded with the last of the beaver pelts, fired the captain and sent the *Little James* back to London with Stephens and Fell in charge.

Not surprising, the beaver skins never reached England. Rumors circulated (probably by Stephens and Fell themselves) that the ship, with its cargo of beaver skins, had been sacked by pirates a short distance from London Harbor, forcing the crew to swim ashore.

Whatever her fate, the *Little James* was never seen again!

Chapter Eighteen "The Letters"

Poor Will had still not managed to get the courage to break away from the town troublemakers, Billington, Lyford and Oldham, but it was a matter that was soon to be taken out of his hands.

Will had been learning a great deal about his companions over the many hours he had spent with them and none of it was *good*. To begin with, John Lyford was actually *Reverend John Lyford,* ordained in the Church of England, but his reasons for coming to America were *anything* but religious! He was an opportunist, always looking to gain from others' misfortunes. Lyford was well- educated and had a good command of the English language, but his lack of ethics would have made him a better politician than a minister. Because William Brewster and the Church of Plymouth had influence over most of the townsfolk, no one took Lyford's preaching very seriously and it provoked him to no end. It occurred to him, that if he defamed Elder Brewster back in England, he might have a chance of feathering his own flock so he took it upon himself to write a series of letters to the investors, claiming *un-Christian practices on the part of Brewster and the other leaders of Plymouth*. One of his claims was that *only sworn members of the Plymouth Church* (which was against the practices of the Church of England) *were given favors when it came to land grants and the division of livestock*. He insisted that his *own dear friend, John Billington, had struggled to build his own house without the assistance of the other colonists and that now his poorly constructed abode was being ridiculed by these so- called Christians.* The truth of the matter was that the men of Plymouth *had* attempted to help Billington build his house, as they did for every new settler, but every day found him drunk and unable to assist in the work. They had finally stopped trying, telling him he would just have to build it himself.

It was the same with the cultivation of his land. Billington, wrote Lyford, *was forced to hire Indians at his own expense, to help him get his crops planted, with nary so much as a finger lifted by his neighbors.* He blamed Elder Brewster's slander as *the reason the people shunned him, leaving his family on the verge of starvation.* He then sealed the letters and sent them off with John Oldham to deliver to Captain Pierce just before the *Charity* set sail back to England. It was clear that he had no qualms about implicating his friends in his dastardly plot. So, when all the messiness of the *Little James* matter had finally been resolved, the governor had yet another situation to unravel.

On an afternoon in mid-August, just before the busy fall harvest came upon them, he called a town meeting and summoned everyone in Plymouth to be present. The whole town filed into the meeting room and those who could not find a seat on the narrow benches stood leaning against the outer wall or squatting in the aisle. Facing them, at a long table in the front, was Governor

Bradford and Elder Brewster, while Captain Standish stood guarding the rear door. Everyone was there including the Hopkins family, with Elizabeth holding baby Deborah and Constance trying to keep Caleb still and quiet. The Snow brothers and their cousin Will were in the back of the room, as was John Billington. No one in the audience had any clue what was about to take place, although everyone had their suspicions; Will Snow was just *sure* it had something to do with the gunpowder and the strange Indians. When the governor first called John Lyford and John Oldham to come forward and testify, the would-be minister and his unfortunate partner stood up nervously and walked to the front of the room, facing the leaders of Plymouth, not knowing they were about to be blind-sided.

What no one in the room knew except the governor and his council, was that Bradford had previously discovered Lyford's plot to discredit the Plymouth leaders and, on a tip from Captain Pierce, he had confiscated the letters as evidence. It was a long time in coming but Bradford welcomed it. It gave him reason to, once and for all, get rid of the two most troublesome people in Plymouth; Lyford for his treason and Oldham for being a generally disruptive person who had, on more than one occasion, scuffled with Captain Standish and, of course, for taking part in the treachery by delivering the letters to Pierce.

The governor was sitting there in his usual starched blue suit and wide brimmed black hat, and he stood up and cleared his throat. "I have called you all together," he began, "so that charges against these men John Lyford and his co-conspirator, John Oldham, may be read and addressed by the general counsel and witnessed by the good citizens of Plymouth."

He paused and began again, speaking to a room as quiet as a crypt except for the fussing of babes in their mother's arms. "John Lyford," said the governor. "You are charged with intent to slander and plot against the colony of Plymouth. John Oldham you are charged with participating and facilitating this plot and for additional acts of insubordination against Captain Standish and failure to follow the laws of our town."

John Lyford was standing very still and appeared to be weaving in place, as if he were about to faint and fall over. *He looks drunk*! Constance thought, in horror. Oldham stood beside him, nervously wringing his hands, as the suspense in the room was building to a feverish but silent pitch.

"Is it true that you, John Lyford, have written derogatory letters to our investors in London?" he asked, staring directly at the accused.

Lyford didn't speak immediately. It appeared he was trying to plan his words carefully. "Is writing letters a *sin* in the eyes of Plymouth Church?" he asked smugly.

"This, Sir, is a *civil* proceeding, *not* the Plymouth Church," replied Bradford. "But, if the letters were written with malice against the good people of Plymouth, I would have to say yes, that *would be* a sin."

This time it was Elder Brewster's turn to look smug.

"I deny these charges," said Lyford flatly. He watched as the governor reached down and produced several documents that appeared to be letters. At that point, his eyes visibly *bulged,* and he and Oldham exchanged worried glances.

"With your permission, Mister Lyford," said the governor. "I shall read these letters for the good people of Plymouth to decide whether or not they constitute *slander.*"

"Those cannot be my letters!" shouted Lyford. "My letters sailed with Captain Pierce weeks ago!"

"I assure you they *are,* Sir," said Bradford. "This is a letter addressed to Master John Sherley." He began reading the letter, as the audience gasped and shook their heads. Finally, the governor paused to catch his breath and finished with, "and I quote: *these so-called saintly people will not assist anyone lest he join the Church of Plymouth.* Are those your words, Sir?"

Lyford hung his head. There was dead silence in the room.

"Stephen Hopkins!" called the governor. "Are you a member of the Church of Plymouth?"

There were snickers in the crowd. Stephen Hopkins' opinions on religion were no secret to the people of Plymouth. Constance watched as her father stood up; on his face was an expression she could not quite read.

"No, Governor, I am not!" he said loudly.

There were more snickers.

"And did the good people of Plymouth *help* you with the construction of your house and in the clearing of your land?"

"Aye, that they did, Sir," answered Hopkins and he sat back down.

"Captain Myles Standish!"

The little captain standing at the rear door straightened his back and stood at attention.

"Are *you* a member of the Church of Plymouth?" asked Bradford, raising his voice to be heard in the rear of the room.

"No, Sir, I am not!" answered the captain.

"And have you always been treated with respect from the good people of Plymouth?"

"Aye," replied Standish. "Except for the two scoundrels who stand before you now!"

There were more snickers in the crowd.

"And you, John Oldham," the governor went on. "Do you deny delivering these letters to Captain Pierce to be sent back to England?"

Oldham shook his head. "But I did not know what was *in* the letters, Governor, Sir," he said weakly. His shoulders slumped and he sat down on the bench, but Lyford remained standing, his eyes circling the audience until they focused on John Billington and Will Snow in the back of the room. "*John Billington! Will Snow! Tell* them I only wrote down the complaints of others!" he pleaded. Then he addressed the audience at large. "*And, what of the crime of stealing another's mail*? Is the governor of this fine colony above the law?"

Governor Bradford looked out over his constituents. "Perhaps," he said, "I can be faulted for opening these letters. And I shall accept whatever consequences that action would bring. But news and suspicion of these men's mischief had reached me from reliable sources and investigations require *investigation!* I could not have made these men answer for their crimes without evidence!"

Lyford then changed his demeanor as quickly as a chameleon changes its color. He turned and threw himself upon the mercy of citizens of Plymouth. "Please," he begged. "I have a family…. *children!*"

"Let it never be said that the town of Plymouth does not have compassion," replied Bradford. "John Lyford, you and your family may remain in Plymouth for a probationary period of six months. During that time, you must not step over the boundaries of the laws of God or Plymouth, or you will be banished permanently!"

"And what of me?" asked Oldham meekly.

The governor looked at him and obviously took pain in the words he spoke. "While it is true we cannot prove *positively* that you had knowledge of the content of the letters, Mister Oldham, in the matter of insubordination and your general disrespect for the law you have continually required reprimand! We must ask you to leave Plymouth immediately. Your wife and children may remain here through the winter or until you have found other accommodations for them. *Wherever* you settle, I hope this matter has taught you a stern lesson." He, then, looked out at the faces in the crowd. "Does anyone of you have any objections to the sentences that have just been issued? If so, please indicate by raising your hand."

Not a hand was raised. The only tears in the room were on the face of poor Mrs. Oldham, who had just lost her husband.

Chapter Nineteen "The Color of a Dress"

The crowd trickled out into the street, tongues wagging in awe of the event that had just transpired. Farmers returned to their fields, masons to their mortar boxes and tailors to their thread and thimbles, their lives not particularly impacted by the sentences that had just been handed down by the governor. The cowardly defendants, Lyford and Oldham, escaped quietly through a back door of the meeting house to avoid attention, while the two unfortunate women who had just witnessed their husbands being shamed in front of the entire town, were left to fend for themselves. Mistress Lyford scuttled her children around her like chicks under a hen's wings and scurried to the sanctuary of her home, where she could shut out the eyes staring at her. Mistress Oldham was even more pathetic still, with tears still rolling in salty sheets over her face and her confused little ones clutching at her skirts, she hurried off down the street.

"I feel so sorry for their wives and children," Elizabeth remarked. "It was a terrible situation these men put their families in."

Stephen nodded his head in agreement.

"We really shouldn't fault their wives," said Constance defiantly. "It's not *their* fault they married such scoundrels!"

"Yes," said Stephen Hopkins, "Elizabeth, my Dear, are you not fortunate that you captured me, *the pillar of Plymouth society*?"

"Father! How you go on about yourself!" said Constance, reaching down to hoist young Caleb up onto her hip.

"I hope you fare as well in your choice of a husband, Constance," he continued. "You must be very selective!"

"Shhhhhh!" Constance said, holding her finger to her lips, afraid her father was going to blurt out his name!

At that precise moment, someone came up behind Constance and spoke to Caleb who was leaning over her shoulder. The toddler was smiling. Constance turned and came face to face with Nick Snow, grinning as he always did, and tickling Caleb's chubby chin. It was to her father, however, that he spoke first. "Was all of this a surprise to you, Hopkins?" he asked.

Stephen shook his head. "Not at all," he replied. "Those two should have been gone a long time ago! I think the governor was far too lenient with them!"

"They could not have just turned their wives and children out in the winter, Father!" said Constance.

"No, not their families, I suppose," said Stephen. He turned and looked at Nick. "But some time spent in the stockade for those two would have been appropriate in my opinion."

Nick joined stride with the Hopkins family.

"We are finished with work for today, Nick. Why don't you come and have supper with us? I'm anxious to hear your version of the *Little James* story!"

Constance held her breath. *At least, she had worn her new blue dress!*

"I would like that," said Nick. "If it wouldn't be too much trouble for the ladies to set an extra place at your table!"

"Your brother and your cousin are welcome, as well," said Stephen looking around.

Anthony, who was walking a few paces behind them, begged off, saying he had promised the Brewsters he would sup with them. "Thank you," he said. "Perhaps, next time."

Cousin Will had disappeared in the crowd.

They continued down the road from the fort, Elizabeth walking along next to Stephen followed by Nick and Constance, holding little Caleb.

"By the way, Constance," whispered Nick. "Your dress is beautiful! You are a very talented seamstress!"

Constance blushed. "It is easy to sew when you have such fine material to work with. I have you to thank for that."

"I must confess," Nick went on. "I did it as much for me as I did for you! It pleasures me to see you in such a fine dress! I could hardly take my eyes off you all through the meeting!"

Stephen turned around with a twinkle in his eye and Constance just knew he was about to say something embarrassing. Instead, he just winked at her and said nothing.

When they arrived at the Hopkins house, Constance put little Caleb down on the floor and Elizabeth retired the baby to her cradle. Stephen pulled up the floorboards in the corner of the room and pulled up a sealed cask of beer from the crawlspace. "Constance, fetch us two mugs from the shelf," he ordered. "You have two thirsty men here!"

I actually feel married! she thought at that moment. *This must be what marriage is like! Fetching food and drink for a husband*. It would have been perfect had the rest of the household members not come barging through the door at that precise moment, ruining the mood. Giles with one of his friends, Ed Dotey and Ed Leister who were engaged in an argument over the outcome of the trial, and Stephen Deane who called to Constance, smiling, "Bring me a mug too would you, Con?"

While the men engaged in their discussions, Constance and Elizabeth quietly began to prepare their supper.

"You should change out of your new dress, Constance," said Elizabeth. "You might get it dirty."

Constance was not about to change into her faded old dress! "I will be very careful," she replied.

"Well at least put my apron on!" said Elizabeth.

The interaction was not missed by Nick Snow, who sat with one ear tuned to the conversation and one eye that never lost sight of Constance. Nor was Nick's attention to Constance lost on her other admirers in the room. Stephen Deane's face reflected a quiet jealousy that brewed beneath the surface, while the two "Ed's" shared an expression of defeat.

By the time the table was cleared, the cask of beer had been emptied and all the men in the Hopkins household were anxious for sleep, Constance was in the yard scraping the dishes off into the dirt for the chickens, with a permanent smile on her lips. The remnants of sunshine were poking through the pine trees, leaving points of light in the strands of her red hair and the evening breeze rustled the skirts of her blue dress. Never had she felt so much contentment.

Nick Snow emerged from the house, having said his goodbyes to Stephen and Elizabeth, and paused at the fence, watching her. When she sensed he was there, she turned toward him, her eyes locking with his silently. "Are you leaving?" she asked.

Nick came around through the gate and took the plates from her, setting them aside and grasping her two hands in his own. The moon that was just beginning to rise had quickly taken the place of the setting sun and the glow on her hair changed from golden to silver. Feeling the warmth of her hands in his, he looked down into her face. "I asked Captain Pierce to bring some more fabric from London," he said.

Constance was pleased but she had to protest to be polite. She could hardly think of anything but the touch of his hands on hers and her mind was spinning. "Nick, you mustn't spend your money on me!"

"I hope I picked the right color this time," he said. "I know very little of such things."

"The right color for a dress you mean?" asked Constance.

"What color do you prefer?" Nick was grinning at her; she could see his teeth white in the moonlight.

"For a dress?"

"Yes, Constance," said Nick softly. "What color fabric would you like for your *wedding dress?*"

She could hardly believe her ears! Her heart began pounding in her chest and her hands started shaking against his. He raised his hands and cupped her chin in them.

Kiss me! Kiss me! Kiss me! she was screaming silently.

And he did; a long, wet, passionate locking of her lips and his, with the tickle of his mustache under her nose and his arms as tight as swaddling around her shoulders. She seemed to be floating on a cloud of emotion and excitement; even after he released her, she felt as if her feet were still levitating off the ground. Nick squeezed her hand one last time before he walked out of the gate into the street. Before she lost sight of him, she suddenly came out of her trance.

"*Nick*!" she heard herself calling after him. When he turned around, she added, *"Any color will do!"*

She heard him laugh as he disappeared down the darkened street.

Chapter Twenty "Will's Confession"

When Nick entered the Snow house, Anthony and Will were already there; Anthony studying at the table and Will with his stockinged feet on the hearth, staring into the fire. They both looked up at Nick and immediately questioned the reason for the broad smile on his face.

"*I'm getting married*!" Nick blurted out.

Anthony threw back his head in laughter. "*You*? The fish that couldn't be caught?" he asked. "That Constance Hopkins must be quite the little angler!"

Will smiled half-heartedly at the news for his mind was filled with other matters. "Congratulations," he said without emotion.

Nick was surprised at Will's lack of interest. "What's the matter Will?" he asked. "Aren't you glad to hear my news?"

Will pulled his knees into his chest and sighed. "I have an apology to make to both of you."

Nick looked at Anthony for explanation but received only a shrug from his brother. "Apology for *what* Will?" he asked.

Will took a deep breath and bit his lip nervously. Confessions and apologies did not come easy for him; *in truth they never came to him at all*! He continued to stare into the fire and spoke directly into the flames, as if they could sear away his guilt. "That could have been *me* today," he began.

He had his cousins' full attention with that statement, and he continued. "I knew all about what Lyford and Oldham were doing! I *knew* and I did *nothing*!"

Will finally turned from the fire and looked directly at them, surprised at the *lack* of surprise in *their* eyes.

Anthony was the first to respond. "We have known all along that you were no longer working for Mister Derby and that you had taken up with Billington and his friends. Did you really think no one in this small town would talk, Will?"

"Did you take *part* in their plot or were you merely a *witness* to it?" asked Nick.

Will shook his head. "I was sworn to keep my mouth shut," he said. "But…."

Anthony's face took on an almost angry expression. "But *what?*"

"There was more mischief going on than what was revealed today, I'm afraid," said Will. "*Much more.*"

"If you know something that will harm the people of Plymouth, Will, you need to say so! Tell us what you know!" said Anthony.

Will went on to tell them about the gunpowder deals between Billington and the Indians. "I was afraid that would come out! I have never been so afraid in my life!" he said.

Nick sat down across from Anthony at the table and clasped his hands beneath his chin thoughtfully. Anthony closed his book.

"You need to go straight to the governor with this information!" said Anthony.

"He threatened me! I don't know what he will *do* to me if I turn him in!" cried Will.

"Now, that you have told us of this, if you don't tell the governor we will be forced to!" said Anthony matter-of-factly.

Will nodded and began to pull his boots onto his feet. He stood up and reached for his cloak that was hanging on the wall. "I am sorry I have been such a disappointment to you," he said. "I never intended to bring shame on our family."

Anthony went back to his book. Nick watched silently as Will walked to the door and then disappeared out into the street.

"What shall we do?" asked Anthony after the door slammed shut.

"It's not up to *us,* is it?" asked Nick. "It's *his* responsibility to report it. *We* didn't witness it so how can we testify to it?"

"It's *hearsay,* you mean?" asked Anthony. "So, we say *nothing*? That's a rather cowardly approach, don't you think?"

Nick didn't want to think about his cousin's problems! He had just proposed marriage to a very respectable woman and now was not the time to stir up a scandal; especially a scandal that involved his own family! "I think we should give him time to handle it on his own," he said.

"That's your answer? When you know he will most likely do *nothing?*" Anthony snapped back.

"I don't know what the answer is," Nick replied. "I have more important things going on in my life just now."

"Well, I guess that settles it then," said Anthony. "I suppose you will want me to find lodging elsewhere as soon as you are married?"

"I had no such thoughts, Anthony! I am sure Constance would not want me to throw you and Will out in the street!"

"I think it would be best if I found other accommodations, Nick. You will want your privacy and room for children that I am sure will follow."

"Are you angry with me, Brother?" asked Nick.

Anthony stood up and walked toward his bed. "No, Nick. I am happy for you. I guess I was a little disappointed. I had always thought it would be *me* that would be the first to marry!"

Nick smiled and slapped his little brother across the shoulders.

"Perhaps you should take your nose out of those books a little more often!"

Chapter Twenty-One "The Heart Breaker"

Will did not return that night. After a week had passed by and no one had seen him, Nick and Anthony assumed he had moved on; just as quickly as their cousin had come into their lives he was gone. Perhaps he had gone north to the Bay Colony or south to Jamestown. Whatever the case, they were soon far too busy harvesting their crops and getting ready for winter to think much about it. He was a grown man and although they wondered where he had gone, they were not going to worry about him. As far as Will's confession and what they had learned about Billington and the gunpowder, they tried to rationalize it out of their minds.

With the help of Hobbamock, they gathered their corn and peas and learned how to dry them in the sun. They trudged into the forest to chop firewood until they had a stack so tall it reached the eaves all around the house.

"You know this wood will be no good to you *this* winter," Hobbamock told his naïve white brothers.

"Are you telling me we did all this work for nothing?" Nick asked.

"This is *next year's* wood. It must be *seasoned*," replied Hobbamock. "It has to *age* in the weather a year before it will burn."

"Well," said Anthony, looking at Nick with a grin. "I had planned to move back to the Common House after we finished the harvest. There is ample firewood there so *I* shall not be cold."

"But what of *this* winter? What will I burn?" asked Nick.

"You will have new bride to keep you warm!" chided Anthony.

This was the first Hobbamock had heard of Nick's pending marriage, and he seemed pleased in his stoic, Indian sort of way. "Is this the same girl who waved to you from the dock? Little Constance Hopkins?"

Nick actually felt his cheeks redden and he mumbled "Yes. That would be the one."

Hobbamock smiled with his eyes and then changed the subject back to firewood. "We will trade some of your green wood with your neighbors who have plenty of seasoned. The Hopkins family has much left of last year's wood. I am sure Hopkins will trade wood with you so that his daughter will stay warm!"

Stephen and Elizabeth were both very happy about the betrothal and, of course, more than happy to see that their daughter's house would have ample wood for the long winter ahead. Stephen took his soon to be son- in- law under his wing and Elizabeth was soon setting a regular place for Nick at the Hopkins supper table. Constance took a quiet pleasure in dishing up his plate and reveled in his compliments about the food she had personally prepared. Sometimes at night, after Nick had left them, she would lie awake on her little pallet on the floor, wondering how everything had happened so fast, thinking of how long she had waited for him to return from his fishing trips and how she had tied herself in knots worrying before the news of the *Little James* had reached them. Love was a marvelous, mysterious thing that just came out of nowhere, sealed with clenched hands and a wet kiss in the moonlight and now her life would never again be that of Constance, the *tomboy*; now she was to be *Missus Nick Snow, a married woman!*

When the discussion about a wedding dress came up one afternoon, as she and her step- mother were alone in the house with just the babies, Elizabeth got up and opened her old trunk, the one she had brought all the way from England. There, beneath all the blankets and shawls and baby clothes, was a beautiful white dress with blue flowers embroidered across the bodice and all around the hemline. "I would be honored if you were to wear the dress I wore when I married your father," she said to Constance.

Constance's memory of the dress and the wedding she could now recollect as a happy event but, at the time, as a young girl, she remembered how she resented her father for remarrying so soon after her mother's death. How horrid she was to Elizabeth in those first few months until she got a little older and realized how lucky she was to have such a wonderful step- mother. She turned to her now and put her arms around Elizabeth. "I was not very loving to you back then," said Constance. "I didn't want Father to marry anyone!"

"I know that, Dear," answered Elizabeth. "And I could fully understand. I never wanted to replace your mother. I only wanted to be your friend."

"And you *have* been, Elizabeth!" said Constance. "You have been wonderful to Giles and me when you did not have to be!"

Both women started to cry simultaneously and then they burst out laughing and began dancing around the room like silly schoolgirls. At that precise moment, Stephen walked in the door, followed by Giles and Stephen Deane.

"Have you two been drinking spirits?" asked Stephen. "What has gotten into you?"

Constance held up the dress and Stephen realized that his headstrong daughter and his beloved wife were sharing a special moment that only mothers and daughters can have.

Giles rolled his eyes. "*Women!*" he said. "I don't think I shall *ever* get married!"

"Oh, yes you *will,* Son," said Stephen. "*When the love bug bites you!*"

No one had noticed that Stephen Deane had turned around and left the house without saying a word.

"I'm afraid you have broken that man's heart, Constance," said Elizabeth. "I believe he has been pining away for you ever since he came to live with us."

"I never made any promises to him," said Constance. "But I never meant to hurt his feelings either."

"Perhaps," replied Elizabeth. "A kind word from you might take away the sting."

Chapter Twenty-Two "A New Home"

They were married a week later in the church room under the fort, where outside there was a layer of fresh snow on the ground and the scent of pine wood burning in the air. The bridal couple made their way up the street; Constance with snow boots on her feet and hiking Elizabeth's dress nigh up to her knees to keep it from dragging in the snow, and Nick walking ahead of her, tromping down a path for her. Nick was understanding about Constance's decision to wear her step- mother's dress, as she knew he would be. He would buy her the cloth anyway, he told her. *No wife of Nick Snow would ever lack for dresses!*

The governor, dressed in his usual blue suit, presided over the ceremony, and Elizabeth cried into her handkerchief when Constance and Nick knelt at his feet and words were spoken that would forever join them together as man and wife.

"I, Governor William Bradford," he said, "publish the bans of marriage between Nicholas Snow of Plymouth and Constance Hopkins of Plymouth. If any know cause or just impediment why these two persons should not be joined in matrimony, ye are to declare it now!"

Constance almost expected her father to say something funny at that moment. She turned around and looked at him; he gave her his usual wink with that mischievous twinkle in his eye.

And it was done! Elizabeth hugged her and Stephen slapped Nick on the shoulder, and they went out in the snow again, where they trudged back to the Hopkins house for supper and a private family celebration.

"It's going to seem strange without you around to pester me," said Giles.

"Why, Giles!" said Constance. "Do you mean you will actually *miss* me?"

"Well," replied Giles. "I'll have no one to tease when you are gone."

"And you'd better be good to Caleb," she said. "No more *smart pill* tricks! I'll only be just down the street. I can still come back and chase you down with a stick!"

"I'm too smart for smart pills now!" said Caleb proudly.

They all knew the story except for the newest member of the family.

"What's this about *smart pills*?" asked Nick.

When Stephen explained it to him all the men laughed heartily.

"Do *all* men share the same *disgusting* sense of humor?" Constance asked Elizabeth.

"Aye," was her step- mother's reply. "I should have warned you!"

Everyone in the room laughed at that.

And, while it was true that Constance was only moving a few doors down the street, she was going to be the mistress of her own house and that delighted her in a strange surreal sort of way. The household chores she had no doubts she could handle; she could grow a garden, she was a good cook, and she knew how to scrub the dirt out of clothes. She looked across the room at her new husband, laughing and talking to her father; *but what will it be like to truly know him in the intimate way a wife knows a husband*? she wondered. At that she would be a clueless novice! At that moment, Nick turned and smiled at her and her worries evaporated. Love would take care of itself!

And it did, at that. When they emerged from the Hopkins house later that night, more snow had fallen, and Nick insisted on carrying Constance all the way down the street to keep her feet dry. Constance had never been inside the Snow house; in Plymouth, an unmarried woman would never visit a single man in his home! So, when Nick finally set her down on her feet in the doorway, her eyes sought out every detail. She crossed the room and touched the rough-hewn table and benches, the farm tools leaning against the wall, the enormous stuffed feather bed in the corner. While Nick went quickly to stoke the dying fire and add another log, he saw his new bride pause in front of the chest of drawers and pick something up in her hands. When he approached her and looked over her shoulder, he could see she had found his old hand mirror which he used to shave and comb his hair. She was staring into it like she had never seen a mirror before and when he touched her shoulders, he could feel she was trembling.

"Are you cold?" he asked her.

"No, I am fine," Constance replied. "It's just that I have not seen myself in a mirror since I was a little girl."

She held it up to see her reflection in the firelight, touching her hair and studying her facial features.

"And now that you have seen how beautiful you are, do you still think I am a suitable husband?" Nick asked, smiling.

"Don't be silly," she said quietly and put the mirror down.

She sat down on a stubby stool near the hearth to remove her snow boots and Nick sat down on the floor next to her and began to rub her feet.

"You *are* cold! Your feet feel like ice!" he said.

She suddenly jerked her foot away from him. "Please, no, Nick! That tickles!" she begged.

"Ah, so my new wife is ticklish, is she?" asked Nick. "Is it only on your feet?"

"Don't you get any ideas, Nick Snow!" warned Constance. "I do not like to be tickled!"

She saw that look in his eye, almost like her father when he had mischief up his sleeve. Nick reached up and grasped her around her ribs, pressing with his fingers, until she shrieked with laughter.

"No, Nick, stop!" she cried.

They wrestled around and she could not escape, for he was much too strong. Finally, they collapsed on the floor laughing. Nick stood up and looked down at her; for a moment she thought about the little mirror, and she suddenly realized nothing would ever make her feel so beautiful as the reflection of love in Nick's eyes at that very moment. He reached down and took her in his arms again, carrying her over to the big bed in the corner where he laid her down gently against the pillows. The firelight flickered and danced magically on the walls. Outside the snow was falling silently, the flakes sticking to the steamy window over the bed. He sat beside her and leaned down to kiss her tenderly.

"Welcome home, Constance," he said.

Chapter Twenty-Three "Strange Bedfellows"

Soon it was spring in Plymouth; the birds heralded its arrival with their song in the trees, the grass and wildflowers announced it with a carpeting of vibrant color on the hillsides and the men went back to the fields, where soon there were fledgling plants sprouting up from the mounds of brown earth. When Constance looked out upon Plymouth from the front step of her new home, it was now with feelings that were a far cry from how she felt in years past, when the whole town was starving and dying from the fever. The memories of those hard days were slowly drifting from her memory, and it looked as though this strange place they called *America* wasn't such a bad place after all. Had she gone back to London as she had desperately wanted to do, she would never have met Nick Snow!

Plymouth's political climate was changing rapidly during this time as well. More ships came every month, bringing a very diverse group of newcomers and, even though the original "separatists" were still in the majority and retained control of the government, Bradford was aware he would have to offer more compromises to those who were of different beliefs to avoid rebellions. The people of Plymouth were demanding to own more of their own land and soon new land grants were awarded; twenty acres to all single freemen and twenty acres per family member for all married men. A new method for dividing up the livestock was also devised, grouping all the settlers into twelve groups of thirteen people each, with each group receiving an equal portion as its share, one share meaning a cow and two goats.

Since Plymouth was outside the jurisdiction of Virginia and had no royal charter to support it, the town continued to self-govern itself, earning a reputation for a having its own unique set of laws, both moderate and modern. While the little settlement on the shores of shallow Plymouth Harbor would never rise to the economic importance of Bay Colony and New York, in its own way, it continued to thrive within itself.

The Common House, with the onslaught of newcomers, was again filling up with single men who had yet to build their own homes. Men usually paired up with their friends to assist each other in the construction work but no stranger set of bedfellows could be found than the two recently displaced men, *Anthony Snow* and *Stephen Deane*. While their friendship appeared to have no basis, for they had no common religious beliefs and no shared preferences for much of anything, they did, however, have one thing in common; both their new circumstances had something to do with *Constance Hopkins*.

Stephen had made the decision to leave the hospitality of the Hopkins household as soon as the engagement of Constance and Nick Snow had been announced. While he still enjoyed a deep abiding friendship with Stephen

Hopkins and they continued to work together in the fields, for his own pride, he just had to distance himself from the girl he thought he would one day marry. Chastising himself, for he had never actually proposed to her, he was surprised when she decided to wed a man she had known for such a short time, when he had been right there living under the same roof since he had arrived on the *Fortune* in 1621. The fact that the Hopkins house was again filling up with children was the excuse he gave for venturing out on his own now that Elizabeth was pregnant again and expected to give birth at any moment. They needed room for their little ones, he told them, although everyone knew the *real* reason he was leaving.

Anthony had moved back into the Common House, as soon as he had helped his brother bring in the last of the crops and they had stored enough wood to last the winter. There was still a slight twinge of jealousy in him. All his life, he had lived in the shadow of his handsome, older brother, who seemed to never have a lack of female companionship, while Anthony was so shy and backward when it came to social graces, he soon faded in the light of his brother's brilliance. Especially in Plymouth, where the single girls were snapped up quickly in matrimony by an over-abundance of eligible men, it all seemed so hopeless. Anthony dove into his scriptures and studied the lessons given to him by Elder Brewster with more vigor than he had ever done before. Marriage, at least for the time being, seemed as if it would never happen for him, so he tried to put it out of his mind.

Little Plymouth was thriving. Not only had the population grown, but the colony's livestock had multiplied as well and that spring there was a division of the new herd; the Snow family and the Hopkins family gained several new cows and calves and two more nanny goats. New merchants and tradesmen were setting up shops; blacksmiths and coopers, butchers and tanners, rope makers and wheelwrights, peddling their goods. It was still a far cry from London, but it was almost a miracle, considering where it began that first year.

Anthony Snow and Stephen Deane were both eager to break ground on their new home, which they had decided they would share until one or the other of them decided to marry. While, in earlier days, the complete construction of a house was completed by the same group of men, now the projects were more organized. They were mass- producing houses in a much more efficient way. First, a team of carpenters went through, raising the entire framework. They were followed by men more specialized in their crafts; door- hangers and window- sealers, masons and bricklayers, roofers and finishers. The houses seemed to be going up overnight and, with each month, more families came to fill them! Within weeks, Anthony and Stephen had moved out of the Common House into their new home.

While the economy in Plymouth was definitely booming, not all the profits came from respectable sources, however. Even though they had seen the last of John Oldham and John Lyford had been laying low and not stepping over the boundaries of the law as far as anyone could tell, there remained an element of the society that lurked in the shadows and on the outskirts of the town engaging in all sorts of illegal and immoral activities. Clandestine meeting places and black-market trading posts sprouted up like mushrooms in rotten soil; where there was silver to be gained, there was no end to the scheming ideas that the scallywags could come up with.

Just outside the legal limits of Plymouth to the north, in an area called Mt. Wollaston, a disgruntled laborer named Thomas Morton, along with several of his friends, put up a trading post and soon went into the business of selling guns and ammunition to the Indians. The place quickly became a gathering place for the worst of the worst; a place where debauchery abounded and drunkenness was common, but also they were intermingling with the female Indians in a most disgraceful manner. When Governor Bradford first heard of what was going on there, he sent word to Morton, demanding he cease doing business so close to Plymouth, but his warnings were ignored. For one thing the land on which Morton's establishment stood was technically *outside* the jurisdiction of Plymouth law. The other dilemma Bradford faced was what to do with him if they arrested him? Plymouth had no funds to build a proper jail in which to house prisoners for extended sentences.

He finally took the matter to the townsfolk, and they responded by collecting enough money amongst themselves to pay Morton's fare back to England on the next ship. So Captain Standish, with eight men from Plymouth as back up, marched into Mt. Wollaston and arrested him, housing him for a few days in the stockade until he was forced aboard a ship bound for England and the trading post was burned to the ground. Plymouth was no different than any other town and it would not be the last time they would have to deal with criminals.

But the year had been exciting in good ways as well. Stephen Deane took up with a girl named Elizabeth Ring, who had come to Plymouth with her widowed mother and siblings, and he married her, leaving the brand-new house he had built with Anthony to move in with her family. Elizabeth Hopkins gave birth to another daughter they named Damaris, after the baby girl they had lost years before to the fever.

And Constance proudly announced that she and Nick would be having their first child in the spring!

Chapter Twenty-Four "A Red-Haired Boy"

A woman's labor is a wonderfully miraculous thing. Apparently, God's plan is to forewarn women of the pain to come by giving them their monthly miseries; conditioning them for years before they will actually give birth to a child. Then, when labor commences, it is a gradual thing, accelerating in its intensity slowly, with short periods of respite, letting her recoup her strength and reassuring her that she can go on! By the time a baby arrives, the labor has been so intense that the actual delivery of the child is anti-climactic. And, when she looks down and sees her newborn for the first time, the memory of the pain is erased from her mind as if by magic. If it were not designed in such a way, what woman would look forward to more babies?

There was no doubt in anyone's mind that Constance was a strong woman; as an adolescent she never complained to Elizabeth of her monthly cramps. Detesting all signs of human weakness, she bravely endured what might have sent weaker girls to their sickbeds. She laughed at the pain she felt when her fingers bled from the goat head thorns in her garden and scoffed at her black eye, when she shot her father's gun for the first time and it recoiled, knocking her to the ground. Now that she was a *married woman,* she took on a new strength; a determination to excel in her new job as a wife to Nick Snow. She had long since mastered all the usual tasks of cooking, cleaning and animal care. Now she was faced with her most daunting challenge yet; the birth of her first child!

She had arrived at the Hopkins front door that mid-morning when the sun had risen almost to the center of the blue sky, glaring down on the harbor and the bustle in the streets was like the low buzz of bees in the wildflowers. From within the house, she could hear her little siblings, five-year-old Caleb and two-year-old Deborah, making their silly baby noises. When she opened the door, they both ran to her clutching her skirts and clamoring to be picked up.

"Children!" said Elizabeth. "At least let your sister get in the house before you knock her down!"

The women laughed and embraced one another.

"How are you feeling?" asked Elizabeth. "You look pale."

Constance kissed the little ones and looked up at her stepmother with an expression mixed of joy and anxiety. "My labor started early this morning," she said matter-of-factly. "I think today will be the day!"

Elizabeth put baby Damaris in her cradle and crossed the room to close the door, dropping the cross bar in place with a thud. "Come," she said. "Sit here. I will get clean rags while you slip out of your under drawers."

Constance sat on the edge of the huge feather mattress and looked around at the room that held so many childhood memories and was now about to witness her most memorable moment of all; *the birth of her first child!*

"Is Sissy sick, Mother?" asked Caleb, a look of concern wrinkling his little brows.

"No, Sweetheart," replied Elizabeth. "She is going to have her baby."

"Oh," said Caleb with a shrug.

Caleb had been only four when his little sister Damaris had been born and he didn't remember much about it all, except that *it took an awfully long time!* He went back to the fort he had built on the floor with his wooden blocks and the game he was playing, pretending to be Captain Standish shooting at the bad Indians.

No sooner had Constance relaxed in the comfort of the big bed she felt her water break and a damp pool puddling beneath her.

"Looks like you came just in time," said Elizabeth quickly changing the rags. "It won't be long now."

She crossed the room and returned with a damp cloth which he folded across Constance's forehead. "Remember when you helped me deliver my babies?" she asked.

Constance smiled. For some strange reason, she thought about her *birth* mother at that moment, silently wishing she could be sharing this moment with her. She loved Elizabeth; of that she had no doubt. Her stepmother had done a heroic job of raising all her children including Giles and herself who came with her father as a sort of *package deal*. Still, there were occasional moments twinged with sadness, when she longed for the woman who gave birth to her.

An hour passed. The sun had changed its direction and was now streaming through from the west. Elizabeth had put little Deborah down for her nap and the toddler was sleeping soundly, with Caleb beside her on his pallet, sucking his thumb and holding onto his ragged baby blanket.

"This baby is going to be a *procrastinator,*" said Constance. "He seems to be taking his sweet time."

"How do you know it will be a boy?" asked Elizabeth, who was sitting in the rocking chair Stephen had built for her, darning her husband's socks.

"I just have a feeling," replied Constance.

She suddenly grimaced when her abdomen contracted.

"Apparently he is listening to you as well!" said Elizabeth.

Constance breathed deeply and prepared herself for another pain. "We have decided to name him Mark," she said. "Nick and I discussed it."

"Mark is a nice name. But why not *Nicholas* after his father?"

Constance had to pause for another pain. "Well, there have already been *three Nicks* in his family. His father and his grandfather. He says that's enough. So, we agreed on Mark."

The pains were coming closer and stronger. Elizabeth got up from her chair and went to her side, holding her hand and looking for the first sign of the baby's head.

"Red hair! I think I see red hair!" said Elizabeth. "Try to push with the next one, Constance."

It came, hard and long, and Constance had no choice but to push as her body seemed to be moving on its own without her help.

"Push!" said Elizabeth again, holding the babe's head gently in her hands. "He's almost here!"

And, with one last contraction, little Mark Snow came into the world, coughing and blinking his blue eyes; wet and slippery as a freshly caught fish, with tiny pink nubs for toes and a rotund little belly. Elizabeth quickly snipped him free of his cord of life with her sewing scissors and wiped him clean with a soft cloth, while Constance continued to push to expel the afterbirth.

Little Mark fussed at being handled; his little arms thrashed about, and he kicked his feet out at Elizabeth, as she swaddled him and handed the bundle to his mother.

On the floor little Caleb awoke at the sound of the baby crying and he sat up, rubbing his eyes.

"Caleb," said Constance, "*Come and meet your little nephew!*"

Chapter Twenty-Five "Nick's *Wyono*"

When Stephen Hopkins came in from the fields that afternoon and flung his hat across the room in his usual fashion, he sensed almost immediately that something was different. His suspicion was validated as soon as little Caleb ran to him announcing,

"Father! Sissy had her baby! She named him Mark!"

Stephen looked at Elizabeth and seeing her smile, reached down and lifted Caleb into the air.

"Is that so?" he asked. "What does he look like? Is he an ornery redhead just like your sister?"

"Yep!" answered Caleb. "He has red hair, but not very much. And, he has long fingernails, Father! And a funny belly button!"

"Well, that *is* news," Stephen said, putting the boy back down on the floor. "And how *is* Constance?" he asked.

"You know your daughter!" replied Elizabeth. "As soon as I had the babe swaddled, she insisted on going home. I wanted her to stay here until Nick returns from his hunting trip, but she said she would be just fine by herself."

Stephen Hopkins chuckled. "Yes, that sounds like my stubborn daughter!" he said walking up close behind his wife and sticking his finger in the pot she was stirring.

"Stephen, you really should wash your hands before you stick your fingers in our supper," she said.

"It's a little too late for that," he said licking his fingers. "Whatever it is, it tastes good. When will it be done? I'm starving!"

"I was going to take some over for Constance and Nick. I doubt our daughter will feel up to cooking tonight."

He encircled her waist with his arms and kissed the back of her neck.

"Stephen!" said Elizabeth. "Go wash up now! And fetch Giles!"

"Giles went along with Nick and Hobbamock. I expect they are lugging a nice fat whitetail toward home by now," replied Stephen.

Only a few hours earlier, Nick, Giles and Hobbamock were still in the woods, crouched down behind a thicket of vines and brush very near the river, where they had seen dozens of hoof prints along the shoreline.

"This is where they drink. We will wait. *Ottucke,*" said the Indian, using the Wampanoag word for *deer*, "always drink from the same spot."

So, they waited and watched in silence. When Giles would forget and start to speak, it only took one look from the Indian and he would close his mouth again. Nick and Hobbamock had their bows ready, with their arrows resting between their fingers. Nick was still in awe of Hobbamock and his knowledge of hunting and fishing and farming. It seemed to Nick that his Indian brother knew something about everything, as much as an old man who had seen many years. But Hobbamock was still a young man, even though it was hard to estimate his age; his hair had no grey, his dark face had no wrinkles, his hands showed no veins, as did most old people. Nick had always assumed Hobbamock was not married, as he spent all his time with the settlers of Plymouth.

All at once, Hobbamock raised his hand and, with his finger, pointed toward the clearing. A lone whitetail buck had silently come to the shore and after taking in his surroundings, cautiously lowered his head to drink. Hobbamock took aim, stretching the bowstring taut, his eyes narrowed as he focused on his unsuspecting prey. With a snap, his arrow whistled through the air and hit the animal just behind the shoulder. The buck's head jerked upward and then it dropped to the ground with a thud.

"Now you can talk, Boy," said Hobbamock.

"Look!" whispered Giles. "There are turkeys over there by that rock. Can I try for them?"

Hobbamock quietly handed his bow to the boy and pulled an arrow from his quiver. Giles narrowed his eyes and watched the birds waddling along the shore. He took careful aim, just as he had watched the Indian do, and released the arrow which flew across the clearing, hitting the rock and splintering, falling onto the ground and frightening the turkeys away.

Giles' shoulders slumped and he pouted. "I was aiming for the turkey," he said.

Hobbamock put his hand on the boy's shoulder. "Next time, maybe you aim for the *rock*," said the Indian, his eyes twinkling.

Hobbamock stood up and went to fetch his *ottucke*. Nick followed with two poles and a roll of twine, and they tied the deer up by his feet to carry back to town. Giles put his hand out and felt the deer's antlers that were fuzzy and bloody.

"What happened to his antlers?" asked Giles, for this was his first hunting trip. For most of his life, he had helped his father in the fields.

"Those are his *new* ones," said the Indian. "He rubs them against the trees to tear away the skin. He gets a new set each year."

"Not anymore, he won't," said Nick. "This set will be going on my wall."

They hoisted the buck up between the poles and walked back toward the path to town. Giles followed behind, carrying their bows and quivers. After a short silence, Hobbamock spoke again.

"We will dress this one for your new wife," he said to Nick. "To honor your new papoose that is coming!"

Nick smiled. Sometimes it seemed unreal that he was going to be a father! "But what of *your* family, Hobbamock?" he asked. "Do you not want to share the meat?"

Hobbamock said nothing for a few moments. Then slowly his words came out, as if each syllable pained him in some way. "My family is gone. My wife and son died of the fever, seven years ago," he said in a low soft voice.

Nick had often wondered about Hobbamock's family and why he never seemed anxious to return to the Indian camp. "I'm sorry," he said. "I never knew."

Hobbamock shook his head. "My wife was named *Pala*," he said. "It means *water*."

"Was she named for Plymouth harbor?"

Hobbamock shook his head and paused, about to share a story he had never told anyone else. *"Pala* loved the water from the time she was a little girl. Her hair was always wet and shining from swimming in the bay or playing in the river. She just loved all water. When we were young, about the age of your boy here, we used to run away into the woods and swim in a little pond she found hidden in the trees. It was her secret place, she told me, where she bathed and renewed her spirit."

Nick could sense that Hobbamock was revealing a very intimate part of himself. "She must have been very lovely," was all he could think of to say.

Although Nick was walking behind the Indian and could not see Hobbamock's face, he knew his eyes were smiling.

"What was your *son's* name?" asked Giles, the tenderness of the moment completely lost on him.

"His name was *Wyono*," he replied. "It means *first born son.*"

They had finally reached the southern road into town and Nick suddenly felt anxious to get home to Constance. He felt pity for poor Hobbamock, who had lost so much and gratitude for his own blessings; a strong beautiful wife, for the Hopkins family who had been so good to him, and for their first child who was to be born very soon!

Just *how* soon he was about to find out!

When they arrived, they hung the deer by its back legs from a rack in the back of the Snow house, to *rest* for a few days before they skinned and butchered it, covering it with a canvas tarp to keep the scavenger birds from picking at the carcass. Giles put down their weapons and hurried inside to tell his sister they were home and to ask if he could stay to supper. He found her lying on the great bed with a tiny, wrapped bundle under her arm.

"Shhhhhh!" she whispered to him. "Your nephew is asleep!"

Giles' eyes got big and round with surprise and he bent over and looked at the tiny face peeking out from the swaddling clothes. "Wow, Con!" was all he could think of to say.

He turned and ran outside again, toward Nick and Hobbamock in the yard. "Nick!" he blubbered. "Constance...she...I mean you have...."

Nick's eyes narrowed and stared at his little brother- in- law. "What are you trying to say, Giles? Whatever is wrong with you?" he asked.

Giles grabbed Nick's arm and pulled him along the path toward the house. When they walked through the door, Giles pointed toward the bed. Nick brushed past him and hurried to the edge of the bed, where he looked down upon his wife, her long red hair spread out over the pillows and his son sleeping contentedly next to her.

"Constance!" he said.

"Sir, may I introduce you to your son, Mark Snow," she said, beaming with happiness.

Nick sat down on the bed gently and leaned over to kiss Constance. "Are you all right?" he whispered. "Why are you here all alone? Did you call for your mother?"

"I'm just fine, Nick," she replied. "Your son is fine, as well."

Giles was leaning against the bedpost, gawking at the new baby. Hobbamock was standing in the doorway.

"Come Hobbamock and see my new son!" said Nick.

The Indian entered the house and approached the bed, padding softly in his leather moccasins. The expression on his face changed and Nick realized it was the first time since he had known him that he had seen Hobbamock actually *smile!* "You have a fine *wyono*" he said.

"Please stay and have supper with us!" invited Nick. "And you as well, Giles! We must celebrate!"

Constance touched Nick's arm gently. "I am so sorry, my Love," she said. "I have nothing prepared! I did not know when to expect you!"

Nick stood up and crossed the room to wash his hands in the basin. "*I* will cook supper tonight!" he said proudly. "Giles, go catch the fattest hen in the yard and bring her to me! I will put the pot on to boil!"

By the time the chicken was plucked and cooking on the hearth and Nick had poured beer for himself, Hobbamock and Giles, the rest of the Hopkins family came knocking at the door, with more food and drink and the walls in the little Snow house were soon reverberating with laughter and conversation. Little Mark woke up, with the new sounds around him, and was passed around the room, staring up at each new face, undoubtedly wondering where he was and who these strange people were who seemed so interested in him. The baby seemed to like little Deborah the best, his little eyes followed after her as if he had a special connection with her!

"Does he have all his fingers and toes?" asked Nick, for only little Mark's face could be seen outside his blanket.

"Of course, he does," said Elizabeth. "He is perfect in every way!"

"His hair looks like it will be red," Stephen remarked. "He'll surely have a temper!"

"That means he will be a brave soldier like Captain Standish!" said Giles, whose mind was always on war and weaponry.

Nick glanced at his wife who was sitting up in the bed. *"He's beautiful just like his mother,"* he said. "I wouldn't want him any other way!"

Chapter Twenty-Six "The Billington Situation"

More ships from England continued to arrive in Plymouth and the little town was growing at an alarming rate. The second ship, Mayflower, tied up in the harbor in midsummer, bringing with it dozens of new settlers in need of housing. Soon, Bradford had to order the building of another Common House for the women and children, as it did not seem appropriate to allow them to live in the same building as the single men. The biggest problem was having enough food to feed them, before they were established and able to grow their own crops. The combined families of Plymouth were asked to contribute to a common storehouse once again. The memories of the old days, when supplies were scarce, had not been forgotten by the old-timers of the colony and they did not take kindly to cutting into their own food supply. They knew from experience, that they were only one failed harvest away from starvation and how quickly circumstances like drought could come upon them. The answer was plain; more land had to be cultivated to accommodate the ever- growing need for food.

The Snow family and the Hopkins family were growing together! Elizabeth gave birth to another little girl named Ruth and shortly thereafter Constance and Nick welcomed a daughter named Mary. Stephen Hopkins hired on some of the new settlers to help expand his fields and Anthony Snow once again picked up his spade and joined his brother to get more acreage cleared before the winter. With so much hard work facing the people of Plymouth, it would seem they had little time for mischief. But that would not be true for everyone.

John Billington, who had threatened their cousin and caused him to run from Plymouth in fear of his life, had managed to escape any complicity in the letter- writing scandal that chastised John Lyford and banished John Oldham's family. In fact, Billington had been lying low, rarely venturing into town on any matter; sending his wife or his Indian servants whenever they needed to buy goods. The strange family who lived out on the bay kept to themselves. While the Indians kept his crops nurtured and Billington went into the woods to hunt occasionally, his wife and children were thin and malnourished looking, without decent clothes. How he was able to pay his Indians was a mystery to everyone in Plymouth except for three people; John Lyford and the Snow brothers.

With the fall came the rutting season, when the whitetails and moose came out of hiding into the open fields to mate. It was the time when all the farmers traded their farm implements for bows and muskets and the woods soon echoed with the hollow sounds of gunfire and moose calls. Storehouses were soon filled with salted venison and the colony collectively breathed a little easier, knowing that, *at least for one more winter*, they would not starve. It was about this time that the *mischief* began.

It began one night under the cloak of darkness. Someone had slipped into the armory on the hill, undetected. Captain Standish had retired for the night, leaving the watch in the hands of one of the newer settlers. Not accustomed to all night duty, he had fallen asleep at his post. When the guard changed the next morning, the captain found that several barrels of gun powder had been stolen and he was so furious he fired the guard on the spot and sent him before the governor for punishment. Ignorant and very remorseful, the man spent the day with his arms and legs in the stocks for everyone to mock. But the matter was not over for Standish, who wanted to know who the thief was and what he was going to do with that much gunpowder!

No one suspected Billington, except for John Lyford, who was not talking, and the Snow brothers, who were still keeping Will's shameful secret. Billington was so rarely seen in town that most folks were beginning to forget what he even looked like. Even though he was a recluse, he still managed to attract the lowest element of people; single, shiftless men who had no families, men who liked to gamble and drink to excess, as well as transients just passing through from one settlement to another.

One of those men was a man named John Newcomen, who had come to town as a man- for- hire and, at one point, had done some work for Billington. He had rented a space to sleep in the town livery, until one day the liveryman reported to Bradford that the man had just *disappeared*. While it was not unusual for men of his rootless existence to just pack up and move on, Newcomen had left all his belongings; a knapsack full of clothes, his heavy winter cloak and his shaving mug behind in the loft of the livery and it looked as if the man had met with foul play.

Standish organized a search for Newcomen and took the liveryman along, beginning by knocking on Billington's door with the governor's warrant in hand. Inside, a musket leaning against the wall was identified by the liveryman as belonging to Newcomen. Indeed, the butt of the gun had the initials "JN" clearly carved in it. Standish arrested Billington immediately, although at that point he could only charge him with petty theft. When the search expanded into the woods, they finally found poor Newcomen, dead with a bullet through his head and the charge against Billington went up a notch to *murder*.

When the news got out, Anthony rushed to Nick's house immediately, insisting they go to the governor and tell him what they knew. They debated the issue at the kitchen table while Constance listened silently, rocking baby Mary to sleep.

"Nick, we simply *have* to tell what we know, even if it *is* hearsay!" Anthony begged his brother. "I would think that you with a family to protect would want to get to the bottom of it!"

"Yes, I agree, Anthony," Nick replied. "Perhaps Hobbamock might be able to help identify the Indians."

He thought for a moment, biting his lip and rubbing the whiskers on his chin. Looking across the room, his eyes met with Constance's, and he suddenly felt an emotion that he had rarely experienced; *what would happen to his family if the gunpowder had gotten into the hands of the wrong Indians? Would they attack Plymouth*?

"Yes, I think you are right," he answered finally. "Hold supper for us will you, Constance?"

"Will you stay and eat with us Anthony when you return?" asked Constance.

"Yes, I would be most happy to," answered Anthony. "After I have cleared my conscience!"

And the brothers went out into the street, headed for the governor's house.

After they had arrived and had told Bradford everything they knew, the governor, while not surprised at the actions of Billington, was very concerned about the whereabouts of the gunpowder.

"The answer lies with those two Indians," said Nick. "I will ask Hobbamock to find out what he can."

"Aye, do that, Nick," said the governor. "I will consult with Governor Winthrop at Bay Colony over this. We have never had a capital offense here in Plymouth. I'm not quite sure how to handle it."

"He should *hang* for this," said Anthony. "The man is a nuisance!"

Nick disagreed. "We don't know all the circumstances," he said. "It may have been self-defense for all we know. We shouldn't rush to judgment."

"*You* were the one who didn't want to tell anyone what we knew, remember?" Anthony shot back at his brother. "If we had *told* someone *then,* maybe this Newcomen fellow would still be alive!"

The governor intervened between the two brothers. "None of that matters now, Gentlemen," he said. "You will let me know what Hobbamock can find out and we will proceed from there."

He showed them to the door and bade them goodbye. Nick walked down the street a step ahead of his brother.

"I'm sorry, Nick," Anthony said, reaching out to touch Nick's shoulder. "I didn't mean to be cross with you."

Nick shrugged and slowed his pace. "You were right. We should have told someone that night. I just…"

"I know, you had Constance and marriage on your mind," Anthony said laughing.

"Now, it's no laughing matter," replied Nick.

Anthony agreed on that score.

Nick paused just before they reached his house. He stared down the street, out into the darkness of the woods. Quietly, his words came steaming from his lips in the cold night air,

"I just hope poor Will isn't out there somewhere with a bullet through *his* head!"

Chapter Twenty-Seven "The Strength of a Woman"

John Billington was hanged a week later; makeshift gallows were erected in the square and almost all the men came out to watch the execution, while most of the women stayed at home, shielding their little ones from the gruesome sight. It was over in minutes and Billington's body was lowered and shuttled off in a crude pine box. The crowd dispersed and went on about their business, with the exception of Mrs. Billington and her children, who walked along behind the wagon that carried her husband's body to the graveyard on the hill north of town.

Constance and Elizabeth were together in the Snow house with their babies, making supper together, for the two families often shared meals.

"I feel sorry for Mrs. Billington," said Elizabeth. "Whatever will she do now?"

"She can get out and work," replied Constance. "She's a *woman*, not an *invalid!*"

"Aye, that sounds like you, Constance," Elizabeth said smiling. "But not all women are as strong as you, my Dear! Some are very delicate."

"Delicate, indeed!" scoffed Constance. "Anyone who can birth a child is not *delicate!* She just needs to pick herself up by her bootstraps and take care of her children!"

Before long, the snows came and the path between the Snow house and the Hopkins house became well-trodden; the two little families had blended into one large family, with two generations of babies growing up together. Anthony Snow, still the lonely bachelor, became a regular guest. The women, feeling compassion for him, mended his clothes and fed him well, as if he were an orphan child they had adopted. It was a lovely winter; the brilliant white snow carpeted the ground and blanketed the trees, the storehouses were full, and the town was, once again, peaceful and serene. Men's beards grew bushy and long and women's hips broadened a little. Children frolicked in the snow, sledding down the main street and having snowball fights in the fields. Families grew closer, babies were conceived, and friendships were forged, as the days grew shorter and the nights became cold and long.

The snow was deep and, by spring, was still packed into the shaded spots. The main street was slick with layers of ice that had been packed down and refrozen night after night, only thawing in the worn pathways the humans had made walking from house to house. On one morning, Elizabeth had sent little Caleb out into the street to borrow some herbs from Constance. The seven-year-old put on his cloak and pulled on his snow boots and walked out into the street to make the short journey to his sister's house, when he came face to face with a huge beast with black eyes and an enormous head.

"Mother!" he screamed, and Elizabeth came running out to find a large moose had discovered the new grass that was sprouting up in the bare path between the houses.

The animal stood there, his massive jowls grinding up the food in his mouth, obviously not the least bit afraid of the human creatures standing before him and not inclined to move.

"What should we do?" asked Caleb.

"Go in and get me my broom," said Elizabeth. "Perhaps I can shoo him away."

Caleb retrieved the broom and stood behind his mother, as she moved closer to the moose.

"Go away now! Shoo!" she coaxed.

The moose just kept on chewing and rummaging for more grass. He took a step closer to Elizabeth without even noticing her.

"Go, you!" she said, raising her voice slightly.

The moose grunted and kept eating.

Elizabeth was terrified of getting any closer to the beast. She retreated backward to the doorway of the house, pushing Caleb inside.

At that moment, the sound of gunfire erupted in the street and the moose fell to the ground with a loud thud. Relieved, Elizabeth looked around to see who had come to their rescue. There, halfway up the street, standing there with a smoking musket in her hands, stood Constance, beaming broadly.

Elizabeth burst into laughter as the neighbors all came out to see what the gunfire was about. Nick and Stephen came running in from the fields and when Nick saw his wife standing over the dead moose with his gun, he shook his head with a smile.

Constance nonchalantly looked up at her husband. "It's not every day your supper comes up and knocks on your front door," she said with the slightest twinge of pride. "I figured we might just as well *eat* him!"

There was meat on the table, not only in the Snow house and the Hopkins house, and Nick had offered shares of the meat to the men working with him in the fields and the women who were helping to plant the already-cultivated plots. It was a joint effort, and, by early summer, the settlers of Plymouth could look out proudly at their crops sprouting green and vibrant in the fields. Then, two things happened in a very short period of time, that brought the town to its knees and nearly brought an end to Plymouth.

First came another drought; this one so severe and long lasting the governor had to forbid any water to be used for bathing or the laundering of clothing. On Sundays, when the church room was packed full of ripe bodies in filthy over-worn clothes, the stench was almost unbearable. It brought back memories of the days spent on the sea, confined to the smelly holds of the ships. Search parties were sent out past the woods into unknown territories to find other sources of water, coming back unsuccessful; the drought seemed to have dried up every watering hole for miles around. Animals were found dead from thirst at the edges of where the water had been. The town brook was reduced to a slight trickle and the Eel River became nothing more than a mire of mud pits full of dying fish. They were beginning to lose hope that they could keep their crops alive when, in late August, a week of rains came, hard and fast, furrowing down the main street of town and flooding the fields. Lids were removed from barrels and set out to collect the precious raindrops; pitchers and buckets were filled and stored away. Water was the source of their survival. Now they were learning to cherish it more than ever before.

With the crops saved Plymouth breathed a collective sigh of relief and everyone went about their business thinking the worst was over. They were wrong.

The next blow came on a hot, September afternoon with a clear sky and a relentless sun beating down harshly on the fields. The sound came, slowly at first; a buzzing, humming sound from the north. The sky began to grow dark; the sun was soon covered by a strange cloud. The people of Plymouth wondered if it was another rainstorm, but the air was still hot and dry, with not a drop of moisture and yet the sky grew darker still. The sound grew louder until it was almost deafening to the ear; like a million crickets rubbing their legs together at the same time.

Locusts! They came in *waves*, rolling over the fields; black torrents of devouring insects that ravished the corn crop, consuming all in their path. The swarmed down the street and took over the little gardens too; no backyard escaped their ravenous appetites. The men were helpless, running into the fields swinging at them with anything they could find. The swarm was too big; for the few that could be swatted away, a thousand more came to replace them. All they could do was sit and watch their crops being devoured.

It lasted for days and then, just as suddenly as the swarm had appeared, it moved on. There was nothing left to harvest; the fields were quickly turned under and another planting was attempted but the growing season was rapidly disappearing. Fall was already in the air and the cold nights were sure to kill any new growth coming so late. They had enjoyed a bounty a year before, *wasted* it actually, and had not worried about rationing when there was such abundance. Now, their larders and storehouses were dangerously low again. Governor

Bradford advised everyone to conserve what they could for what was promising to be a long, hard winter.

As the weather grew colder, Nick and Stephen took to hunting, with Hobbamock helping them to find rabbits and squirrels, for the deer and moose had moved south for the winter. The men came back, day after day, with barely enough meat to feed the children. They went ice fishing on the bay with little success. To add to their troubles, the colony's shared bull had suddenly died, and they were waiting for Captain Pierce to bring a new one from England, but he wasn't expected until the spring and the udders of the unbred cows were quickly going dry. Mothers were forced to water down what little milk they had left for their babies and some of them grew sickly and weak. Not wanting to butcher their breeding stock, they tried to stretch the bones from the calves into soup but without vegetables it was nothing more than flavored water and offered little nutrition. The only milk left was from their nanny goats, who all had hungry kids at their sides, competing for the milk.

Nick took the whole situation *personally.* "I promised myself I would not have a family until I was able to provide for them," he told Constance one night, after the babies had gone to sleep. They were lying on the big bed, watching the fire in the hearth and listening to their bellies rumble from hunger, for they hadn't had a filling meal in a long time. "If I hadn't been so generous with that moose meat, we would have it for ourselves now!"

"It's not your fault, Nick," said Constance. "I certainly don't blame you for those horrible bugs eating all our crops!"

"I am worried about you and the children. How will Mark and Mary survive without milk? Without vegetables?" Nick asked.

He reached out and took Constance in his arms. When she looked up into his face, she could see tears clouding his eyes.

"We will get through this," she comforted. "*We are not going to just give up and die*!"

Chapter Twenty-Eight "The Honey Satchels"

Constance refused to give up. While the men were out hunting and fishing with mixed results, she often left little Mark and Mary in Elizabeth's care and went out on her own, scouring through the woods for winter berries and pine nuts in the snow. She planted seeds in pots that she put in the windows of their little house in the daytime to absorb the sun and moved them to the hearth at night to keep them warm. Nick was amazed at how she could coax the little bean plants and carrot tops to grow in cups of melted snow. Soon, the inside of the house had a dozen green plants started that she had fooled into thinking it was spring!

The hardest part for Constance was hearing her babies cry; she knew they wanted milk, but she couldn't breast feed them both. They needed something to keep them satisfied in between to give her breast milk a chance to replenish itself and the longer she went without food herself her milk stream became less and less. On one of her excursions into the woods, she discovered a beehive in a dead tree and an idea came upon her. She knew nothing about bees but the bees that were clinging to the hive didn't seem very threatening; they seemed almost lethargic. She stepped closer and slowly reached her hand into the hive; she could feel the stickiness of the honeycomb on the tips of her fingers, and she grasped it in her hand and gently pulled it out. Still the bees did not seem agitated; she was able to flick them off with her fingers and she wrapped the gooey comb up in a handkerchief she had in her pocket and took it home.

When she arrived home, she found an old piece of cloth and cut it into pieces. Then she took the pieces of cloth and placed a section of the honeycomb on each one and tied them up with twine, like little satchels. When she went to the Hopkins house to fetch her youngsters, she tried one on little Mary; the baby immediately thrust the little "satchel" into her mouth and began sucking. With the moisture from her saliva the cloth became damp, and the taste of the honey soon came through the cloth. When the baby had her first taste of the sweet honey, she sucked more vigorously to get more.

Elizabeth was amazed and soon her own babies were sucking on the little honey *satchels.* "You are ever so clever!" she told Constance. "I would never have thought of it!"

"Well, it's not *nourishment,* exactly," replied Constance. "But at least it will keep them happy in between their meager meals."

Nick and Stephen were both in awe of the ingenuity of their little Constance as well when they came in that night.

"Remember that first year, Con?" asked Stephen. "We thought we would never make it, but we did! I know we will this time!"

"We just have to pray," said Elizabeth quietly.

Stephen shook his head. "I can't wait on the Lord," he said. "I will keep hunting and fishing all winter."

"Aye," agreed Nick. "But I want you to be more careful, Constance. You shouldn't be going into the woods alone."

"I don't see why not," replied Constance. "What have I to be afraid of? I shot that moose, didn't I? Is there anything bigger in the woods than that?"

Nick and Stephen exchanged glances.

"There could be *Indians* in the woods."

Constance rolled her eyes. "I'm not afraid of *Indians*. I've been around Hobbamock and Samoset for so long, they are like my family," she replied.

"Yes, well there are other tribes of Indians, like the Narragansetts, that are dangerous," said Nick. "They will have your long red hair decorating their belts, if you aren't careful!"

He knew he couldn't frighten her. *Nothing* frightened his wife; she was the bravest woman he had ever met. "Just promise me you will be careful," he pleaded.

"Oh, I will," she said.

When they returned to their home that night, Nick tried one of her honey satchels. "These are quite good!" he said, laughing.

"You and that sweet tooth of yours!" replied Constance. "Someday you'll have no teeth, for they will all be rotted away from sweets!"

"And will you love me when I have no teeth?" he asked, cornering her against the bedpost.

Constance's eyes danced back at him. "Well," she said, "I'll have to see how *funny* you look!"

With that he began to tickle her, and they ended up laughing and falling into each other's arms. Locked in love's embrace, for a night at least, everything seemed possible!

Chapter Twenty-Nine "A Ship in the Nick of Time"

At least the firewood is holding out, Constance thought to herself, as she melted a pot of fresh snow in the kettle and chopped some dried herbs to season the broth. She wasn't stupid enough to think it was *really* broth but if it could fool her children for a little while, it would have to do. She wiggled her fingers that were still frozen from scooping up the snow in front of the fire but there wasn't much pleasure warming one's hands near the hearth when one's stomach was gurgling and growling, begging for food! Who would have thought, after ten years, the town of Plymouth would be starving again? She stared at the shelf and reached for the meager ration of dried lentils she had left and scooped out barely a teaspoon-full, adding it to the pot. What she wouldn't give for a slice of venison roast or a bite of goat cheese, instead of the squirrels and rabbits Nick was able to trap on *good* hunting days!

The honey satchels had run out and there would be no more honey until the bees awakened in the spring. Now, when her babies cried out for their sweets, she could only cradle them close until they fell asleep in her arms. When she changed their nappies, she felt their soft, little tummies that were no longer round and supple and the ridges of their little ribs sticking up through their skin. She no longer had milk in her breasts to give them; she, herself, had grown gaunt and weak, as did her poor husband, who went out every day with Hobbamock, promising to bring back meat for supper. The other colonies had experienced the locusts and the drought along with them and they were all suffering the same misery, so there was no one they could turn to for help. If the coming year wasn't better, Plymouth would only be a colony of bones. Their only hope was for a ship with provisions to arrive soon from England!

While the *broth* was simmering, she pulled the can down that held what was left of their corn flour and measured a cup of it into a bowl. She added the morning's egg to the flour and a bit of water and began to stir when she noticed the flour was *moving*; she had stretched it for so long, the weevils had finally found it and now she would have to throw it all away, wasting the last egg they would have until tomorrow! Constance was angry and she slammed the spoon down and took the bowl of wiggling corn batter out to the yard for their last pair of chickens to eat. She was not about to feed her family corncakes with *weevils* in them, no matter *how* hungry they were!

"God!" she cried, shaking her fists angrily and staring upward. "Why have you forsaken us?"

She thought about Elder Brewster and how he had continued to lead his parishioners in prayer, but she knew even the godly minister's heart must be breaking every Sunday, as he promised them that the good Lord would provide for them. Where was their good Lord now when her babies were starving and malnourished? Why had He let their bull die? Why had He sent the locusts? Constance had so many unanswered questions, she wanted to scream! Who could continue to have faith under such conditions?

She went back into the house and put the children down for their naps. They didn't cry; Constance was afraid they were becoming too *weak* to cry. She took a sharp knife from the drawer. Pulling her cloak over her head, she opened the door and went back outside in the cold air. She walked slowly and hesitantly across the yard and stood for a moment, staring at the livestock; the dry cow nibbling at a patch of green grass that had sprouted up from the leftover snow and the nanny goat, with her twin kids, warming themselves in the sun. She had killed all but the last breeding pair of chickens, who were now pecking and scratching the dirt for bugs. Now, there was only one thing she could do to assure her babies would have milk. It was her last resort.

She approached the goats quietly and the kids came to her, burying their noses in the folds of her skirts, looking for scraps which she had frequently brought them back when they had food to spare. The kids, one black and one white, looked up at her and begged with their baby goat voices. She sat down on a stump Nick had put in their pen for them to climb on and the white one jumped up into her lap, digging his sharp little hooves into her thighs. She petted him on his head, feeling the little nubs of horns that were coming through and he rubbed against her wanting her to scratch some more. While the nanny goat paid little attention, Constance pulled the knife slowly from her pocket. The blade glistened in the sunshine. She kept scratching the kid's head and spoke to him in a low reassuring voice. "I'm sorry, Little One," she whispered.

With one swift and silent stroke, she slit the baby goat's throat. The blood spewed onto the ground and the little goat went limp in her arms. Still, the nanny goat didn't suspect anything was amiss. Constance stood quietly, holding the bleeding kid in her arms, and opened the gate to the goat pen. At that point, the mother goat saw her baby being taken away and she began running up and down the fence calling to him. Her kid could not call back. He was on his way to the pot on the Snow hearth; tonight, his tender baby meat would simmer with nourishment for her family.

She butchered him around the corner of the house, out of sight of the mother goat. She had watched Nick and Hobbamock as they skinned and gutted deer many times and she tried to do everything exactly as she had seen them do. It wasn't as easy as the men had made it look; the skin did not come off as readily and she found it very difficult to cut *around* the goat's entrails without cutting *into* them, with the knife that was way too big for the task. Unfortunately, Nick always took his hunting knives with him, and she had to make do with her big, clumsy kitchen knife.

By the time she had the carcass down to bare meat and bone and had sawed it into manageable sized pieces, she took the meat into the house and laid it out on the cutting board. The skirt of her dress was drenched in blood, and she removed it and set it to soak in a pail of cold water. Changing into clean clothes and washing her hands and arms thoroughly, she again went to the yard; this time with a clean pail in which to hold the goat milk.

When Nick and Hobbamock returned from the woods that evening, with two rabbits in their bag, they were surprised at the aroma of simmering meat in the house. Nick peered into the pot and turned to Constance curiously. "Which one did you kill?" he asked.

"The white one," replied Constance. "And now her mama can spare enough milk for *our* babies."

He looked very sad, not for the goat, but for himself, as if he had failed in some way. Sometimes, he thought Constance was a much stronger person than he was. She was always amazing him with her strength and will to survive in any circumstance and he loved her for it. It was just his pride that suffered, when it wasn't *he* that was bringing home decent food for his new family.

"I had to do it Nick. Mark and Mary must have milk and you need real meat in your stomach too," she said.

For the first time in a long while, the Snow family went to bed with full bellies.

When morning came, Nick was up and out again with Hobbamock, this time with fishing poles in hand. Constance watched them as they disappeared down the street toward the harbor.

"Bring me a big, fat fish!" she called after them and Nick nodded and waved to her.

She went about her usual chores and at least she could smile at her babies, who had bellies full of goat milk. Today she felt like she could almost sing a song, for she felt happy, and she wasn't sure exactly *why.* She knew the goat meat would not last forever; she knew the nanny goat's milk would soon dry up, as she weaned her remaining kid. No, there was just something in the air today. It wasn't because her stomach was full of food. It wasn't because her heart was full of love and her arms were full of babies. *It is going to be a good day* Constance thought to herself, and she truly believed it!

She stepped outside the house and let the morning sun kiss her face. The snow was almost gone, and the hills were becoming green with spring grass again. She let her eyes scan the horizon. What a beautiful place Plymouth was in spring! She was feeling new hope; it came from somewhere deep inside of her, filling her spirit just as the air filled her lungs. The ocean was blue and beautiful and there was no morning fog, so she could see all the way to

Cape Cod. Her eyes blinked and she refocused; then, they teared up and she felt her feet bouncing up off the ground. With her outstretched arm, she pointed to the east. *Did no one else see it? Was she hallucinating?*

"*A ship!*" she heard herself yell. "*Look! A ship is coming!*"

She began to run down the street and soon there were others running behind her.

It was indeed a ship arriving! It was Captain Pierce returning from England!

Chapter Thirty "The *Real* Thanksgiving"

Plymouth had never seen such a celebration! It overshadowed even that first supper they had all shared back when the Mayflower had first arrived from England! Even serious Elder Brewster was seen dancing with Missus Brewster in the street! When Captain Pierce jumped up onto the dock, women were kissing him, and men were shaking his hand and slapping him soundly across his shoulders. Nick and Hobbamock came running up from the beach. Everyone came out to welcome him and Pierce could see that *he had come just in time*.

They unloaded barrels and crates full of supplies, shuttled poultry and pigs off to their pens, and, lastly, brought ashore the bull they had been waiting for! The governor tried to organize the frantic settlers, so that everyone would get a fair share of the food and Captain Standish had to help him push everyone back to the edge of the dock to have room for the cargo being unloaded. He had his clerk fetch his record books and began to dole out the rations fairly, as he always did, based on the size of the family. The head of each family was given his share. For the rest of that day, no one thought of hunger or work or sadness for lost loved ones. Bradford had tables set up in the Common House and his wife supervised the cooking of the food for a grand banquet. Anyone who owned a musical instrument of any kind came to play. The children were led in games. The tables were set with a cornucopia of food and drink.

"I knew the Lord would provide!" said Brewster as the entire community bowed their heads in prayer. "But I must admit that even *I* was beginning to lose hope!"

The party lasted well into the night and Captain Standish informed Bradford he was *taking the night off* and was *not going to arrest anyone for drunkenness!* It was a wise decision on his part; there wasn't a sober man in Plymouth by nightfall. Nor was there a man's head that wasn't aching the following morning, when the roosters from the new flock began to crow. The governor and the elder concurred that the day would be a holiday and the feasting continued.

On the third day, the men returned to the fields and their trades, with a renewed sense of purpose; a more forceful stride in their step, a more strenuous heave in their thrusts and more silent hope in their hearts. The Snows and the Hopkins' families resumed their habit of supping together now that they finally had enough food to share! Anthony was included in the family gatherings more often now, Constance and Elizabeth conspiring to find him a suitable wife once and for all! Many more acres of land were cleared that year; more fishing shallops were built and their armory was fortified. Even though there had been no trouble with Indians, Captain Standish wanted them to be prepared for the worst. The harvest that year was the most plentiful ever, for the men were more determined than before to never again see their families go hungry and by the end of fall *both* storehouses were filled to the brim with food.

Constance gave birth to a second daughter in the spring, and they named her Sarah; a little, blond-haired imp with big blue eyes like her mother and a talent for enchanting her father with her baby smiles. Nick loved all three of his children equally, but his little Sarah was the one who tugged on his heart the most. From the day she was born, she had a special connection with him, a bond that would last a lifetime.

Captain Pierce had sailed again, as soon as the thanksgiving feast was over, travelling south to the West Indies to pick up supplies that were not readily available in London, such as sugar cane and bananas. When he returned to Plymouth, he had a new cargo that was welcomed by the women of the colony, especially Constance Snow; it was the first shipment of cotton fabric! Nick traded the captain several fox furs for a bolt he gave to Constance for her birthday, and she made him a new shirt, dresses for the girls and a little shirt for Mark.

"Next time, I want you to make *yourself* a new dress!" Nick scolded, even though he secretly loved the feel of his new shirt. The fabric seemed to keep him cooler while he was laboring in the fields; the weave allowed his skin to breathe.

She promised she would, but with three children and a husband, Constance didn't think about things for herself much anymore.

When the winter of 1633 arrived, the storehouses were again full, and Plymouth seemed to be in a period of peace and prosperity with no sickness to speak of and no troublesome criminal activity afoot.

"If only life could remain just as it is now," remarked Constance to Elizabeth one day as they set the tables for a shared family supper. With eight children between them, their husbands were forced to build a second table for the children. The Hopkins' brood, eight-year-old Caleb, seven-year-old Deborah, four-year-old Damaris and two-year-old Ruth sat on one side, while three-year-old Mark Snow and his sister one-year-old Mary with baby Sarah on the other side.

"Aye," replied Elizabeth in a strangely sad tone.

Constance knew the sound of her stepmother's voice and felt something was wrong. "What is it, Mother?" she asked. "Are you not feeling well?"

"Oh no, I am fine, Constance," Elizabeth said. "It's just that I think my *change* has come upon me and there will be no more babies for me."

The change? thought Constance. *It can't be true! The change is for old women and Elizabeth is still young!* "I don't believe it! You are still a young woman!"

Elizabeth smiled. "It has been three years, now, since Ruth was born. And, my body feels different, like it is drying up somehow. I haven't had my monthly misery in ever so long. I can't explain it, Constance. But I know what I *feel.*"

"Well," said Constance. "The four little ones you have should keep you busy for years to come. If ever you feel the need to hold a babe in your arms you can hold one of your grandchildren, for I plan to have many more!"

"Yes," said Elizabeth. "You and Nick are raising a fine family."

Stephen and Nick came through the door at that moment, followed by Anthony.

"Where is Hobbamock? Isn't he having supper with us tonight?" asked Constance, who had developed a warm friendship with their adopted Indian brother.

"He said he didn't feel well. He went to the Common House to lie by the fire."

Constance went outside and called the children in from the yard. "I shall take him a plate of food," she said, "once the children are all fed."

Later, she went out into the winter night, bundled up in her heaviest shawl and cap. It was the clear, cold kind of night that always came before the first snow. As she hurried along, she could hear gray wolves howling from beyond the palisade, for they were one of the few animals that remained active in the winter. She had covered the plate of food tightly with a rag, hoping it would still be warm by the time she reached the Common House.

When she arrived and entered the building, she saw Hobbamock lying near the fire, wrapped in his woven Indian blanket. His eyes were closed, and he was rolled over toward the fire when she touched his shoulder. When he turned toward her, she could see his face in the firelight; it was drawn and pained. She reached out and touched his forehead which was blazing hot. "You have the fever," she said. "I have seen it before."

Hobbamock tried to sit up.

"Stay right where you are," she said. "I will go get cool water for you to drink. You are burning up!"

She took his supper and hurried outside, back to the house, where she dipped a pail of water from the cask, grabbed some clean rags from the drawer and exchanged his supper plate for a bowl of clear broth.

"What's wrong?" asked Nick.

"He has the fever," Constance replied. "His body is on fire!"

She ran back outside and down the street. For over an hour, she sat with him, the once- strong Wampanoag, who usually stood so tall and showed so much life, was now weak, burning with fever and shivering with chills. She sponged his forehead and spoke to him gently. "You must rest and stay warm," she said, giving him sips of water and spoonfuls of broth.

When he finally fell asleep, she left him and returned to the Hopkins house.

"Nick took the children home to put them to bed," said Stephen. "You take care that you do not get sick yourself!"

"*Someone* has to care for him Father," she answered. "He has no wife or family."

"I know that, Love," replied Stephen. "Just take care of yourself. You have a family that needs you too."

She hugged her father and Elizabeth and went home, where Nick was sitting by the fire, waiting for her to return. He, too, was concerned about his wife's health.

"I don't know what I would do if you got sick," he said. "Poor Hobbamock! Is there anything I can do to help?"

"You can help me with the children, while I try to get him well," she said. "He has been a good friend to us."

"Yes," said Nick. "He has at that. He is like a brother to me."

Chapter Thirty-One "God's Justice"

By the week's end, a dozen more settlers had come down with the sickness. Governor Bradford declared that the Common House would serve as a temporary hospital, as it had done in the past and soon the pallets on the floor were filling up with feverish patients, tended by a group of women, including Constance. Elizabeth took over the care of the Snow babies in the daytime and five-year-old Mark went to work every day with Nick, while Constance cared for their dear friend, Hobbamock, and the others who had fallen ill. Since she had already been exposed and thought herself to be immune, she agreed to stay on and help with the new patients that were arriving every day.

The town had one trained physician, Samuel Fuller, who instructed the ladies on what to do, although the mere sight of an Indian in amongst the patients seemed to unnerve him. Not all of Plymouth were as open minded as the Hopkins and Snow families and many moved their pallets as far away from poor Hobbamock as possible, as if *his* sickness was somehow *different* than their own.

"Do you not think he would be better off back home with his *Indian* family?" the doctor whispered to Constance on that very first day.

"We *are* his family, Sir," she replied haughtily. "His own wife and son died from this very illness."

"It is just that his presence makes the other patients a bit uncomfortable," replied the doctor.

Constance glared at him. Her nostrils flared and her lips pursed. "I will *not* move him until he is well!" she fired back. "He has done as much for the people of Plymouth as *you* have!"

"Well," said Fuller. "Perhaps, I should take it up with the governor."

"Yes, perhaps you should!" she said and turned her back on him, to go back to her nursing.

When she returned home that night, she found poor Nick trying to prepare supper for the children; the house was strewn with toys and clothing and the children running amuck in the middle of it all.

"Here," she said, taking over the supper preparation. "Let me do that."

Nick went about the room picking up things and clearing the table. "I don't know how on earth you manage to keep the house so tidy with three little ones under your feet all day," he said with a look of admiration in his eyes.

After Constance had the supper prepared and simmering over the fire, she sat down and gathered her little ones around her. "I've missed you children!" she said, kissing their faces and smiling.

"Are you taking care of Hobbamock?" asked Mark.

"Yes, Dear, I am," she replied.

"Is he getting any better?" Nick asked with sincere concern.

"Perhaps a little," said Constance. "Doctor Fuller thinks he should go back to the Indian camp and be cared for by his own kind! I was so angry with him, Nick, I wanted to pummel him!"

Nick shook his head.

"He said he was going to take it up with the governor," Constance went on.

"If it weren't for the children, I would bring him here!" replied Nick. "Maybe I should speak to the governor as well! I heard from Samoset today that they have the sickness in the Indian camp as well."

"That's not good," replied Constance. "Doctor Fuller will surely blame the Wampanoags for bringing it into Plymouth!"

"We interact with them every day, Constance. Who is to say *who* infected *who*?"

Constance put the supper on the table and then bundled her little ones into their beds before she collapsed herself from the long day.

Nick slipped off her boots and began to rub her feet.

"No tickling!" she said smiling. "I don't have the strength to fight you off tonight!"

"I hope you are not working so hard you get sick yourself!" said Nick.

Constance looked up into her husband's eyes. "I have no time to be sick," she said. "I have to nurse Hobbamock back to health and get back to my work here at home, before you and the children have it in shambles!"

Nick nodded sheepishly and leaned in to kiss her.

"Besides," said Constance, "The only thing *I* seem to catch is *pregnancy!*"

Nick's mouth fell open and his eyes stared at his wife, who was smiling with all the enthusiasm her tired body could muster.

"Yes," she said. "We will have another baby in the summer."

They fell asleep entwined in each other's arms that night. Constance was so exhausted she slept until the sun's rays coming through the window and little Sarah's fussing in her cradle awoke her. Nick was already up and dressed.

"I have to go," he said almost apologetically. "I hate to leave you."

Constance chuckled. "Do you think I will collapse from hard work? Surely you know me better than that, dear Husband!"

"Aye," replied Nick. "You are far stronger than I could ever be. Do you want me to take the children to Elizabeth for you?"

"They haven't had their breakfast yet, silly. No, I will take them after they have had their breakfast and I have washed them properly. The work at the hospital will still be there an hour from now."

The children were always anxious to visit their grandmother, for it meant getting to play with little Ruth and Damaris. They were not concerned at all to see their mother go off down the street to nurse the sick in the Common House.

That morning Constance did a lot of thinking as she made her way. *What if Doctor Fuller convinced the governor to force Hobbamock to go elsewhere? Where would he go*? She knew she couldn't bring him home and risk him infecting the children. She remembered all too well the horrible deaths of her siblings, Oceanus and Damaris. There had to be a way to protect them and still care for Hobbamock! She absolutely abhorred the ridiculous prejudice others had against the Indians!

After a deep breath and a renewal of her determination to defend their Indian friend, she marched in through the doors of the Common House and looked around for her nemesis.

One of the women rushed up to her immediately. "Constance!" the woman said, "The *doctor* has taken ill! We will need you to tell us what to do!"

Her eyes searched the room and found him lying on a pallet nearest the windows, set off by himself. He was turned toward the wall, and she could not see his face. *'Twas God's justice as sure as the sunrise*! she thought smugly and, just as soon as she said it, in her mind she reprimanded herself. She went first to check on Hobbamock, who was sitting up and looked much improved.

"How are you feeling this morning?" she asked him.

"Feeling much better," replied Hobbamock. "You have nursed me well and I thank you."

"Well, it is easy to nurse one who is so strong!" said Constance.

"I must get back to work with your husband today," he said.

"Perhaps you should take at least one more day to rest. I will make you a good breakfast and then you can decide how you feel."

She poured some thick gruel into two bowls and took one to Hobbamock. Then she approached the doctor and tapped him on his shoulder. The doctor turned toward her, and she could see he was in great misery.

"I have brought you some breakfast," she said.

"No," replied the doctor. "I don't want anything."

"Perhaps some broth then. You must at least take liquids, Doctor."

"I was wrong in what I said yesterday," he said weakly. "It would be un-Christian to turn *anyone* out who feels like I do right now, no matter whether he is white *or* savage! Can you forgive me, Constance?"

Constance's face had a look of surprise that quickly turned to shame. "Only if you can forgive me for being pleased at the news of *your* illness," she replied.

The doctor half smiled and closed his eyes. "I can't blame you for that. It was surely my comeuppance."

She brought him his broth and raised his head so that she could spoon it into his mouth. She sponged his head and chest until he fell asleep and then she went on to care for the other patients.

When she went back to check on Hobbamock, she found the Indian was gone.

Chapter Thirty-Two "The Kennebec Incident"

It had now been a month since the outbreak of the sickness that crippled Plymouth and it finally seemed as if the height of the epidemic was over. Hobbamock was back working and hunting with Nick. Word from the Wampanoag village was that they too had seen the worst of it. Constance was relieved of her duties at the hospital and the governor couldn't thank her enough for her brave service. There had been twenty deaths, including those of the Indians, but it could have been far worse. The one death that strangely affected Constance the most was that of Doctor Fuller. She had discovered his corpse early one morning, lying on his pallet in the corner of the Common House, curled into a fetal ball. After his honest apology, she felt like he had begun to turn away from his prejudice against the Indians. Apparently, God had not been quite so forgiving of his intolerance.

As her belly grew with another new life inside her, Constance learned that Elizabeth, the wife of her spurned admirer, Stephen Deane, was also pregnant with their first child. She was happy that he had at last gone on to have a happy life without her, and, although she had never told him as much, the Deanes were still regular guests in the Hopkins house. Their babies were born within a few weeks of each other; the Deanes welcomed a little girl whom they named Susannah and Constance gave birth to a son named Joseph. Then the news came, sudden and heartbreaking; Stephen Deane had been killed by a falling tree while lumbering in the woods and his widow was left with a brand-new baby and no family except her aging, widowed mother. That death had an impact on Constance as well; she asked herself over and over why she had never apologized to Stephen for disappointing him when she had up and married Nick. She told herself she had no way of knowing how he felt but she knew deep down that was a lie. Constance was racked with remorse over his death for some time to come.

Summer was winding down in Plymouth and yet the building and trading continued every year up until the first snowfall. The town was still growing, stretching its boundaries beyond those originally staked out in the early days. But even though it continued to grow, Plymouth remained a little sister to the larger colonies to the east, who often bullied the Plymouth governor and frequently took advantage of the smaller colony.

 Early on, Plymouth had staked its claim to the Kennebec River, just north of town. They had built a trading post on the riverbanks and hired Plymouth colonist, John Howland, to manage it. This particular summer, trouble came from the Piscataqua settlement, another colony to the north, under the leadership of John Hocking. Hocking himself sailed up the river and anchored his ship just downstream, competing defiantly with the Plymouth post and ignoring repeated warnings from Howland to move along. Finally, Howland became so frustrated with the violation of their trading boundaries, he sent his assistant, Moses Talbot, and some others to cut the moorings from Hocking's ship, hoping to send it adrift down the river. When Hocking came upon Talbot in the act, he shot and killed him. The other men from Plymouth retaliated and killed Hocking.

Neither Piscataqua nor Plymouth were under the jurisdiction of the bigger Bay Colony but the governor there, John Winthrop, nevertheless decided to meddle into the affair. John Alden, husband to Constance's dear friend Priscilla Mullins, had been visiting the trading post on the day of the incident and was arrested by the constable of the Bay Colony for complicity in the murder. When word of his arrest arrived in Plymouth, the new governor, Thomas Prence, who had replaced the retiring William Bradford, sent a scathing letter to Governor Winthrop delivered by Captain Standish. Standish was called to testify, and Alden was released but the matter was far from over. More letters were fired off by Governor Prence, stating that the Bay Colony had absolutely no jurisdiction over the Kennebec River and accusing them of sheer arrogance by putting themselves in the position of judge and jury over the matter. When tempers finally cooled, the two governors put their heads together and it was decided to put an end to the whole affair, since any further discord between the two colonies could prompt their investors in England to send a "general governor" to oversee *all* the English settlements, not an attractive proposition for any of the colonies!

Constance gave birth to another son whom they named Stephen, just when the leaves on the trees were beginning to change color. The little house suddenly seemed to be bursting at its seams with little ones, so for much of the fall, Nick spent his time building a loft so that the older children could sleep upstairs. They borrowed Elizabeth's cradle for the new baby since little Ruth Hopkins had outgrown it. But, although it was very crowded, it was a happy time for the Snow family; the children were healthy and there was ample food in the storehouse. Hobbamock visited often and the children seemed to be fascinated by their big, dark- skinned friend who would sit cross-legged on the floor with them, as he related the legends of the great Wampanoag tribe. They especially loved the story of *Moshup the Indian Giant,* who once lived on Cape Cod and who could catch whales and uproot trees with his bare hands. From the expressions on their faces, the children seemed to believe *Hobbamock was the giant himself*! Constance would watch him with her children with a twinge of sadness that he didn't have children of his own. Hobbamock had become as much a part of both the Hopkins and Snow families as if he had been their own blood.

All of Plymouth did not approve of the Hopkins and Snow families integrating the Indian into their homes, however, and it was planting seeds of resentment. The sentiment of others, while not always voiced, was apparent in the cold stares Constance and Elizabeth received in the street and the children of the other settlers often had unkind words for the Snow and Hopkins children. There was still an ordinance that prohibited serving or selling spirits to the Indians, even the friendly Wampanoags, but frequently Stephen Hopkins ignored the warnings of his friends and would share his beer with both Samoset and Hobbamock when they came to visit.

 "I am concerned about Father's drinking," Constance told Elizabeth in confidence one afternoon, as they were washing clothes together behind the Hopkins house while the children played together in the yard. "Does he fall asleep in his chair every night from too much spirits?"

Elizabeth nodded sadly. "If that were the *only* problem, I would be most happy," she said.

Constance's eyes narrowed as she looked at her stepmother, waiting for her to explain.

"Come with me," said Elizabeth.

The women put down their laundry and Elizabeth led Constance across the yard toward the little shed that had once served the Hopkins family as a chicken coop.

Constance noticed that her father had installed a door on the shed.

"How *ever* do the chickens get to their nesting boxes?" she asked.

"They don't," replied Elizabeth. "I have to search for eggs all over the yard since your father decided to start his own beer- brewing business!"

Elizabeth opened the door a crack and the pungent aroma of fermenting grain hit Constance in the face with a strong punch. Inside the little shed were casks of soaking grain, amidst bottles and other brewing equipment.

"He used to only make enough for himself," said Elizabeth. "Now, he has started *selling* it."

Elizabeth closed the door and the two women returned to their laundry.

"Can he *do* that? I mean is it *legal?*" asked Constance.

"Making beer for one's own use is not against the law," replied Elizabeth. "But----"

"But *what?*" asked Constance fearfully.

"I am afraid he will be arrested for serving it to Samoset and Hobbamock when they come for supper. They never drink too much, and I know they would never say anything to get your father into trouble. I am afraid someone who does not understand our friendship with them will report us. I am afraid they will think he is selling it to the other Indians. I don't know what I would do if your father were imprisoned or sent back to England!"

Constance could not believe her ears! *Her father was not a stupid man! How could he do something that so dangerously jeopardized his family? Had his consumption of alcohol so clouded his mind that he was not thinking rationally? Even if he did have a good rapport with the new governor and was a longtime friend of Captain Standish, he was still treading on shaky ground by taking such liberties!*

"I will speak to him tonight," she told her stepmother. "I am not afraid to tell him what a ninny he is making of himself!"

Returning home Constance prepared supper for her family and sat silently at the table, choosing the words carefully that she was going to say to her father.

"What are you thinking about?" Nick asked.

"I spent the afternoon with Elizabeth," she replied. "I am going to go speak to my father about his drinking after I have gotten the children settled in."

Nick shook his head. "Are you sure that is wise, Constance?" he asked.

"Poor Elizabeth is beside herself with worry, Nick!" replied Constance. "Someone has to talk some sense into him!"

Nick was not at all sure she was doing the right thing, but he did not stop her when she put on her shawl and went out into the night.

She stopped for a moment on the front step of the Hopkins house and collected herself. She knew she often spoke her mind and was later sorry for it. She knew also that her father was every bit as stubborn as she was and not likely to agree with her. She didn't care about that. She wanted to save her father from trouble with the law! *Surely*, she thought, *that is reason enough to speak firmly with him even though he is my father!*

Elizabeth answered the door and let her in, just as the family was finishing their supper and her father was heading toward his chair to remove his boots and rest after a hard day in the fields.

"Well, Constance! I am surprised to see you here at this hour!" he said cheerfully. "Why aren't you home preparing supper for Nick and my grandchildren?"

She took a deep breath that did little to bolster her courage. "Might I have a word with you, Father?"

"Uh oh. I know *that* tone of voice," said Stephen. "What have I done to displease you this time, Love?"

"Father, it's about this new *enterprise* of yours," Constance began.

Stephen dropped his boots on the floor and shook the dirt out of his socks as Constance continued.

"You must know how dangerous it is! You must realize you are putting your entire family at risk of being shamed in front of all of Plymouth!"

There was a silence that enveloped the room. Stephen was searching for words. "Everyone in this colony drinks beer, Constance," he said quietly. "And it is really none of your concern, anyway."

Constance tried hard to restrain herself, but her frustration seemed to burst forth from her lips. *"None of my concern?"* she asked sharply. "If you get yourself arrested, it will affect all of your family! Do you want your children and grandchildren to pass you in the street, while you are chained up in the stocks? Do you want to get Samoset and Hobbamock banished from Plymouth, after all they have done for us?"

Stephen sat down in his chair and stared at the floor. "Tom Prence would not do that do me!" he said. "He lived under our roof when we first came here, or have you forgotten?"

"Tom Prence is the *governor* now and he has to uphold the *laws* of Plymouth," snapped Constance. "You are pretty sure of yourself, if you expect him to bend the laws for *your* sake!"

Elizabeth was standing near the hearth, listening to the conversation and finally had to stop her stepdaughter, fearing she would say too much.

"Constance is just concerned for your safety, Stephen," she said. "And, for the family's reputation."

Stephen stood up then and leaned down to kiss his daughter on the top of her head. "I am a grown man, Constance. You needn't worry about me. Go take care of your own family now and let me rest. It has been a long day."

Constance shrugged with exasperation, before she stormed out of the door, fuming all the way back to the Snow house on the corner. When she opened the door, Nick could see that it had not gone well.

"My father is impossible!" she said. *"There is no reasoning with him!"*

Nick was holding baby Stephen in his arms and the other children were sitting at his feet. Looking at the scene, she was overwhelmed with love and pride for her husband who had become such a good father and who had never given her the slightest bit of worry or unhappiness.

"I am so blessed to have you," she said, as the children ran to greet her.

"Your father is a good man, Constance," he said, handing her the baby. "Even if he *does* like his spirits."

"He is going to get all of us into trouble," replied Constance. "I just know it."

"I don't see how it would have anything to do with us," Nick replied. "We have our own life to live."

He went across the room and retrieved a cloth bag from beneath his cloak. "I almost forgot to give you these," he said. "Captain Pierce arrived today from Jamaica."

Constance took the bag and peered into it. Inside were what looked to be three strange red tubers. "What are they?" she asked.

"They are called *sweet potatoes*," Nick replied. "The captain says they make delicious pies!"

Constance put the bag down and threw her arms around him. "I am glad the only thing you desire in excess is *sweets*!" she said later, as they put the children to bed. "If only my father…."

Chapter Thirty-Three "Cole's Inn"

It has often been said that when a door closes the Lord opens another. For Stephen Hopkins the Lord changed the sequence ever so slightly. The door that first opened was one made of ruggedly- hewn oak planks. It opened with a hefty iron ring in the middle and rubbed back and forth across the floor so often that the marks of its path were permanently etched in the entry way to Cole's Inn.

James Cole, the proprietor, had arrived in Plymouth from London in 1633, with his wife on his arm and a bundle of cash in his briefcase. It didn't take long for the wealthy investor to choose the parcel of land he wished to purchase; it was clearly visible from the docks and made an excellent location for Plymouth's first public house. It was erected on the little hill at the foot of the main street, recently christened *Leiden Street,* where it overlooked the harbor and was the first place disembarking passengers would see as soon as their feet touched solid ground.

Cole was a vociferous character, stout and sturdy, who smelled of the tobacco he always had tucked away in his cheek, perfectly suited for a man who frequently had to extricate intoxicated patrons from his establishment. For the council of Plymouth, he was a bit of a dilemma; the town desperately needed Cole's money and they all agreed that having an inn for travelers would be a boon to their economy. Still, they worried that giving him license to sell alcohol was a gamble. They ultimately decided to throw the dice and take their chances.

Stephen Hopkins was ecstatic when he first heard the news that an inn was being built and he wasted no time in contacting Mister Cole, offering to supply the beer for the inn. They agreed on a price and the operations in the Hopkins' former chicken coop was soon ramped up to a feverish pitch. Neighbors began to tell jokes about the Hopkins' chickens being seen swooning in the yard and that they had started laying eggs with pink spots! Stephen, of course, was oblivious to the ridicule, while poor Elizabeth tried to ignore it; Constance was livid about the reputation she believed her father was imposing on his entire family.

Also arriving with Captain Pierce from Jamaica was a merchant by the name of John Tisdale; a purveyor of rum, who was also interested in supplying Mister Cole with liquor, and, after a taste of his wares, Cole agreed to contract with him as well.

Soon the inn was ready for business, boasting four comfortable rooms with feather beds upstairs over a fully stocked saloon and dining room on the first floor. Stephen Hopkins was one of Cole's first customers and continued to be a most regular guest, when he wasn't toiling away in his backyard chicken coop-turned-distillery. He increased the production of barley on his land, which Giles and Caleb tended to in their father's absence. Stephen had only two complaints about the inn;

that Indians, including his friends Samoset and Hobbamock, were not allowed to set foot inside and that the inn was closed on Sundays, rules that seemed frivolous and petty to him.

John Tisdale usually travelled back and forth with Captain Pierce, peddling his rum, but he remained in Plymouth for several months to be sure Hopkins did not interfere with the deal he had cut with Cole. Cole retained a friendly relationship with both Tisdale and Hopkins but, being a wise businessman, did not allow it to become anything beyond that of a customer and a vendor.

The problem started on a Saturday night, when many of the men had stopped off at the inn for a drink of liquor before going home to their families. Stephen was there, sitting on a stool between his competitor, John Tisdale, and his friend, Captain Pierce. Their conversation was pleasant and jovial at first, singing sea shanties together and telling stories that stretched the boundaries of the truth, as men will often do without their wives present to contradict them. The room was foggy with pipe smoke and humming with the guttural laughter of the men that resonated out into the street when, suddenly, John Tisdale held up his drink to propose a toast to his new friend, Stephen Hopkins.

"Here," said Stephen. "Have a drink of my beer!"

"And you taste my rum!" replied Tisdale, with a slight slur to his words, for the two men had been drinking for quite a while.

As soon as the beer touched Tisdale's tongue, his expression changed, and he rudely spat it out on the bar. *"What rot is this?"* he bellowed. "Is this what you call *beer?"*

The room fell silent as Stephen put his drink down on the bar and turned toward Tisdale. The captain, sensing trouble afoot, put his hand on Stephen's shoulder to calm him.

"What did you say?" demanded Stephen, looking at Tisdale with rage in his eyes.

"Why, it's no better than strong water with nutmeg for coloring!" said Tisdale. "And, selling it for two pence is highway robbery! It isn't worth a penny!"

He rose from his stool awkwardly and turned away from Stephen.

"You come back here and say that to my face!" shouted Stephen, rising himself and pursuing the rum merchant across the room and finally grabbing him by the neck, spinning him around.

"All I said was...." Tisdale started to say before Stephen swung wildly, his fist connecting squarely with the other man's jaw and knocking him to the floor.

By that time, Cole had come running from behind the bar, taking Stephen by the arms and pinning him against the wall. Poor Tisdale was helped to his feet, his nose bloodied and a bruised eye that was surely to be black by morning.

"Someone call Captain Standish!" yelled Cole. "*I want this man arrested!*"

Captain Pierce tried his best to come to Stephen's aid, suggesting a good night's sleep was all his friend really needed. "He'll be paying penalty enough when he wakes on the morrow with an aching head," said Pierce. "Why don't you let me take him home?"

Cole refused. "No," he replied. "This man will pay for his actions in the stockade!"

When Standish arrived and shuttled Stephen off to jail, Captain Pierce took it upon himself to pay a visit to Elizabeth, to inform her where her husband would be spending the night.

"Thank you for telling me Captain," Elizabeth said sadly.

"I am sure Standish will allow you to see him. Do you want me to escort you up the hill?" the captain asked.

Elizabeth smiled slightly, her presence unruffled. Calmly she replied, "That won't be necessary, Captain. My husband will just have to suffer through this night on his own."

Chapter Thirty-Four "A Helping of Crow Pie"

Stephen Hopkins opened his eyes and blinked them several times before he remembered where he was; lying on a hard, canvas cot under a window, through which the morning sun was shooting directly into his face like a hot dagger. His head was on fire and his mouth felt like it was full of cotton bolls. He needed a drink!

Captain Standish was sitting behind a small desk in the adjoining room, separated from him by iron bars, eating the breakfast that his wife Barbara had brought for him. A plate covered with a white linen napkin sat on a chair next to the cell.

"My wife brought you some breakfast too, Hopkins," said the captain, pointing at the plate. "You'd better eat it before it gets cold."

Stephen raised his head slowly and tried to focus on the room around him. "Don't feel much like breakfast," he said. "Can I get a drink?"

Standish stood up and dipped a tin cup full of water from a small cask in the corner and brought it to his prisoner.

"Water is all I can give you," he said, passing it between the bars to Stephen's shaky hands.

There was a pause while he drank the water and the captain returned to his breakfast.

"What am I going to do with you, Hopkins?" asked Standish. "If the members of our own council can't abide by the laws, how are we ever to have peace in this town?"

Stephen shook his head. "I'm sorry Myles," he said. "How badly did I hurt Tisdale? I don't remember hitting him but once for that crack he made about my beer."

"Apparently that was all it took," replied the captain. "He is on his way back to Jamaica on Pierce's ship, with a shiner and a swollen nose. And I expect you will be banned from the inn for a good long time."

Stephen sat back down on the cot and held his aching head in his hands.

"Was it really worth it?" asked the captain.

"Has Elizabeth been to visit me?"

"Pierce offered to bring her here and she refused," said Standish. "She is a fine woman, your wife. But even the best wives have their limits."

Stephen stretched out again and hid his eyes from the sun. He could hear footsteps and voices from the church downstairs and realized it was Sunday. Elizabeth and the children would undoubtedly be sitting right under him, singing and praying and trying to hold their heads high, while the head of their family was sitting above them in a jail cell.

"How long must I stay here, Myles?" he asked, not bothering to open his eyes.

"You can go home tomorrow," he said. "The governor wanted you to stay at least two nights, so it didn't look like we play favorites."

"Tom knows about this?" asked Stephen.

"Of course. I had to ask him what he wanted me to do with you! You are lucky he didn't want me to put you in the stocks! You are an embarrassment to a lot of people right now!"

Stephen rolled toward the wall to try to go back to sleep. "I know, I know," he mumbled as he drifted off again.

At that very moment, Elizabeth bravely entered the meeting room downstairs, with all her children following in her footsteps. Several women's hands reached out to clutch hers as she passed and Elder Brewster came up to her as they took their seats and planted his bony hand on her shoulder.

"God bless you, Elizabeth," he whispered. "You are truly a brave woman and an example for your children and grandchildren."

She didn't feel brave, however. Inside, her stomach was tied in knots, wondering what the other parishioners were thinking but not saying. She looked up at the ceiling and wondered if Stephen was awake and what was going to happen to her husband. *Perhaps*, she thought to herself, *I have been too lenient with him*! Perhaps she needed to be more like Constance and speak her mind! Constance and Nick arrived with their children and sat down behind the Hopkins family. Elizabeth was thankful that her stepdaughter had chosen such a fine man as Nick Snow to marry. When the elder began to preach, she tried to put her mind on the sermon, but his words drifted in through her ears and very little of it registered in her head. It was going to be a long, long Sabbath!

When they finally returned home, Constance and her family joined them, as they always did on Sundays; she sent little Mark home to fetch the sweet potato pie she had prepared, and the other children ran out to play in the yard.

"Have you heard what they will do with Father?" Constance asked.

"No," replied Elizabeth. "I haven't asked."

Constance put her arms around her stepmother. "You are doing the right thing, Mother," she said gently. "He has gone too far this time and he must deal with the consequences of his actions."

"I didn't even take him anything to eat," said Elizabeth.

"I am sure Barbara Standish is feeding him well," replied Constance. "And I hope it is a big helping of *crow pie!*"

Nick chuckled. "You women are cruel! Maybe I should pay poor Stephen a visit and let him know he hasn't been forgotten!"

"Don't you *dare* go visit him, Nicholas Snow!" said Constance. "Not until he has apologized to this family!"

When they all sat down to eat their supper, the children were unusually quiet, glancing up from their plates toward the Stephen's empty chair.

"When will Captain Standish let Grandfather come home?" asked little Mark with the innocence of a nine-year-old.

"He will be home soon," said Nick. "Now you finish your supper. *There is pie for dessert!*"

Chapter Thirty-Five "The Jailbird"

As promised, Captain Standish released Stephen that Monday morning. Stephen had slept through the Sabbath and into the night. When he *did* wake, it was to semi-darkness in the little cell, with only the flicker of an oil lamp burning behind the captain's desk, where the night guard, a young lad not much older than Giles, sat reading a book. He had laid there for several hours, thinking about his predicament, rehearsing the words he would say to Elizabeth and the children. He could feel his hands shaking; he could not remember the last time he had gone so long without a single drink. He finally fell back into a fitful sleep full of dreams, until the sun woke him again, poking him rudely in the eye.

In the morning, when they changed the guard and Standish came on duty, he noticed that his prisoner was awake. He retrieved his key and opened the cell door. "You are free to go, Hopkins," he said. "As soon as you have paid your fine."

Stephen sat up. His head no longer ached, and his stomach had settled. "Might I have some water?" he asked.

The captain pointed to the cask sitting in the corner of the room. "Help yourself," he said.

"So how much do I owe?" Stephen asked.

"Five pounds to the colony. Forty shillings to Tisdale, as restitution," was the captain's reply.

"*What?*" shrieked Hopkins. "*That is outrageous! And what of Tisdale?*"

"Tisdale didn't throw a single punch, Stephen. I can hardly fine him for that!"

Stephen shook his head and started for the door. "I don't have that much on my person," he said. "Will you trust me to go home and return with the money?"

Captain Standish smiled and crossed the room, where he took Stephen's hand in friendship. "Of course," he said. "Stephen, it's nothing *personal,* you understand. I am bound by the law!"

"Aye," replied Stephen, as he walked out of the door out onto Leiden Street.

He hurried along, staying in the shadows of the houses, hoping not to meet anyone along the way. It was mid-morning, and he could see the men in the fields and the merchants in their shops. Quietly, he approached the front door of his house and opened it quickly. Elizabeth was seated in his chair, with her sewing in her lap and she looked up at him, with no expression in her eyes. He went to her side and knelt on the floor beside her, burying his head in her lap. "Can you ever forgive me, Elizabeth?" he whispered.

Elizabeth laid her hand on her husband's head and stroked it. "Yes," she said curtly. "*As long as it never happens again.*"

Stephen looked up at her startled at the defiance in his wife's voice. "*You have been coached by Constance! Those are her words, as sure as I am standing here!*"

Elizabeth shook her head. "In the first place, you are kneeling, not *standing,*" she replied. "And, no, those are *my* words! And, I mean them, Stephen! Never again will you shame our family in such a way!"

He was taken aback by the stern tone in her voice. Was this *his* gentle Elizabeth? He stared at her for a moment in disbelief. *This is my daughter's doing*! he thought to himself. "Did Constance tell you not to visit me?" he asked sarcastically.

"No," she said. "I refuse to bring my children into a jailhouse where criminals are kept!"

"The only *criminal* there was *me*, Elizabeth," said Stephen. "What do you suppose people think of a wife who doesn't even have enough compassion to visit her poor, imprisoned husband?"

Elizabeth put down her sewing and pushed Stephen aside as she stood up. "Perhaps," she said with quiet defiance, "They will think I am a woman with high moral standards!"

With that said she marched out and slammed the door. He sat down in his chair, reeling from the tongue lashing he had just received from his once sweet and understanding wife. How could she have changed so much in only two days? He knew it was because of Constance's influence. He would have words with his daughter; it was one thing to be a hard-headed and stubborn child, but he would *not* allow her to meddle in his marriage!

He looked around the room. He needed a drink! Just a little to calm his nerves! He hurried to the corner of the room and lifted the floorboards over the little crawlspace, only to discover Elizabeth had thrown out the last of the beer! Suddenly, he panicked. What had become of his brew house in the backyard? He ran out of the door and saw it was still standing and, relieved, he rushed across the yard and reached for the door only to find it was locked with a large iron padlock.

By now he was furious! He ran back through the gate and up the street, toward the Snow house, seething with anger and ready for a fight. Not bothering to knock on the door, he burst into the room where Constance and Elizabeth were sitting at the supper table.

"Are you looking for this?" asked his wife, holding up a brass key.

Stephen stared at her and then he turned toward his daughter. "I hope you are happy with yourself, Constance!" he said sharply.

"Your daughter has nothing to do with this," responded Elizabeth. "She has been nothing more than support for me during a very difficult time that *you* caused."

"And I suppose she is not counseling you now! I notice that you ran to *her* first!"

Constance, showing remarkable restraint, had not said a word.

"*What? Nothing to say*?" he fired at his daughter. "*Tell me what have you two been talking about?*"

Elizabeth stood up from the table. Constance reached out and squeezed her stepmother's hand affectionately. Stephen watched as his wife bent over and picked up the cradle that she had loaned to Constance for baby Stephen. Holding it under her arm and anchoring it on her hip, she started for the door. She turned and looked into her husband's eyes. "We were discussing which one of us would need the cradle *first* since *both* of us are expecting a child in the spring!"

Chapter Thirty-Six *"Catone* and the Berry Wine"

Hobbamock bent his towering frame slightly to enter the door and Stephen, Nick and Giles followed behind him into the *wetu.* The fires were burning brightly with flames popping and snapping up toward the opening in the hickory wood shingles and the embers were disappearing out into the night sky. It was an honor to have been invited to the Wampanoag harvest celebration and the three were most humble, sitting down cross-legged in the dirt that was packed and smooth from many before them. The *sachem* sat in the center of the round room on a mat of rabbit skins, so his height was not apparent, but Nick remembered that when he stood upright, he was several inches taller than even Hobbamock. The brown muscles of his arms were showing from under his sleeveless vest and a wide beaded band was wrapped tightly around his forehead, with a single black and white eagle feather protruding up from the crown of his graying head. He wore a simple chain of white bone beads around his neck and his face was well oiled and painted red with mulberry. The *wetu* was full of men, dressed and faces painted much like their sachem, and women, in simple deerskin dresses and woven hemp belts. After the women brought in the food in huge wooden bowls and clay pitchers, they took their places beside the men. *In the Wampanoag tribe,* Hobbamock explained for the benefit of his white brothers, *women are equal* to *men; they possess the land on which their families live.*

"Our Constance would surely be in favor with that custom!" remarked Stephen, winking at Nick and Giles.

A hush came over the room when Massasoit began to speak, and the Englishmen could only understand a few of his words but the passion with which he spoke was not lost upon them. With Hobbamock whispering translations to them, they listened as the tribe prayed to many *gods,* most importantly *Mother Earth,* for nurturing their crops and the *Three Sisters, Corn, Beans and Squash,* for their abundance. They passed around ears of raw corn, of which everyone took a bite and then threw the bare cobs into the fire. They drank the bitter tobacco drink and then a sour wine made of fermented blackberries; Nick realized he could stomach the tobacco if he washed it down quickly after with the wine.

They sang songs in the *Wampanoag* tongue, while several men beat on drums made of stretched deer hides and held together with deer bones. They thanked the deer, the rabbits, and all the birds who supplied them with meat. On the sachem's right, sat his brothers, *Quadequina* and *Akkompion* and, on his left, were his three sons, *Wamsutta, Metacomet* and *Sonkanuchoo* and his daughters, *Amie* and *Diguina.* Surprisingly, another white man whom Hobbamock later introduced to them as *Gabriel Wheldon,* the husband of *Diguina,* sat next to his wife with their daughter, a lovely olive-skinned beauty named *Catone*.

After the prayers, there was conversation and laughter and more drinking of berry wine and tobacco tea. Hobbamock introduced his white brothers to all the Indians who had names too difficult to pronounce and when they finally came to Gabriel Wheldon it was with relief to finally speak to someone who understood English!

"Where are you from?" Nick asked him. "I don't believe I have ever seen you around Plymouth."

Wheldon was well versed in both English and Wampanoag and frequently broke into one or the other language, depending on whom he was speaking with.

"I settled up in Maine when I first came from England. I am a fisherman by trade," he replied. "I fish off Cape Cod and Chappaquiddick mostly now."

"I find it interesting," said Stephen, "that the Wampanoags so readily accept the marriage of the sachem's daughter to a white man."

"Indeed," added Nick. "In Plymouth they would have whipped you through the streets!"

Wheldon shrugged. "The Wampanoag accepted me right away. But my English brothers were not quite so tolerant. Now, I spend most of my time here among my wife's family."

"Strange, isn't it?" remarked Nick. "How humans can be so ignorant? Can you see our *red* cows refusing to mate with our *black* bull? Or the *white* goats turning their noses up at the *brown* ones? We humans are, after all, of the same species, are we not?"

"And, yet the white tail do not mix with the mule deer, do they?" asked Stephen. "At least, you never see them running together."

Hobbamock shook his head. "It happens," he said. "But not very often. I saw an *ottucke* once with a big white tail, no antlers and fat hind- quarters like an English mule. Hobbamock paused and added, "He tasted just fine."

The men laughed.

The conversation, at that point, was lost on Giles. His attention had been on one particular person in the *wetu* from the moment he had set eyes on her. Never had he seen such a beauty! Her hair was long and like shiny silk, her eyes were deep like black holes in her face. He waited breathlessly until Hobbamock introduced her, and then forgot everything he had wanted to say, just standing there like a blubbering fool, watching her walk away. He had never felt that way about *any* of the girls in Plymouth! He remembered his father's words about getting bitten by the *love bug* and now he could understand. Giles was hopelessly smitten with *Catone…. the half- Indian granddaughter of the great sachem!*

The four men finally said their goodbyes to Massasoit and his family and started out on the long walk back to Plymouth, wavering in the moonlight from the berry wine and still singing the Wampanoag songs. Giles and Hobbamock each held one of Stephen's arms, maneuvering around the ruts in the road and Nick, the soberest among them, walked alongside, wondering what Constance would have to say about her father's intoxication.

"Enough of Wampanoag songs!" Stephen suddenly blurted out. "Let's sing an English tune for a change! What was that one we used to sing on the Mayflower, Giles?"

Giles' mind was blurry, more from the sight of Catone than from the wine, but he humored his father and tried to remember the words,

Across the rolling windswept sea,

For months we've sailed along,

I see a land that's new to me,

Against the blue horizon.

He couldn't remember the rest.

"I think we had better stop our singing," said Nick as soon as he saw the lights of Plymouth ahead of them. "Captain Standish will surely arrest us all for public drunkenness!"

And, sure enough, the Snow house was just ahead, with a single lamp glowing in the window.

"Constance must be waiting up for me," he said. "Can you two get Stephen home all right? Try to keep him quiet so he doesn't wake our neighbors!"

"Excuse me, Nick, but I do believe I am capable of finding my own way home," Stephen replied. "I want to sing some more!"

"Shhhhhh!" said Nick. "Constance will hear you!"

"We will get him home," said Hobbamock, holding tightly to Stephen's arm.

Nick slipped into his house quietly and Giles and their Indian brother continued up the street toward the Hopkins house, trying to direct Stephen's teetering steps. Although they had stopped their singing, Elizabeth immediately opened the door.

"Bring him in and put him in his bed," she said.

Giles let go of his father's hand and the huge Indian scooped Stephen up in his arms and carried him across the room. As soon as he laid him down, Stephen sat up and started singing again.

"Giles, you need to go to bed! It is late!" she said. "You are welcome to sleep here by the fire, Hobbamock." She turned to Stephen who was still singing. "And you, *hush*! You are going to wake the dead lying in the cemetery!"

They all fell silent and looked at each other when they heard someone pounding on the door. Elizabeth went quickly to open it and came face to face with Governor Prence and Captain Standish. As they stepped into the room and saw Hobbamock sitting on the floor they exchanged looks.

"I'm sorry, Elizabeth," said the governor. "I really don't want to arrest him again."

"No apologies are necessary, Tom," she replied. "Take him! Perhaps I shall get some sleep tonight after all!"

"Hobbamock, I am surprised at *you,*" said Standish.

"The fault is mine," said the Indian. "I invited him to our harvest celebration. I am afraid he was not accustomed to our spirits."

"Stephen knows the law about drinking with the Wampanoags. I will have to take him in."

Elizabeth stepped forward. "Surely, you are not going to arrest Hobbamock too!" she said.

"No," replied Standish. "He may stay, for it looks as if he has his wits about him. But your husband is coming with us."

Chapter Thirty-Seven "Elizabeth's Blackmail"

When morning came, Elizabeth got up and went about her usual chores without variation. She prepared breakfast for Hobbamock and the children, then she put on her bonnet and laced up her boots. "Giles, will you please watch over the children for a little while?" she asked. "I have something I need to do."

"Of course, Mother," said Giles. "But where are you going so early in the day?"

"It doesn't concern you, Giles," she said matter-of-factly and disappeared out of the door and headed up the street toward the stockade.

When she reached the building on the hill, instead of climbing the stairs to visit her incarcerated husband, she entered the church meeting room and sought out Elder Brewster. After a few words were exchanged, she and the reverend marched back down the street toward the governor's house and knocked on his door. They were there for the better part of an hour before she thanked them both and returned home. Giles and the children were waiting for her.

"Has Hobbamock gone?" she asked Giles.

"Yes, Mother," replied Giles. "He was going to chop firewood with Nick today."

"You are free to go now, Giles," said Elizabeth. "I shan't need you to care for the little ones anymore today."

Giles was intrigued by his mother's mysterious demeanor, wondering how she was keeping her composure when Father was locked up in the stockade. "What are you up to, Mother?" he asked. "You have a strange manner about you."

"Your father's behavior has me a bit upset," she said. "But I think I have resolved the problem now. Go on now! You must have work to do!"

The rest of the day was uneventful. While Stephen was still sleeping off the berry wine in the stockade, Constance came with the children in the morning, having heard the news of her father's arrest. "I think it is unconscionable what Father is doing to this family!" she told Elizabeth.

Elizabeth smiled. "I think everything will be under control now, Constance," she said. "I have a plan."

"Do tell, Mother! What are you going to do to him?" shrieked Constance.

"You will have to wait and see," said Elizabeth, in a most provocative tone.

When Nick and Hobbamock returned from cutting wood and they all finally sat down to eat at the Hopkins supper table, the empty chair where Stephen usually sat loomed in the room like a ghost. No one mentioned him, not even the children. And, still, Elizabeth was being evasive about her "plan."

The rest of the week raced by for the family, for there was always more work to be done and never enough time in which to do it. The hours passed very slowly however for Stephen, who was now wide awake and anxious to go home.

"I say, Standish!" he said. "When are you going to let me out of this cage?"

Captain Standish repeated what he had been saying all along; *that he wouldn't know until the governor had made a decision.*

"Well, that's gratitude for you!" said Stephen icily. "And to think I opened my home to him! When I get out of here, I will have a few choice words for *Tom Prence!*"

"Seems to me, this is the time for you to be on your best behavior!" replied Standish.

Another day passed without issue. Elizabeth and Constance did laundry together as usual, while the men stacked firewood and the children played in the autumn sun. Still, there was a sense of foreboding in the air; something looming over the horizon. The family got no answers when they asked when Stephen would return. Elizabeth just continued to wear her never- wavering expression and changed the subject, whenever her husband came up in conversation.

"I cannot believe they have already kept him in jail almost an entire week!" Constance told Nick in the privacy of their home. "Elizabeth is planning some type of punishment for him when he comes home! How long can they legally imprison a man for drunkenness anyway?"

Nick swore that he was as much in the dark about the matter as was the entire family.

Several more days passed, until early on Sunday morning, when Elizabeth laid out clean clothes for all the children and told Giles to get them ready for church. "I have something I must do," was all she would say. "You can take the children up the hill at the proper time and I will meet you there."

At that moment, up the street, two men entered the stockade where Stephen was still sleeping; Tom Prence and Elder Brewster were both dressed for the Sabbath. They sat down in silence until Elizabeth arrived, before anyone spoke.

"Hopkins!" shouted Standish. "Wake up!"

Stephen stirred on his cot and rolled over, staring in surprise at the group of people standing outside his cell. "What is going on?" he asked, the instant he saw Elizabeth.

"Hopkins," began the governor. "There has been a consensus of opinion regarding your sentence."

Stephen rolled his eyes suspecting a conspiracy. "Indeed?" he said. "Where is my daughter? Surely she has something to do with this!"

Elizabeth stepped forward and peered between the iron bars at her husband. "Constance does not know anything about this," she said. "Only the people in this room know what is going on."

"Hopkins, you are to have a choice of your punishment. You may either serve out your term of one year in the stockade or…." began the governor.

Stephen stood up then and approached the bars of his cell. *"One year?"* he said curtly. *"Have you all gone mad? One year for drinking the Indian's berry wine? Ha! What is my other choice?"*

Elder Brewster stepped forward. "You will join the Plymouth Church and attend services every Sunday, until the end of your sentence."

The room was silent. Stephen stared at them in disbelief. He couldn't believe his ears. *"You can't be serious!"*

"We are *very* serious, Hopkins," said Prence. "It's *your* choice! What will it be?"

Stephen wanted out of the little cell. He wanted to sleep in his comfortable feather bed. He wanted to be with his family again. Still, who were they and what right did they have to force him to join a church against his will? It was nothing short of blackmail!

"I have no other choices?" he asked, knowing what the answer would be. "Very well, Tom! But I shall remember this!"

So, they all marched downstairs and into the church, that was by now full of parishioners. Elder Brewster came in first, with his Bible in his hands, and silently took his place at the pulpit. Governor Prence found the spot his wife was saving for him in the front row. Captain Standish took his usual post beside the door.

And, then a hush came over the room, as Elizabeth and Stephen Hopkins entered together and walked down the aisle. Constance and the rest of the family looked up at them in disbelief as the two sat down beside them.

"We have a new member joining our church today!" said Elder Brewster. "*Please welcome Mister Stephen Hopkins!*"

The applause was so deafening, and it shook the walls of the room with such intensity, some said that *God himself* was clapping along with the congregation that morning!

Chapter Thirty-Eight "The *Miracle* Baby"

That very night there was a knock at the door of the little house on the northern outskirts of town that belonged to Edward Doty, the former bondsman for Stephen Hopkins and spurned suitor of Constance Hopkins. When he had finally recovered from the shock of Constance's marriage to Nick Snow, Doty had proposed to the first girl who had shown him any attention at all and married her immediately. For several years now, the couple had been farming and raising a passel of children, rarely coming into town and never attending services at Plymouth Church. While his wife was tending to their latest newborn, Doty picked up his axe for protection and went to the door, straining his eyes out into the darkness to see who was calling. The Dotys were not accustomed to visitors.

A vaguely familiar- looking man stood on the front step; a bedraggled- looking fellow with a ragged pack slung over his shoulder and a walking stick in his hand.

"What do you want?" barked Doty, expecting the man to be a beggar looking for a handout.

"I am looking for work, Sir," said the man. "And perhaps a place to sleep in your barn?"

Doty squeezed the tobacco he had been chewing between his tongue and his cheek and spat a puddle of brown juice onto the ground, very near the man's dusty shoes. "Do I know you?" he asked of the stranger.

"I have been away for a long while," said the man. "I used to live in Plymouth, with my family."

"Why don't you go to them for a job, then?" Doty asked sharply. He didn't need any vagrants hanging around his place looking for things to steal!

"My cousin was getting married and there was more no room for me," said the man. "I was hoping to find a job and lodging elsewhere. Perhaps you know him...*Nick Snow?"*

"Aye," said Doty sourly. "*I know him.*"

Doty was not at all keen on hiring this man and *especially* if he was related to *Nick Snow,* the scoundrel who had stolen Constance Hopkins right out from under his nose! While he was silently debating with himself over the issue of helping the Snow family, his wife spoke to him from across the room, "Edward, do you not have a section of land that you were hoping to get turned under before the snow?" she asked.

Doty sighed and twisted his face, spitting his tobacco juice again onto the ground. He looked the man up and down. *He certainly looks sturdy enough for field work*, he thought, *but only if I can get him at a bargain price.*

"Can't pay you much," he said to the man. "Room and board and a penny a day."

The man broke into a broad smile and reached out to shake Doty's hand. "That would be just fine, Sir!" he said. "I can start right away! Thank you, Sir! *Will Snow's the name!*"

Faith Doty came up behind her husband and smiled at Will over her husband's shoulder. "You must be hungry. Wait there and I will make you a plate before my husband puts you to work!"

"Thank you, Mistress!" said Will. "It has been a long while since I have had anything to eat!"

"Humph!" grunted Doty. "Hardly seems fittin' to *feed* him before he has done a lick of work!"

When she brought him a plate of beans and corn, with a tiny morsel of meat no bigger than a walnut in it, she whispered, "Don't mind my husband. He sounds fierce but he is really a good man."

Will thanked her again and took his dinner out to the one-stall barn that was no more than a three-sided lean-to behind the house and found a spot next to the family cow in the straw to eat his food.

"*Plymouth!*" he thought, while he savored the vegetables on his tongue and pulled his wineskin from his pack. It had been a long time, *thirteen years actually,* since he had seen his cousins! He began to wonder if Anthony had married and how many children Nick and Constance would have by now. He wondered if his old companion, Billington, was still up to his scheming ways and if his cousins had ever revealed what was going on between him and the Indians. Realizing he could have a warrant out for his arrest, he planned to lay low for a while, put a little money in his pocket, and find a way to see his cousins without calling unwanted attention to himself.

Will had spent most of his absence on fishing boats out of Bay Colony, figuring he was less likely to be found on the open sea. In retrospect, he could now see the absurdity of his own life; the insincere promises he had made both to himself and his cousins the day he had climbed aboard the *Anne* back in London. How he had fretted over the English constable following him, when he only got himself into more *serious* trouble in Plymouth! *Forgiveness*, he reasoned, if he was forgiven at all, was more likely to come from Nick than from Anthony, who would have no such compassion for him. What did it all matter now, anyway? Even if his cousins no longer wanted to have anything to do with him, *for the moment at least,* he had a job, a roof of sorts over his head and food in his belly! He glanced up at the cow standing beside him as he made his bed in the straw, thinking *Anthony's God* must surely be watching over him, no matter what opinion his cousin had of him, for tonight he felt quite blessed indeed!

When morning came, Doty rousted poor Will out of the straw, poking him in the back with the friendly end of a pitchfork and slapped a spade into his hands before he summoned him down the road and pointed to the land that needed to be cleared. "Want to get as much turned under as I can before the snows come," said Doty. "I expect a full day's work out of you, so don't think you'll get away with sleeping under a tree. I'll be watching you!"

"No, Sir," Will said humbly, staring out at the field of weeds and brambles. "We'll have this field done before you know it, Mister Doty, Sir!"

With that, Doty marched off down the road and Will did not see him again until nightfall but, somehow, he was sure the man was spying on him from afar as he worked. He bent over and began shoveling the hard clay. His muscles had strengthened a bit from all the years he had spent shipboard; the daily hoisting of lines and repetitive climbing aloft on the shrouds had left him in better physical shape than he had ever been in. At about the time the sun first appeared over the treetops to the west, Faith Doty came up the road carrying a plate of food for him.

"My husband is a stern taskmaster," she said. "Sometimes he forgets about breakfast!"

"I thank you, Mistress," said Will, taking the plate from her.

"Supper is at sundown," she said. "You just come on down to the house and I will set a place for you."

She was a plain woman, slightly pear- shaped, with sagging breasts and a large bottom that filled out her long dress, and she wore a perpetual look of fatigue on her face. She seemed happy, however, even in her shabby faded clothes and content with her lot. For a man who had lived all his life pursuing money for a living, Will was beginning to see that life was not all about how much silver he could put in his pocket. No, there were little, more important things, like having a wife and family, and he almost envied Doty!

As he worked the earth into long horizontal furrows that morning, Will had no way of knowing that he was not the only member of the Snow family who was beginning life anew that day! A few miles away, within hours of each other, two babies were coming into the world. With fourteen-year-old Deborah Hopkins acting as midwife to both her mother and her sister, running back and forth between the two houses on Leiden Street, and her older brother, Caleb, supervising all the other children as they played in the Hopkins' backyard, it was turning out to be a most memorable, frantic sort of day.

Little *John Snow* entered the world first, at half past ten in the morning, with his mother's red hair and his father's strong lungs; a robust, chubby boy whose voice could be heard all the way to the Common House!

His infant aunt, *Elizabeth Hopkins*, named after her mother, arrived just two hours later; a tiny, tow-headed cherub who would thereafter be known as the Hopkins' *miracle baby,* for she came after many barren years, and she was to truly be *the last child Elizabeth would ever bear!*

Chapter Thirty-Nine "A Ticklish Affair"

 Within the next few weeks, *the subject of Indians* was on the tongues and in the minds of almost every adult in the town of Plymouth, mostly because of two events that happened almost concurrently, but neither having anything to do with the other. One concerned a woman by the name of *Mary Mendlove* and the other a situation involved *Giles Hopkins*, younger brother of Constance Hopkins.

By 1639, the relationship between the Wampanoag tribe and the settlers had grown stronger than ever. In addition to Hobbamock and Samoset, who had lived among the people of Plymouth for many years, there were dozens of their brown-skinned brothers working alongside them as well; cultivating crops in the fields, leading hunting parties into the woods and even working as household servants to those who, like the Hopkins and Snow families, had shed their prejudices enough to allow the *gentle savages* into their homes. Some, like Nick Snow and Stephen Hopkins, truly considered the Indians to be as much brothers as the men back home in England, regardless of the color of their skin.

There were still a few, however, who did not exhibit such tolerance, who thought of the Indians as second- class servants, refusing them a voice the affairs of the colony, even though they had been instrumental in building it. It was apparent also that when the men on the Plymouth council determined there had been improper behavior between the Indians and the English, there was a vastly different *double standard* in the way the offenders were punished. It soon became common for decisions to be made for *political* reasons rather than *ethical* ones.

Mary Mendlove had come to Plymouth from England with her husband Robert on one of Captain Pierce's later voyages and had settled on a parcel of land to the east of town, out toward the old Billington place. The Mendloves were, from the very beginning, reclusive; they did not mingle with the townsfolk at all but kept to themselves on their land. Mary was very young, at least twenty years her husband's junior, which might have accounted for their private natures; women in the colony could be especially harsh when it came to men marrying much younger girls. Mary was also very beautiful, with long, flowing hair and a handsome figure, which might have been her husband's motive for keeping to themselves.

Whatever their reasons were, Robert Mendlove soon found himself in need of help in his fields and came to town one day, inquiring about hiring an Indian to work for him. The next day, a young Wampanoag named *Tinsin* appeared at the Mendlove front door, ready to go to work and, after that, Robert and *Tinsin* could be seen every day digging side by side. They were an unlikely pair, the bare-chested Indian in his doeskin loincloth and his employer, a middle-aged man with a belly paunch and a receding hairline. It didn't take long for the tongues of Plymouth to begin wagging with gossip.

Just what was going on no one really knew, except the Mendloves and *Tinsin* himself, but it made good fodder for conversation. The day Robert Mendlove came into town to buy lumber to build a loft in their house for *Tinsin* to sleep, the rumors took off like wildfire and there seemed to be no end to the stories. That is until one day in October, when Robert once again appeared in town, this time to speak to the governor about obtaining a divorce. It was true, he told Tom Prence, he had caught his wife red- handed, dallying with *Tinsin* in his very own house! Accompanied by Captain Standish and the governor, in his official capacity, Mendlove returned home, only to find that his young wife and her lover, *Tinsin*, had *vanished*.

An official warrant was issued, and it was only a matter of days until the couple was found in the northern town of Duxbury and were both dragged back to Plymouth to stand trial. The entire town came out to witness the proceedings, for no one could resist the temptation of such a scandalous story! Two witnesses were called to testify; the wronged husband and a livery man from Duxbury who had found the couple sleeping in his hayloft. Mendlove's divorce was granted on grounds of adultery. As for the two accused, little Mary Mendlove was sentenced to be whipped in the street and as further punishment was required to wear a badge on her sleeve, identifying her as an adulteress. Even though the whipping seemed to be enough punishment in itself, the poor girl was threatened that if she was ever found *not* wearing the shameful badge in public, she would be burned in the face with a hot iron! It was no wonder Mary Mendlove soon disappeared and was never seen or heard from again.

Her lover, *Tinsin,* however received a much less brutal sentence; while he too had to endure a whipping, it was not a public event and he received his stripes in the privacy of the stockade and then was quietly sent back to the Wampanoag camp.

At about the time the gossip was dying down over the Mendlove affair, Giles Hopkins stirred up an even bigger controversy. It began one evening at the Hopkins supper table and quite out of the blue. While Stephen Hopkins was fully aware of his son's friendship with Hobbamock and knew that his son visited the Wampanoag village regularly, Giles had been keeping a secret from his parents and the rest of the family.

"Father," he said on this particular night, while Elizabeth was clearing the supper dishes and Stephen had settled in his chair, "I want to marry *Catone.*"

The name did not register to Stephen at first. "Who?" he asked.

"Catone," replied Giles. *"Massasoit's granddaughter. Remember? You met her at the harvest festival!"*

The room was silent for what seemed like a very protracted moment. Stephen cleared his throat, while Elizabeth set the dishes down and waited silently for her husband to speak.

"Father?" asked Giles, *"Did you hear what I said?"*

"Yes, Son," replied Stephen.

"Well," said Giles, seating himself on the bench very near to Stephen's chair. "What have you to say about it?"

"Well," began Stephen, "have you spoken to her *father* about it?"

Giles nodded. "Catone's *father* is an Englishman too and he likes me. And Massasoit himself has given us his blessing!"

Elizabeth sat down at the table across from her son. She reached out and took his hand. "Surely you know this marriage would not be accepted by many of our neighbors, don't you, Giles?" she asked. It was not from prejudice that she was speaking; she wanted to protect her child from the cruelty that came from human ignorance.

"Mother," said Giles. "I am surprised at you! Bending to the hypocrisy of people who think it is perfectly acceptable to have Indians cultivate their fields but think their roofs will fall in if they invite them inside for supper!"

Stephen defended his wife. "I am sure your mother is not bending to *anything*, Giles," he said. "She just doesn't want to see you hurt. Have you so quickly forgotten what happened to the Mendlove woman? Have you had any thoughts of what the governor will have to say about this? They could banish you from Plymouth altogether!"

"This is *nothing* like the Mendlove affair!" replied Giles angrily. "That was nothing more than a disgusting scandal! Surely the governor can't arrest me if we marry *legally*! As long as both our families accept, us we don't need the approval of others."

Stephen shook his head. "I am afraid you *will* need the approval of the Plymouth council if you intend to go through with this! You know your mother and I have no objection to you marrying the girl. We have always believed that Wampanoag blood is red, just as ours. But you must be prepared for the opposition and ridicule you will undoubtedly receive from others. You must be prepared for the consequences this marriage might bring. That is what your mother is trying to tell you."

Giles reached across the table and took Elizabeth's hand in his. He had thought about it in recent weeks; in fact, he found it difficult to think of anything else. His love for Catone had grown with every visit he made to the Wampanoag settlement and when he had finally made the discovery that she favored him as well, he knew he had to marry her. Surely, his mother could understand that! "I love her, Mother," he said. "She is unlike any of the girls in Plymouth."

"Very well then, Giles," said Elizabeth. "We will support you. But you must go immediately to Tom Prence and seek his approval. You can do nothing before you do that!"

It was a long, suspenseful walk to the Prence house and Stephen accompanied Giles in silence. He was not eager to cross Tom Prence again, especially now while he was still serving his own "sentence" for misconduct! Perhaps Tom would banish the entire Hopkins family from Plymouth! While he would have expected surprises such as this from his head-strong *daughter,* never in his wildest dreams could he have imagined *Giles* to do anything so outrageous!

Tom Prence invited them both in and they sat down in the two chairs that faced the governor's desk.

"Giles has something he needs to discuss with you, Tom," Stephen said anxiously.

The governor looked at Giles with questioning eyes and a smile. "What can I do for you, Son?" he asked.

Fear suddenly struck Giles in his gut, and he began to tremble. *Would they throw him in the stockade for just asking permission? Would they run him out of town*? Up until this moment, his love for Catone had masked all his other emotions. Now, panic took over and he stood mute, unable to utter a word.

Stephen broke the awkward silence. "Giles wants to marry an Indian girl," he said bluntly.

Tom Prence leaned back in his chair in a most thoughtful pose. "Is that so?" he said, looking at Giles.

Giles nodded his head.

"The girl is *Massasoit's granddaughter*," said Stephen.

The governor's eyebrows arched in a look of surprise. "Well Giles," he said. "You certainly started at the top!"

"Yes sir," he said.

"And what does the Wampanoag chief say about this?"

"He has given us his blessing," Giles answered proudly. "Catone's father is English too and he lives among them."

Tom Prence was never one to make quick decisions; he liked to ponder on things and approach matters with a well thought out decision. "I would like to discuss the matter with the council," he said, finally. "Can you give me a day to give you an answer, Giles?"

"Certainly, Sir," said Giles, rising from his chair and shaking the governor's hand. "Thank you!"

Chapter Forty "Dancing Snowflakes"

When Tom Prence, Captain Standish and Elder Brewster finally sat down that afternoon to discuss the new "Indian" matter, the seriousness of the situation was not lost on any of the men. The relationship that Plymouth had enjoyed with the Wampanoags had, on more than one occasion, saved the colony from peril. They knew that they needed the protection of the friendly tribe against their common enemy, the Narragansetts. They also knew without the Wampanoags' labor in their fields, their harvests would suffer. Coming so soon after the ugly Mendlove affair was an unfortunate coincidence. With the image of Mary Mendlove being whipped in the street still fresh in the memories of many, would it bring questions in the minds of the people about the fairness of the judicial system of Plymouth? Would Giles Hopkins be considered as guilty of improper conduct as Mary Mendlove and *Tinsin*? It was a difficult decision for the council to make and they debated the issue for several hours. By the end of the day one thing was certain; *whatever* they decided to do about the marriage of Giles Hopkins and the granddaughter of Massasoit, the main objective was to not offend the *great sachem.* Finally, they all agreed they had no choice but to allow the wedding to take place.

The day of the nuptials was unlike any wedding ever seen in Plymouth. Far from being the quick civil affairs presided over by Governor Prence, the joining of Giles Hopkins and Catone Wheldon was turning out to be quite a spectacle. The preparations began early on that October day; a special *prayer alter* was constructed by several Wampanoag men in the middle of the Hopkins' bare corn field. They brought in bales of straw and covered them with beaver pelts for the *sachem* and the bridal couple to sit on. They decorated the altar with strings of purple and white clam shells, the Indians called *wampum,* and fans made from hundreds of eagle feathers. The women of the tribe came with baskets of food and clay pitchers of berry wine and Governor Prence had the men of Plymouth kill and skin a deer, placing it on a large spit over a fire they had built in the square for the occasion.

Constance and Elizabeth had been cooking pies and cakes all morning, setting them out on the tables Nick and Stephen had carried from the Common House.

"It would all be so much easier if we had the wedding *inside*," whispered Constance. "Rather than to drag the food out here in the dirt!"

"Your brother says the Wampanoags want it this way," replied Elizabeth. "They want to be sure the sun god can bless their union from the sky."

"I just hope their *sun god* stays with us," said Constance, for there were dark clouds off to the east that looked mildly threatening and the air had a chill that felt like snow could be coming. "But, why must they have the wedding in the middle of Father's cornfield?"

Hobbamock, who was helping Nick carry benches into the square, overheard her question.

"The cornfield is where they are closest to Mother Earth and from her all blessings flow," he explained to her.

"Oh, I see," replied Constance, not *seeing* at all!

To Constance it was all very confusing; the Sun god, the Moon god, Mother Earth and the Three Sisters! So many gods! She loved her brother dearly and she was thrilled that he was getting married at last, but she just couldn't see the necessity of all this ceremonial *pomp*. *Let the sachem say the words and get on with it*! she thought impatiently. She had six restless children at home, whom she was trying to keep clean long enough to attend their uncle's wedding!

She hadn't long to wait. The procession from the Wampanoag village soon appeared on the hill above town. The settlers gathered along the roadside to watch as the great Massasoit made his regal and rare entrance to Plymouth. Even without the parade of Indians that followed him, the *sachem* alone would have been a sight to behold! Standing almost seven feet tall, he moved with the grace of a deer and the confidence of a bear; he wore his usual doeskin vest and breeches but had adorned himself with dozens of strings of *wampum* and had painted his face with brilliant orange stripes made from the clay cliffs off the Gay Head coast. Over his shoulders, hung a full- length bear skin that hardly covered his massive body and barely touched the ground, and on his huge feet he wore high moccasins laced up to the knee.

Beside him, walked the bride, wearing a raccoon skin robe over her deerskin mantle and skirt and leggings secured with ties made from hemp. Her hair was unadorned and shining, braided down her back and her face was scrubbed clean and oiled with bear fat, so that she literally *glistened* in the October sunshine that was darting in and out of the clouds.

Giles joined them on their walk as they made their way up Leiden Street. He was wearing a white linen shirt that

Constance had sewn for him and calf hide breeches that were freshly brushed. He took Catone's hand and joined the procession and the families followed them to the square, where the governor and Elder Brewster officially welcomed them.

"This is a special day," Prence said loudly and cordially and extended his hand in friendship to the great *sachem.*

"We join our houses!" said Massasoit in his broken English. *"It is good, Tom Prence!"*

Constance was standing behind Giles and Catone, watching the interaction of the leaders of the two settlements with interest. Massasoit towered over both the governor and the minister; as she looked over the crowd that had formed for the occasion, she realized he towered over every man there! She watched her brother look lovingly into his bride's eyes and almost started to cry it was so sweet; her ornery, younger brother was now a man*! How extraordinary!*

The group followed Massasoit up the street and, by the time they reached the altar in the cornfield, most all of Plymouth had joined the wedding procession, watching as Massasoit took his place sitting on the covered bales of straw and the couple sat at his feet.

In the language of the Wampanoag, with his words repeated by Hobbamock in English for the sake of his white brothers, the *sachem* held up his massive arms and began to speak, his deep voice was almost musical; the guttural foreign words were delivered with such strong passion Constance felt her arms ripple with gooseflesh. Everyone there was in awe of Massasoit!

He thanked the *Sun god* for its warmth and asked that *Catone* and Giles would always have the warmth of love in their hearts.

He thanked the *Moon god* for the tides and the blessings of the ocean and for bringing Giles and his family safely to Plymouth.

He thanked the *Three Sisters* for their abundant harvest and asked that Giles' and Catone's family would always be well-fed and healthy.

He removed the strings of wampum from around his own neck and placed one on the bride and one on the groom, asking *Mother Earth* to bring much prosperity to the couple for as long as they would live.

Finally, he held up the fans of eagle feathers, waving them in the wind and prayed that no matter where the couple travelled that all the *great winged gods* that flew above would watch over them from the sky and protect them from all harm.

Just at that moment, something very strange and magical happened. With the sun still shining down from between the clouds, like so many silver spears shooting from heaven, suddenly delicate snowflakes began to fall, twinkling and dancing in the sun's rays and melting as they touched the earth. There was no doubt that *all* the gods were pleased that day!

Chapter Forty-One "Just Like Having Twins"

"I don't know about *you*, Mother," said Constance, after they had cleaned the last table and carried all the leftover food back to the Hopkins house, *"But I am exhausted!"*

Elizabeth nodded and smiled a very tired smile in agreement. "Yes, it was quite an occasion!" she replied. "I am so happy for Giles."

Nick and Stephen were toting the tables and benches back to the common house and the children were running in and out of the house, still excited about seeing all the Indians, as were all the children in Plymouth. After all the eating and drinking and merrymaking, the Wampanoags had left, walking slowly back up the road in silence.

"I am glad we had the wedding in Plymouth!" Constance remarked. "I know I would never have able to make that journey twice in one day with all the children!"

She looked across the table at her stepmother and noticed that Elizabeth had closed her eyes momentarily, as if she were falling asleep. "Mother, are you feeling all right? Do you want me to stay and put the baby to bed?"

Elizabeth shook her head and opened her eyes. "You have *six* little ones to care for, Constance. You go on home now. I know you are as tired as I am."

Constance rounded up her brood, carrying one-year-old John in her arms, and kissed her stepmother on the cheek, before she went out into the street toward home. She looked up at the sky that was very near dark by then and noticed that not a bit of the afternoon flurry had stuck to the ground, The chill in the air told her there would probably be more snow by morning. It was just at the hour of day when the sun was going to sleep behind the tall trees to the west of town and the oil lamps and candles were being lit in the windows up and down Leiden Street. House by house, there came a flickering of yellow light through the shutters as the fires were rekindled in the hearths and all of Plymouth took on a warm glow. She looked up the road and thought of her brother, who would be living with the Indians in a *wetu* for a while, at least, until he could build a proper house in the spring. How strange it seemed that her annoying little brother was now a *married man!*

They met Nick just coming around the corner from the Common House and the children rushed him, dangling from his outstretched arms like so many puppets. He was a good man, the man Constance married; a loving husband and a devoted father and she couldn't have asked for a better life companion. He kissed Constance over the tops of the children's heads, before they all hurried inside the house and Nick kindled the fire in the hearth, while the little ones were scuttled off to their beds.

"Can I sleep in the loft tonight?" asked four-year-old Stephen, for it was a privilege only granted to the older children who could navigate the narrow ladder easily and sleep without falling from the open ledge.

"I suppose it will be all right for this *one* night," said Constance. "Mark and Mary, you be sure he sleeps between you, so when he wakes, you can help him down."

Nick laughed. "I may have to build extra supports under the loft if you *all* intend on sleeping up there!" he said. "Or the whole lot of you is liable to come crashing down on us!"

"It's going to snow tonight, Father," said Mark. "So, build a big fire tonight, will you?"

"I will," replied Nick. "You get in your beds now. Your mother looks worn out and needs her rest."

Constance bundled baby John up in a woolen blanket and tucked him into the well-worn cradle that all their children had slept in and began to rock him to sleep as she did every night.

"I say," said Nick. "I can't remember the last time it snowed this early in the year can you, Constance?"

"Yes," she replied, nodding her head slowly. The painful memory that had once been vivid in her mind, seemed to be fading a little with every year that passed. But how could she ever forget that very first winter, when they had arrived from England? The snows had come early *that* year too, when Constance had been imprisoned with all the other women and children in the stinking, freezing Mayflower. She remembered the ship bobbing up and down in the harbor, while her father and all the other men struggled against the icy winds on shore to build the first Common House. How could she forget those months of brutal cold when there were icicles hanging from the yards of the ship and the snot in her nose froze so she couldn't breathe? She could still see the faces of tiny Oceanus and Damaris, her baby siblings who had died soon after, and poor Mistress Bradford, who had fallen silently overboard and drowned in the frozen water of Plymouth Harbor. *So many faces that were now gone forever!*

"Constance?" It was Nick speaking to her, awaking her from her memories.

"Are you all right?" he asked. "What on earth are you thinking about?"

"Oh nothing," she answered. "But you can be sure when it snows this early, it will be a long winter."

When the baby had finally drifted off to sleep, Constance reached down and pulled off her boots. Nick walked up behind her and began to rub her shoulders.

"Let us not worry about the mess tonight, Constance," he said. "Let's just go to bed."

Suddenly it seemed there was a knocking at the door. Constance opened her eyes in the dark room and looked over at Nick sleeping beside her, not even able to remember getting into bed.

There was another knock, more persistent.

Was she dreaming? Was it morning already? *Who would be at the door at this hour?"*

"Nick! Wake up!" she whispered.

She heard a voice then, her father's voice, and she jumped from the bed and ran to lift the bar stretched across the door.

Stephen took one step inside and almost fell into her arms sobbing.

"Father! What on earth is the matter?" she asked. She had never seen her father so upset!

"It's your mother," he blubbered. *"She's dead, Constance!"*

Constance steered her father over to the nearest bench and sat him down. By that time, Nick was awake, putting a robe around himself, and came to sit beside them.

"She was sleeping, just sleeping…." her father kept muttering over and over. "I couldn't wake her up!"

"I must go see her," said Constance, not able to believe the word her father had used…*dead*! *She couldn't be dead! Not Elizabeth*! "Nick, will you stay with him until I return?"

"Aye," replied Nick. "I will take care of him."

She pulled on a heavy cloak over her nightgown and stepped into her snow boots, even though there wasn't any snow yet. As she hurried out into the street, the flakes were just beginning to fall softly around her and she ran to the Hopkins house, not stopping to catch her breath until she reached the front door. All the older children were asleep in the loft, and she found Elizabeth lying in her parents' big feather bed. When she lit the lamp on the table, she reached out and took her stepmother's hand and felt the cold lifeless flesh in hers; she touched her mother's face, her forehead, her other hand, desperately wanting to feel the slightest bit of warmth, an inkling of life still existing somewhere in her body but there was none. Tears overcame Constance then, and she wept long and hard, resting her head on Elizabeth's breast, squeezing the hand of the *second mother* she would have to bury in her lifetime.

Baby Elizabeth stirred in her cradle and Constance got up and tucked the warm blanket around her, rocking her until she fell back to sleep. Her mind was racing. Would her younger sisters be capable of running the household? Would they need help? What about the baby's needs? Her sisters would, no doubt, be able to take care of the baby with one obvious exception; Constance would have to suckle her little sister to gradually wean her off her mother's milk. She still had plenty for her own baby. *It would be no different than having twins to nurse*, she told herself. She could do it! She *would* do it! Elizabeth would have done the same for her if the situation were reversed. She dried her eyes. It wasn't as if she hadn't seen death before and she was sure it wouldn't be the last.

She gathered her wits and her cloak around her and went back home to comfort her father, leaving all the Hopkins children sleeping soundly.

"I must be there in the morning when the children wake up," she told Nick. "Father is in no condition to explain this to them!"

"Yes," said Nick. "That is probably a good idea."

"*And Giles! I almost forgot about Giles! He must be told!*" Constance said.

"Hobbamock has gone to fetch him already," replied Nick.

So, for the first night since their marriage, Nick would not have his wife sleeping beside him.

Chapter Forty-Two "Only God Knows Why"

They planned to bury her that afternoon, in the little cemetery on the hill above town. It had been a very long night for Constance; she hadn't slept much, as evidenced in the dark shadows around her blue eyes. Just being back home in her father's house seemed strange enough but to have her stepmother's corpse right there with them made everything seem so surreal. When the children awoke, they were confused to find their big sister preparing their breakfast over the hearth.

"Where is Mother?" asked ten-year-old Ruth.

Caleb, who was standing behind his sister, looked over toward his parents' bed and saw the covers drawn up over the pillows and the obvious form of a person under them.

"I want you all to sit down with me," said Constance when they had all risen and she gently explained to them that their mother was dead.

The three girls began to cry and hold on to each other. "Where is Father? Is he dead too?" asked Damaris.

"No," Constance reassured her little sisters. "He is resting with Nick at my house. This has all been very upsetting for him. You will all need to be very good and helpful to him now."

Ruth looked over toward the bed. "I want to see her," she said solemnly. "I want to kiss her good-bye."

Constance walked with her sisters to the bedside and pulled the quilt down, so that they could see their mother for the last time. Each girl approached Elizabeth and kissed her, which prompted another outpouring of tears.

"What about the baby?" cried Ruth. "We can't very well nurse her!"

"I will take care of that," said Constance. "I will take little Elizabeth home with me. You will still see her every day, Girls! And she can come home and be with you again when she is a little bigger!"

"Why, Constance?" asked Deborah. "Mother wasn't sick. *Why did she have to die?*"

Constance had asked that very same question over and over in her own mind. There seemed no reason for God to take their mother so soon; just when she finally had her miracle baby that she had lost hope of ever having, just when her Father seemed to have mended his ways and settled down. *Why take her now?*

"I don't know, Deborah," she told her little sister, sadly. "*Only God knows why.*"

Caleb seemed remarkably brave and stoic with the news. At sixteen, he was almost a man and Constance knew it was probably his masculine pride that was holding back his tears. She knew, at some point, her little brother would have to break down and cry too.

Constance did not want to leave her siblings alone with Elizabeth's corpse, so she stayed until Nick and Anthony could come and take her body away to the Common House and secure a coffin for her. Then she changed the bedding, while Ruth and Damaris cleaned up the breakfast dishes. When she returned home, she found her father sitting at the table with his grandchildren. His face looked drawn and seemed to have aged overnight.

"Everything is going to be all right, Father," she said, trying to comfort him. "We shall bury her this afternoon. Nick will pick the highest spot on the hill, where she can see the cape and the ocean beyond it and feel the ocean winds on her face! The children are taking it very well. You'll see. Everything is going to be fine."

"I don't know what I will do without her, Constance," he said with a note of finality in his voice that worried her. She would not allow her father to give up and follow his wife to an early grave. She would be cheerful and encouraging, something she had not always been in her adolescence.

"Perhaps we should hire you a woman to supervise the household," she replied. "The girls are quite capable of *doing* the work, once they are told *what* to do."

"Do you mean they are not like *you* were at that age?" asked Stephen with a sad smile.

"No," replied Constance. "My sisters are not nearly as hard-headed and stubborn as I was!"

She held him then, her strong father, wrapping her arms around the big shoulders that they had all leaned upon for so long, as if she were cradling a babe and they cried again together.

When the news got out, most of Plymouth came to offer their condolences; Elizabeth was well-known, and it seemed that she was loved by all who knew her. Her gentle spirit had comforted many during the difficult years of Plymouth's infancy and there was a long sad line of mourners following her coffin up Leiden Street that afternoon. Even Elder Brewster had to wipe his eyes while giving her eulogy. Poor Giles and Catone, the unfortunate bridal couple, arrived with Hobbamock, to spend the first day of their married life in mourning.

The family gathered at the Hopkins house afterward. Their neighbors brought food that Constance and her sisters stored along with the leftover food from the wedding feast. By the time Constance and Nick finally returned home with their six children plus little Elizabeth in tow, even the children were exhausted and ready for sleep. Nick carried the extra cradle inside and placed it next to little John's beside their bed, where Constance sat, coaxing her little sister to nurse at her breast. After so much excitement and confusion, the baby was fussy and restless, but she finally settled down and suckled, staring up into the blue eyes of someone who looked and smelled *nothing* like her mother. Nick was in awe of Constance; not merely because of the love she was showing for her little sister but because it seemed so selfless what his wife was trying to do, giving so much of herself to one that was not her own.

"I think what you are doing is wonderful," he whispered to her, as she put little Elizabeth down and tucked her in for the night.

"It is the *least* I can do," she replied. "She is my little sister!"

"And you are an amazing woman!" replied Nick, as they put out the light and clung to each other together under the covers.

The next day, Constance spent most of her day running back and forth between the Hopkins and the Snow house, keeping an eye on the toddlers, assigning chores for her sisters and finding time to nurse the two babies somewhere in the middle of it all. Stephen was still in a state of confusion over what to do and she convinced him to go to work in the fields.

"You need to get out of this house, Father," she scolded him as gently as she knew how. "It will be *good* for you!"

"I cannot leave all the household chores to you, Constance!" he protested. "You have a household of your own to run!"

"We have to make do for now," replied Constance. "Believe me, I will find work for my sisters! We will find a woman who can help out soon."

She handed him his cloak and pushed him toward the door. She had been so busy she hadn't even noticed the people in the street all walking in the direction of the square.

"What is happening?" she asked her father. "Where is everyone going?"

They had been so occupied with burying Elizabeth and taking care of the children, the affairs of the town for the last several days had been lost on them.

"There is to be another hanging!" said one of the neighbors in passing. "Arthur Peach is being executed for murdering that Indian in cold blood!"

Constance hadn't seen Hobbamock and Samoset since her mother's funeral!

"*What Indian?*" she asked frantically.

"Don't know his name," replied the neighbor. "He was from one of the tribes up north."

"Oh, *my*!" Constance replied and quickly gathered all the children together, away from the sight of the gallows, until the horrific event was over.

Chapter Forty-Three "If Only She Could Swear"

Later that afternoon, after she had put all the little ones down for their naps and Constance finally had a precious moment to herself, there came a sudden knock at the door.

A young woman was standing there; a petite thing with long, curly, brown locks and a face that was tear-streaked and most forlorn.

"May I help you?" asked Constance, not recognizing the woman's face.

"My name is Dorothy Temple," the woman replied. "'Twas my fiancé they just hung in the square."

Constance was at a lack for words; what on earth did this woman want from *her?* Didn't she have enough needy persons in her life already? Was God expecting her to help them *all?*

"We were going to be married tomorrow," the woman continued. "Now, I don't know what I will do. I have no money to go back to England and no family here. The reverend said you might be needing someone to help your father, with the recent passing of his wife."

Constance was at once relieved that she wasn't being called upon for more help. A servant for Father! She didn't know the woman personally but if she came at Elder Brewster's direction, she assumed she must be trustworthy. Perhaps, God was looking out for her after all! "Can you come back this evening?" she asked. "I will have to discuss it with my father and see what he thinks of the matter."

Dorothy Temple thanked her and walked away.

When Stephen returned from the fields that night, Constance mentioned the woman's visit just as they were sitting down to supper.

"I think I have found you a housekeeper, Father."

She went on to explain who the woman was and why she needed a job.

"I'm not sure about it, Constance," he said warily. "A complete stranger to be taking care of the baby?"

"Well, I will have the baby close to me for a while. But she seems quite nice, Father," replied Constance. "And Reverend Brewster sent her to me. You know he would not send someone who was not reputable."

Stephen stared into his plate and Constance saw tears slowly trickling down his cheeks.

"Perhaps it is too soon to talk about it," she said apologetically. "We can discuss about it later when you feel better."

"No," Stephen said finally, after several moments of silence. "I cannot ask you to take care of two households in addition to nursing two babies! We will hire this woman and make the best of it!"

Dorothy Temple returned to the Snow house that night, with a small traveling bag in her hands and eager to start her new position in the Hopkins house. Constance led her up the street, where she took her in and introduced her to her sisters and Caleb and finally to her father.

"I thank you, Sir," said Dorothy. "For giving me employment. I will work hard for you!"

Stephen nodded and quickly walked out of the house, without a single word, leaving Constance with the task of giving the woman her instructions. She suspected his heart still was not ready to acknowledge that Elizabeth was truly gone and having another woman in the house just made it all too real for him. So, after discussing what needed to be done and lecturing her sisters on the subject of idleness, she showed Dorothy where she would sleep in the loft with the girls and left the house to look for her father.

When she found him sitting in the yard looking a bit like a lost child, she approached him and gave him a loving hug around his shoulders. "It will get easier," she promised him and kissed the top of his head.

And, indeed, it *did* get better over the next few months. The girls and Dorothy seemed to get along very well, for she was very young herself and perhaps filled the vacancy their older, wiser sister had left when Constance had married Nick. Stephen did his best but still remained slightly aloof, spending much of his time outside, until the freezing temperatures forced him to come inside, where he would sit by the fire and doze in his chair. It wasn't long before young Elizabeth was weaned and came home to take her proper place in the Hopkins family and Dorothy seemed to take instantly to the baby. Stephen still mourned, however, often climbing the hill to the cemetery and spending hours there, in silent conversations with his dead wife. But life, for the most part, had returned to its normal routine.

Soon the brown earth that had been frozen finally turned green; the men went back to the fields and the women were once again tending their gardens in the spring sunshine. The cows bore many new calves and the goats dropped a score of new kids. The construction of more houses began, with the sounds of hammering and sawing, and a new dock was built to accommodate the many ships that were now passing through the harbor. The wheels of life began to turn, unburdened from layers of snow and ice, and the blood began to pump again in the heart of Plymouth.

It seemed to Constance that the worst was over; they had surely learned their lessons about famines and fevers and both storehouses were now kept full in case of disaster. The town had remained peaceful and there had been no trouble of any consequence except for the hanging of Dorothy Temple's fiancé.

 The Snow children were growing rapidly. Their firstborn son, Mark, was already eleven years old and almost as tall as his father, marching off to work in the fields every morning with Nick and Anthony. The girls, Mary and Sarah, were big enough to tend the backyard gardens and Joseph and Stephen cared for the animals, with a little help from their big sisters. It was only baby John who remained in the house, keeping Constance company during the day now and they were alone that day when Deborah Hopkins came knocking on her sister's door.

"Deborah!" said Constance. "What brings you calling so early in the day? Have you left all the work for poor Dorothy and your little sisters?"

Deborah stepped inside and looked around the house as if to see if they were alone. "Oh, Constance!" She spoke the words as if they pained her greatly. "I *have* to speak to you!"

"What is it? What has happened? Is Father ill?" Constance asked, wiping her hands of flour and leaving her bread dough resting on the board.

"It's not *Father*," Deborah replied. "It's something else and I was afraid to tell him. *You know how he gets!*"

"For goodness sake, Sister!" Constance snapped. "What is it? *Quit beating around the bush!*"

Deborah sat down at the table and began to explain. "It's Dorothy," she said. "I went out to collect the eggs this morning and I found her behind the chicken coop......."

"Tell me!" Constance practically screamed.

"She was puking in the grass, Constance."

Constance narrowed her eyes and stared at her sister.

"She has gained weight too."

It all became perfectly clear to Constance what Deborah was trying to say.

"You don't mean......?"

"Yes, dear Sister, I do," replied Deborah. "She is unable to hide it now, although she tries underneath her skirts and I think she knows that I suspect something."

All at once Constance thought of her father. She knew her father well enough to know he would never do anything so shameful as to have an illicit affair with his housekeeper, but she also knew he would be the first suspect when fingers began to point. Who else could they blame but the man who lived under her very roof?

"Deborah, you mustn't mention this to anyone else," she said. "I want to speak to Father and Nick first."

Deborah looked relieved to have been unburdened of the unpleasant responsibility. "Thank you, Constance," she whispered, hugging her sister tightly. "I knew you would know what to do!"

I will know what to do? thought Constance, after Deborah had left. *Why me*? For once in her life, she did *not* know what to do! Just when things seemed to be going so well, when the pain of Elizabeth's death was finally subsiding, when her father was getting back to his old normal self, just when……she paused and clasped her hands over her stomach…. just when she was expecting another baby of her own*! Oh, I wish I could swear!* thought Constance. *Just this once!*

Knowing she would surely burst if she didn't talk to her husband about the matter, she called Mary in from outside and asked her to watch the baby. Then she put on her bonnet and started walking down the road to the river. She had to share it with Nick, for he always made her feel better. Nick saw her coming down the road and ran from the fields to meet her, worried that something might have happened to one of the children. When she told him what the matter was, he was much calmer about it than Constance expected.

"Things like this happen, Constance," he said. "She will have to go before the council, and they will undoubtedly punish her.*"*

"I am not worried about her!" said Constance. "It's *Father* I am worried about! What if this has been her plan all

along? What if she set her sights on Father the minute Elizabeth was dead?"

"Seriously," replied Nick. "Reverend Brewster surely would have seen through that scheme."

"What shall we do? I hate to get Father upset all over again!"

Nick left her side and ran to Anthony in the field to tell him he had a matter to attend to in town. When he returned, he took Constance's arm under his and led her back toward town.

"We will tell the governor first, before any gossip gets started," he said. "Surely, that is the best plan."

Chapter Forty-Four "A Cunning, Little Vixen"

Tom Prence was silent for several long moments when he heard the news and sat staring blankly into the empty space above his head, while Nick and Constance were nervously awaiting his response. Finally, he spoke, very slowly and very articulately. "I will have her brought before the council so that she may be questioned on the matter," he said. "Thank you both for bringing this to my attention."

Nick stood up and was happy to leave the whole affair in the governor's able hands, but Constance wanted more.

"Will my father have to be involved in the matter?" she asked. "He has been through so much lately I fear that this will depress him even more than he is now. I hope you can settle it without dragging him into it."

The governor sighed deeply. "I will try to keep Stephen out of it as much as possible," he replied reassuringly.

Nick went back to the fields and Constance returned home, trying to put the matter out of her mind. Deborah came running to tell her immediately when Captain Standish had taken Dorothy into his custody and yet the afternoon wore on without a word from the council.

When Stephen returned from the fields that afternoon and found Dorothy gone, he immediately went to Constance for an explanation.

"None of your sisters want to talk, Constance," he said when she opened the door and invited him in. "What in the world is going on?"

Constance sat down with her father and explained it as carefully and calmly as she could. When she was finished, Stephen stood up and kissed his daughter.

"We will manage without her," he said. "You needn't worry about us any longer, Love."

By suppertime, there was still no word, and Constance felt like she would go out of her mind if they didn't say something soon! The children could sense something was wrong and even Nick's humor could not break the tension that was building in his wife's mind. Finally, at long last, there came a welcome knock on the door. Nick opened it to find Tom Prence standing on the doorstep; on his face was not the expression of one bearing good news. When he came in and sat down, his words hit Constance as if someone had slapped her soundly. "She admits she is carrying a child," he said. "But she refuses to tell us who the father is!"

That could only mean one thing! Constance thought bitterly.

"What does that mean?" Nick asked.

"Well," continued Prence. "We can only assume the man she has been living with is responsible, that is, until she will name someone else. I am afraid we must put your father on house arrest for now, until she is willing to talk!"

Constance's eyes grew dark, and a quiet rage boiled within her. She stood up and went to the window, staring out into the street.

"Well, we thank you for letting us know," said Nick, as the governor turned to leave.

"You can't possibly believe my father had an affair with that woman!" said Constance, spinning around. "He has just lost his wife and you are going to add to his grief by giving substance to this woman's lies? *Tom please don't do this! He is your friend for God's sake!"*

"I am sorry, Constance, but I must follow the law," Prence said and hurried out the door. "There will be a trial next week. Perhaps, by then, she will be willing to talk."

The week that followed seemed endless. Constance checked in with her father every day, trying to assure him that justice would prevail, that the woman would come to her senses and do what was right. Inside, she wasn't so sure. *What did they know about this woman who mysteriously showed up on her doorstep, anyway? Was she a cunning, little vixen just looking for a lonely old man to cloak her sins for her? Had they all, including Reverend Brewster, been fooled by her innocent act?*

They attended the trial held in the church room, where Constance sat holding her father's arm tightly and holding Nick's hand on the other. When they called Dorothy Temple to testify, there was not so much as a cough to break the silence in the audience. She stepped forward, now obviously heavy with child, and hung her head, refusing to make eye contact with anyone.

"Dorothy Temple," said the governor. "Are you now willing to testify as to the identity of the father of your unborn child?"

Without uttering a word, she shook her head.

At that point, the room was a sea of muffled whispers. Dorothy Temple was told to take her seat.

"Stephen Hopkins! Please come forward!" called Prence.

Constance released his arm and watched her father walk slowly to the front of the room, his shoulders slumped, and his head bowed.

"Do you acknowledge that this woman, Dorothy Temple, has been employed by you for the past six months?"

Stephen nodded. "Yes, Sir, I do," he said quietly.

"And can you tell us who the father of her unborn child is?"

There was nervous laughter in the audience.

"Well, Tom," said Stephen. "I don't know the answer to that, but *I can assure you it is not me!!*"

Tom dismissed him to go back to his seat. He whispered something to Reverend Brewster and then he addressed the crowd. "If there is anyone else in this room who can shed light on this case, let him please come forward now!"

No one spoke. No hands were raised.

"In that case," continued Prence. "The defendant will remain in custody until the birth of the child and at such time she will receive her punishment of a public whipping in the street. Stephen Hopkins, you are to remain under house arrest, until the paternity of the child can be determined and are not permitted to leave Plymouth for any reason whatsoever until the council releases you."

Chapter Forty-Five "Pounds for a Parasite"

Exactly four weeks later, in the holding cell above the church, a male child was born to Dorothy Temple. Barbara Standish had assisted the birth and reported to her husband that the baby was quite healthy and normal, *with only one exception*. Holding steadfastly to her silence as she was marched out onto Leiden Street that morning to finally receive her punishment, Dorothy Temple's tears of pain invoked no sympathy from the crowd that had gathered to watch her humiliation.

Immediately after the whipping, Tom Prence called another public meeting to announce the final resolution in the case. This time the entire Hopkins family sat in the front row in support of their father. Behind them the Snow family took their seats silently; Constance sat immediately behind Stephen, holding onto his shoulder tightly, as the governor began to speak. "This has been quite an unusual case from the very beginning," he said. "This woman, Dorothy Temple, arrived in Plymouth less than a year ago, with her fiancé, Arthur Peach, and very soon thereafter, Mister Peach was found guilty of murdering a northern Indian and was hanged for the crime. He, too, offered no explanation for his offense."

Constance did not know where Tom was going with this, unless he was trying to tie this Peach fellow to the child, which would make perfect sense, if only the woman would talk! She knew everyone in Plymouth believed her father was innocent and the Temple woman was trying to blame him for monetary gain.

"What is interesting," continued Prence. "Is that it appears that we can now solve *both* of these cases with a *single piece of evidence*."

The whispering stopped, along with the breaths of every person in the room.

"Bring the baby in," the governor said, and Captain Standish appeared with a small bundle wrapped in a blanket.

 All eyes were riveted on the infant as Standish peeled back the covering and revealed the small, very *dark* face and coarse black hair of an obviously half-breed Indian babe!

Dorothy Temple looked up at her child and realized her shameful secret was finally exposed. The Indian murdered by Arthur Peach was obviously the father of her child! And, more important still, Stephen Hopkins could be absolved of all guilt in the matter.

"However," said Prence, "The fact that Stephen Hopkins was under contract to employ Dorothy Temple for the period of two years, the court finds that he will be given the choice of two resolutions. First, he may take the mother and child back into his home and provide room and board for her until the end of her indenture, or, second, he may pay for her sustenance in someone else's home.

Constance felt like her heart kept starting and stopping, bursting and plummeting in her chest. She felt her father move under her hand, as he stood up and spoke directly to the governor.

"I refuse to allow this *jezebel* back into my home! I only wish I could whip her myself!"

"Is there anyone else who would be willing to take this woman and her child in?" Prence asked.

There was an awkward silence followed by more whispering and finally a man stood up in the back of the room. "I am John Holmes," the man said. "I am in need of a servant. I will only charge Mr. Hopkins three pounds to take over the term of her indenture."

Stephen's face went livid. *Pay a price for the woman who had blackmailed him*? he thought. *Never*!

Before the words were formed in his mouth and he could spat them out, Constance stood up behind her father. *"I will pay the fee, Governor!"* she shouted. *"If only to free my family from this parasite once and for all!"*

Chapter Forty-Six "The Book Worm Gets His Wings"

Anthony Snow rose from his bed early that morning and looked around at the strangers sleeping on the floor near the hearth. After his partner, Stephen Deane, had married and moved out of the house they shared, Reverend Brewster had seen fit to offer the extra space in Anthony's home as shelter to just about every penniless beggar who passed through Plymouth and could not afford to stay at Cole's Inn. At first, Anthony didn't mind it, for some of the fellows were quite personable. But, lately the stream of vagabonds was getting rougher and more disagreeable. While the good elder assured him he was *doing God's work*, caring for the homeless and helpless, Anthony was beginning to grow weary of the sounds and smells of the strangers who warmed themselves by his fire every night, finished off the food on his table and then continued down the road, out of Plymouth, never to be seen again.

Anthony had advanced only slightly in his position with the Plymouth Church. Brewster now considered him competent enough to send him out every evening, when he had finished his work in the fields with Nick, to call on families who were not "of the faith", making him a sort of traveling evangelist to draw the unfortunate and the misguided into the flock. Anthony also paid visits to families who were recently bereaved, to offer the church's condolences, and to those who were experiencing some other type of misfortune. This particular day, the Lord saw fit to finally bestow upon Anthony a reward for his years of good works.

The Warren family consisted of the widow Elizabeth Warren and her children; five daughters and two sons. Elizabeth's husband, Richard, had recently died and Elizabeth was doing her best to carry on without him. She was an outspoken and independent woman with the unique distinction of having a law passed by the town council specifically in her favor. The transfer of a deceased husband's estate normally passed to his eldest sons, but Mistress Warren convinced them that she should be the sole beneficiary. When he visited them for the first time that evening, Anthony learned that, surprisingly, they had been passengers aboard the *Anne* the same year of his own crossing, although he had to admit he didn't remember them.

"We remember *you*," said Mistress Warren when she invited him in, and they all sat at her table. "*You were the bookworm! Remember girls?*"

Her five daughters giggled, and they all nodded their heads. *They remembered him too;* sitting all alone on the deck of the ship, with his nose buried in his scriptures, for almost the entire voyage.

"Have you read the holy book all the way through?" one of the girls asked him.

"Not quite," Anthony replied. "Reverend Brewster gives me assignments that are not necessarily in biblical order."

As it turned out, Mistress Warren *had* indeed read through the holy book from *cover to cover* and had many questions for the young minister, before she would consider joining the Plymouth Church. When the boys, Nathaniel and Joseph, came in from working in the fields, the entire family took pleasure in sitting around the fire, listening as Anthony read to them and debating theological issues with their mother. The evening seemed to fly by, and it was with disappointment that Anthony put on his hat to bid them goodbye.

"I shall look forward to regular visits," said Mistress Warren. "We enjoy your company, Anthony!"

And a regular visitor he became; over the next few months he was frequently invited for supper with the Warren family, and he called on them often at other times as well. He found Mistress Warren to be very intelligent on matters not relating to the scriptures and quite capable of carrying on a lively conversation on most any subject. The boys were quite friendly and hospitable, and the girls were much like their mother; warm and well-educated. It became apparent before too many visits had transpired, that Anthony was looking upon one of the girls, in particular, with much interest. Abigail, the oldest of the sisters and by far the prettiest one, had stolen his heart!

Of course, Nick was delighted with the news.

"Finally, Brother!" he remarked, when Anthony told him one day while they were working together in the field. "I was beginning to think you were going to be a monk and never marry!"

"I'm not quite sure how to tell Reverend Brewster," said Anthony. "I will no longer be able to offer my house to the poor transients he sends my way!"

"It's high time you used that house for its proper purpose!" Nick replied. "There is nothing better in the world than the sound of your little ones laughing and the smell of your wife's cooking when you come home every night!"

And the good elder was not upset in the least on hearing Anthony's news. "It is *good* for you to marry," he assured his protégé, adding as a postscript, with a slight twinkle in his old eyes, "and I will look forward to seeing the *entire Warren family* in church from now on!"

And, so they were married, quickly and quietly, as were all the marriages in Plymouth, in the church meeting room; a marriage that had been long in coming for both Anthony and Abigail. She was delighted, of course, to finally move into her own home and Anthony was ever so pleased with the grace she brought to the previously dreary, masculine household.

Chapter Forty-Seven "The Prayer of Jabez"

Constance had given birth to six children; all healthy babies who came into the world without too much trouble on their mother's part, but *this* pregnancy was somehow different. Constance could *feel* it. In the first place, she hadn't gained nearly as much weight as with her previous children and when the pains came prematurely that afternoon, almost a month too early, she *knew* something was dreadfully wrong! The children were very helpful, and Nick was especially sweet and kind, when she took to her bed, hoping to thwart the early labor and keep the baby warm and safe in her womb for a little longer.

It was not to be, however. With ten-year-old Mary acting as her midwife, the labor continued long and hard through the night, giving her much more pain than her other babies. By morning light, she had given birth to a tiny, underdeveloped baby girl; a pale and gaunt- looking infant, unlike her brothers and sisters who had come into the world looking like plump little cherubs. The baby hardly cried when she was swaddled, making only mouse-like squeaks, and she went instantly to sleep when Constance held her in her arms for the first time.

"I think I will name her Elizabeth," said Constance, looking down on her newborn. "Because she is soft-spoken just like her grandmother was!"

"That would be a most appropriate name," said Nick, as he sat beside her on the bed, almost afraid to hold his fragile new daughter. Constance could see the look of worry in her husband's eyes.

"She will be fine," she assured him. "She just has a little catching up to do!"

Nick never failed to be amazed at his wife's confident demeanor. Even when circumstances were at their worst, she always seemed to have a positive viewpoint and was never one to give up! He leaned over and kissed the top of the baby's soft silky head and touched her tiny hands that were clenched above the swaddling cloth.

For the first few weeks of her life, little Elizabeth's little mouth seemed to have difficulty latching on to Constance's' breasts and had to be fed with a rag soaked in her mother's milk. Because she consumed such a small amount, Constance's nipples became sore and painful. No sooner had she finally learned to suckle properly, the poor little thing came down with a cold, wheezing and coughing and feverish for several days. She carried her everywhere in a cloth sling she tied around her shoulders, afraid to put her down in the cradle, for fear she would stop breathing. For the first few months of her life, the tiny girl slept in between her parents in the big bed tucked up under her mother's chin, with her recently- discovered thumb in her mouth. By that time, transitioning her to her cradle was a challenging test of wills. But by the time she was six months old, even though she would always be smaller in stature than her siblings, little Elizabeth seemed to have overcome the difficulties of her untimely birth and had permanently taken her rightful place in the Snow family.

Exactly thirteen months after the birth of little Elizabeth, Constance went into labor for the eighth time in her life and brought into the world a little boy they named *Jabez,* after hearing Reverend Brewster recite the *Prayer of Jabez* on the Sabbath the week before. The sermon had so moved Constance, who had been praying fervently for the health of her children ever since the birth of little Elizabeth, that, after hearing the reverend's words, she instantly knew the child she was carrying would be a boy. She had already chosen his name, before he ever made his entrance into the world. He was blond haired and blue eyed, like his father, and took to walking and talking very early. As he continued to grow healthy and strong, for the first time in her life, Constance truly felt the power of her prayers!

Life was once again back to a normal routine. By this time the three older Snow boys, Mark, Joseph and Stephen, were old enough to accompany their father every day working in the fields and hunting in the woods. In addition to their survival skills, Constance was teaching the girls to read, practicing every day with books she had borrowed from Captain Standish, who, she had discovered, owned quite an extensive library. She was determined that her daughters would be intelligent and worldly; never ignorant, simpering cows like some of the girls she had grown up with, just waiting for a husband!

With eight children in the house, it was difficult to find a quiet moment at all, let alone time to read a book for herself or bathe in peace; it reminded her of her childhood when the Hopkins house had been packed so full of people. Although she loved her family dearly, she occasionally felt the urge to take a long walk, on the shore or in the woods. But it was only after Mary had turned fourteen, that she felt comfortable enough to leave her in charge of the babies, so that she could once again spend time in the sunshine.

It was a summer day, so bright that everything seemed to glisten from the silver mirage on the surface of the harbor to the new growth on the pine trees. Constance left the children and went walking in the woods, with her berry basket in her hands. The canopy of trees above her seemed sparser than she remembered, undoubtedly from the increased demands for lumber by the growing colony. The old pathways were worn smooth from the trodding of many feet over the years and, with more sunlight filtering through, the woods were thicker than before with ferns and berry brambles. She filled her basket quickly with juicy blackberries. *Nick will be most pleased*, she thought, *to have a fat blackberry pie on the table when he came in from the fields.*

She passed the old beehive, now abuzz with life, and she couldn't help recalling that winter she had gone in search of food for her babies. She sat down on a stump, left by the men who lumbered in the woods, to listen to the birds' sounds in the branches above her; the dull hammering of the woodpeckers and the melodious tunes sung by the songbirds. It wasn't long before she left her basket on the stump and went searching out the secret place that she had not visited since her marriage to Nick; her private bathing pool hidden in the denseness of the woods.

It had been so long, and the underbrush had grown so thick, she could scarcely remember its location, but she kept pushing branches aside to look for it. *How many others had discovered her private place since then* she wondered? *Probably many now that Plymouth was home to so many*. After all, they weren't *her* woods! In quiet times like today, however, it almost seemed like they *did* belong to her alone. She found the spot finally, after much searching, still hidden away in the brambles; the delightful little hidden pool she had visited so many times as a young girl.

Much to her surprise, however, just as she set foot into the tiny clearing, she realized *she was not alone.*

Chapter Forty-Eight "A Funeral Pyre"

Earlier that morning, to the east in the Wampanoag camp, Hobbamock approached the *wetu* that he had once shared with his wife and son. The home where his wife *Pala* and his son *Wyono* had died from the fever, was set apart from the other *wetus* in the camp for a reason. his family had been isolated, to keep the dreaded fever from infecting the others in the tribe. Now that he lived among the settlers of Plymouth, he rarely visited it; the memories of his lost family being too painful, it sat, vacant and devoid of life. For years, no one dared enter it except for Hobbamock, for it was thought to be *cursed*. Now, he stepped into the little hut, brushing the cobwebs from the doorway and kneeling on the dusty reed mats that covered the floor.

He had not been feeling well; for several days the strong Indian had felt weakness in his legs and arms and strange pains in his chest. He had no appetite and whenever he tried to stand up after sleeping, his vision would be blurred, and he would have to sit down until the world around him stopped spinning. Nick had noticed the Indian's signs of weakness as well and had suggested that Hobbamock take some time off to rest and restore himself.

From a basket on the floor of the *wetu,* he pulled out two items; a small pair of moccasins that had belonged to his son, *Wyono,* and a string of wampum that his wife, *Pala,* had worn. The giant Indian held them both cupped tightly to his face and breathed in the scent of his lost family. From the moccasins, he found comfort in the warm smell of deer hide coupled with his son's sweat. From the necklace, there was the slightest hint of the bear fat which his beloved *Pala* used to soften her skin. Tears came to his eyes, for he missed them greatly and yet he felt gladness in his heart, for he knew they both were now sleeping with the gods. Then he rose to his feet, lowered his head and left the *wetu,* silently and softly, walking slowly down the road toward Plymouth.

It was still early in the day and Nick and Anthony were not yet working in the fields when he passed by their plot of land and he took the shortcut to the woods, stopping several times to rest along the way. The sun was on his back, warm and comforting, and he felt a small burst of energy from it. He hastened his steps until he reached the edge of the tall trees and followed the path he had travelled many times; the path to the secret pool where he and *Pala* had shared precious moments of love and contentment. There, he reclined at the water's edge, to rest on a soft bed of new spring grass that had sprouted, and he removed his bow and quiver from his shoulder. Putting the moccasins and the necklace over his heart and holding them tightly in his huge hands, he closed his eyes to renew his spirit, breathing in the cleansing freshness of the forest air deeply into his lungs.

By the time Constance found him there, lying beside the water, his eyes were still closed, and he appeared to be sleeping peacefully, still holding the small moccasins and the string of wampum beads. His bow and quiver lay at his side. Hating to wake him from his sweet repose but not wishing to startle him too suddenly, she stepped softly into the clearing. *"Hobbamock,"* she whispered.

The Indian did not respond, so she whispered again, more loudly.

"Hobbamock?" she said, her voice shaking. She studied the Indian's chest in the filtered light from above and could not detect any signs of movement. At that point, she hurried to his side and gently shook his taut, toned arm, until the moccasins fell from his hand onto the bank of the pool. She reached out and touched the smooth brown surface of his forehead tenderly, feeling beneath her fingertips the same cold, clammy skin that she remembered from the night she had found Elizabeth dead in her bed.

"Oh no!" Constance cried out among the tall trees, where her voice echoed back to her with no one else to hear.

They came for him, two young Wampanoag men, with a litter made from deerskins and pine wood poles, after Nick had delivered the sad news of his wife's discovery to Massasoit himself. As they dragged him back on the litter through the town of Plymouth, many came out to pay their respects to their Indian friend, for there were not many who had not benefited from Hobbamock's wisdom and kindness over the years.

They put his body high on a funeral pyre, made of wood and draped with animal skins, on the outskirts of the Indian camp. Covering him with his blanket, they let him "sleep" there for nine days, with his family's belongings surrounding him. On the tenth day, all the Wampanoags painted their faces black with charcoal from the fire pit and formed a circle around the *pyre.* The women brought food in Hobbamock's own bowl and placed it beneath him, so that he would have food in the afterlife. His bow and quiver were laid at his feet. Everyone from Plymouth was welcomed by Massasoit, for the great *sachem* knew that Hobbamock was greatly loved among his white brothers. Nick, Constance, Stephen, Anthony and Abigail came, as did the governor, Reverend Brewster, Captain Standish and several others, to pay their respects. Giles and Catone were there to greet them. They sat on the ground amongst the Indians, as the *pyre* was lit on fire and the body of their friend was consumed and rose to the sky in a spiral of black smoke. What was left when the embers had finally died down was covered with a great mound of earth, over which Massasoit said a prayer to the gods, asking for them to open the skies to their honored son, so that he might join his family.

And Hobbamock was gone.

Chapter Forty-Nine "The Prodigal Returns"

The Snow and the Hopkins families were the last to leave the Wampanoag camp on the day of Hobbamock's funeral, taking the opportunity to visit with Giles and Catone and their two little ones. Constance realized how much she missed her brother, as she watched him bouncing his children on his knee and listened to him tell of his experiences living with the Indians, when it seemed like only yesterday that he had been an annoying little beast who delighted in teasing her. It made her quite emotional when they finally said their goodbyes and she hugged him for a long, tender moment.

"Are those tears I see, dear Sister?" Giles said, in his usual teasing manner. "I thought you would be glad to have rid yourself of me!"

Constance laughed and gave her brother a playful push, but deep inside she felt sadness at leaving him. "Indeed!" she replied, smiling. "Thank you, Giles, for reminding me! I had almost forgotten how much trouble you were!"

The relationship between Constance and Giles would never be viewed by others as one of deep affection, but, inside, they both loved each other very much.

It was nigh on to dark as they finally started out on the road to Plymouth, walking toward the sun as it disappeared behind the tall trees. How strange it would be to no longer have Hobbamock as a part of their family! No longer would the gentle Indian sit by the hearth, telling his stories to the children; no longer would he labor in the fields with the men. Nick probably felt the loss more acutely than the others; they had spent so many hours fishing and hunting together. Hobbamock would be missed greatly, in so many ways.

As they rounded the bend in the road and Plymouth came into view, in the warm glow of many lamps in the distance and the twinkling of the summer sky, the silhouette of a person appeared, walking up the road toward them. At first, he was not recognizable, but as he approached them, there was something familiar about his walk and the outline of his body in the twilight. Nick strained his eyes against the darkness and recognized him.

"*Will!*" he called out and ran ahead to greet his cousin, embracing him warmly.

"It is our long-lost cousin," Anthony explained to Abigail, without his brother's enthusiasm.

Nick brought him forward, his arm firmly around Will's shoulders, and introduced him to the women. For a moment, Anthony was at a loss for words. "At least you are alive!" he finally said flatly.

"Yes," replied Will. "You will be pleased to know I have mended my ways, Cousin! Haven't had a drink in a good while now!"

"Is that so?" asked Anthony, not at all convinced.

"I've been working out at the Doty place for the last few years," said Will.

"Edward Doty?" Constance asked incredulously. "Father's old bondsman?"

"One and the same," answered Will. "He's a stubborn old coot but he has been good to me. I finally have my own house and livestock now!"

There was so much to talk about, and they had only just gotten started when they reached the Snow house at the edge of town.

"You must come in and meet my family!" Nick exclaimed happily.

"That should keep you busy for tonight," said Anthony. "There will be time to meet mine later."

Will did not push the matter; he had dreaded the first meeting with Anthony for some time. He was just pleased to be welcomed warmly by Nick and Constance. "I hope to see you soon then, Cousin," Will said, waving as Anthony and Abigail continued down the road. Stephen Hopkins bade them goodbye as well.

"Eight?" Will asked when Nick had finished introducing all the children. *"That's extraordinary!"*

"Aye," replied Nick. "Five boys and three girls so far! The boys are a great help to me in the fields."

Will laughed. "*Help*? You have your own crew with this lot!"

Constance laughed. "I am hoping our next child will be a girl. It's a contest between Nick and I, you know! So far he is winning!"

"And what of you, Will?" Nick asked. "Have you any children yet?"

Will shook his head. "No," he said. "I haven't met many ladies. To be honest, Nick, I was a bit worried about coming back to Plymouth after that Billington affair. I'm not looking forward to meeting him again."

"Then, you haven't heard?" Nick said. "They hanged Billington for killing a fellow who worked for him."

Will took a deep breath and shook his head slowly, realizing his fear of the man had been justified after all! "And what of Lyford? Is he still up to his old tricks?" he wanted to know.

"We rarely see him," said Nick. "We finally went to the governor when someone stole gunpowder from the stockade and told him about Billington's Indians. Hobbamock looked for them for years and he never could figure out who they were. They just seemed to have disappeared!"

"*I* would recognize them," replied Will. "I still have nightmares about them."

"Well, if you ever see them again, you can go to the governor. He harbors no ill will against you, Cousin!" Nick said, adding, "I am so glad to hear you are doing well!"

They sat and shared stories long into the night and invited him to the family supper on the Sabbath. The bridge between Will and Nick had not been broken and, while getting back into Anthony's good graces might take some time, it was with lightness in his heart he returned to his little house on the Doty farm. He slept more peacefully that night than he had in many years!

When they had all the children finally settled in their beds, Constance extinguished the oil lamp on the table and climbed into the feather bed. She sensed her husband's happiness at seeing his cousin again; the reunion seemed to have eased the blow of Hobbamock's death but somehow the darkness brought him to Nick's mind again.

"He told me a story once," Nick began, and repeated what the Indian had told him about the secret pool in the woods. For a moment she was silent in her surprise.

"Oh Nick! I have to tell you something that I have never told *anyone*," she finally whispered.

When she had finished her confession about her "secret bathing pool" he was speechless too.

"I always knew it was a special place," she said. "But I never knew *why*. Now, I know what drew me to it."

"I will surely miss him," Nick said just as his eyes closed in sleep.

Chapter Fifty "A Year of Mourning"

The family had seen good years and bad years; periods of famine and drought and disease, some overlapping in an unfortunate *combination* of nature's scourges. But, beginning just on the heels of Hobbamock's death, 1644 was destined to be one of the worst in terms of *losing their loved ones.*

It began in April, just when the new growth of spring was appearing on every patch of bare soil and the colony's livestock all had newborns cavorting at their sides. Anthony and Nick had finally cultivated the last strip of their raw land, laying bare the brown furrows and sifting through the undergrowth and rocks, down to the rich loam along the riverbed. With the help of young Mark, Joseph and Stephen, they were feeling very optimistic about the coming harvest. On that very day, when their spirits were soaring at their highest, William Brewster's son, Jonathan, came walking up the road from Plymouth, with a message for Anthony.

"My mother asks that you come right away, Mister Snow, Sir," the young man said urgently. "It is my father. He has fallen ill."

Anthony had accompanied him back to town and, after stopping to change out of his dirty work clothes and washing the dust from his face and arms, he rushed in haste to the Brewster house. When he arrived, Mistress Brewster led him to her husband's bedside, where his seventy-eight-year-old mentor was lying, his Bible clasped in his frail hands and his face drawn and pale.

"Thank you for coming, Anthony," said Brewster, his voice was raspy and barely above a whisper.

"What can I do for you, Sir?" asked Anthony, for he really knew nothing else to say.

"Keep doing God's work, Anthony," Brewster murmured. "I trust that you will be of great help to our new minister."

The man of God spoke as if he knew he was going to die!

"I will do all I can, Reverend," he replied, a bit surprised at the finality in his voice. He was, at the same time, secretly relieved; for a brief moment, he had worried that he might be asked to fill the elder's shoes, which he knew he was not *remotely* qualified to do. Not only did the job require endless hours of service, it also constantly tapped into the vast knowledge that Brewster possessed. Anthony was the first to admit he was still just a student of the scriptures and a helpful assistant, at best.

"I'm not sure who it will be," said Brewster. "Governor Prence is considering several candidates. But, whoever he chooses, do I have your promise that you will help them?"

The elder paused and his breathing became labored as if speaking exhausted him. Whatever his illness, it had come on very suddenly, for Anthony had noticed no change in him in recent days.

"Of course, Reverend," Anthony replied. "I will help in any way that I can."

"He should probably rest now," Mistress Brewster said quietly, as she showed Anthony to the door. The entire Brewster family had gathered there, and Anthony knew, by the expressions on their faces, no one expected him to live through the night. Just before he left, Mistress Brewster whispered to him, *"The governor will deliver his eulogy, Anthony," she said. "If you can do anything to assist him, I would be most appreciative."*

He returned to his house, where Abigail was waiting for him with his supper still warm on the hearth.

"Is he *very* ill?" she asked him as he sat down at the table to eat.

"Yes," replied Anthony. "He has seemed a little tired lately, but nothing to speak of. I am shocked that this came upon him so suddenly."

"Well, he is getting on in years, "Abigail replied.

"Aye," said Anthony. "Seventy-eight he is. He is just one of those people you feel will live forever!"

Sure enough, with the morning light, came another message, this one delivered by the governor in place of Brewster's son, who was in mourning for the passing of his father.

"We will have the funeral tomorrow afternoon," said Tom Prence. "I know how close you were to him, Anthony. Would you like to say a few words at the service?"

"Oh no, Sir," Anthony replied. "I am not very good at public speaking."

"Very well then," replied the governor.

The next afternoon all of Plymouth crowded into the meeting room beneath the stockade. There was not a single family in the colony whom he hadn't touched; not a child who had not been baptized at his hand, not a man or woman who had not been counseled and blessed in some way by the little, white-bearded man from Scrooby. He had seen Plymouth through its darkest days with a faith that was strong and true. Many people stood up to speak about him, but it was the words uttered by the elder's closest friend, the former governor William Bradford, that remained with Anthony for the rest of his life.

"For the government of the church," said Bradford, "he was careful to preserve good order in the same and to preserve purities, both in the doctrine and communion of the same; and to suppress any error or contention that

might begin to rise up amongst them; and accordingly God gave good success to his endeavors herein all his days, and he saw the fruits of his labors on His behalf."

They buried his body on the hill above the town, overlooking the harbor, and just when they had placed him gently in the ground, they could see a ship sailing around the cape. Captain Pierce had returned from England and the saddened faces relaxed a little and their tears evaporated for with the ship they knew would come needed supplies and letters from family.

And indeed a letter had arrived from London, in their little sister, Mary's, hand, telling Nick and Anthony that *their mother Lizzie had died earlier in the spring.*

Chapter Fifty-One "A Hard Decision"

Grieving is perhaps easier for those who are a great distance from a loved one who passes; they have not the constant reminders in their surroundings, and they do not have the grave nearby over which to mourn. But they grieve, nonetheless. Anthony and Nick's lives had been so full with hard work and growing families over the years, that they did not think about their mother on a daily basis; now that she was gone, however, they both felt the emptiness just as strongly as they had when their father had died in London. They each had to fight the seeds of guilt that wanted to take root in their minds; guilt over abandoning her and their sister in their quest for adventure in Plymouth. But life goes on, both the good and the bad, and the Snow brothers both resumed their lives, feeling the worst of the year was over.

Babies always bring happiness and Constance gave birth in the summer to another girl they named Ruth and Abigail presented Anthony with a son they christened Josias. Both families were growing and prospering. Nick had expanded the loft in their house, until it covered the entire room below, with a small hatch in the corner for the ladder. Because of the pitched eaves, it did not have nearly the space of a room with four square walls, so the older children had to crouch to avoid bumping their heads. Anthony followed his brother's lead, and he too built a loft in his house, so his small family still had room to grow. Now the logistics alone of planning their Sunday suppers together, with the Hopkins brood and the Snow household, was becoming quite difficult, especially now that several of Constance's siblings, Caleb and Deborah, were married with families of *their* own. In the summer, when the weather was warm, they could move the tables and benches outside and have their supper in the yard, but in the winter months the cold drove them inside and apart.

Constance was determined to have the family together for Christmas that year, despite their lack of space. Giles and Catone came to stay with their little ones and bunked in the Hopkins house. Will came and Anthony, who had extra space, was talked into putting his cousin up over the holidays. The women baked pies and cakes and the children played outside in their mittens. The men went into the woods to hunt before the arrival of the first snows. Everything seemed perfect; the family was intact, everyone, even Anthony and Will, were getting along famously. *What could possibly go wrong*? Constance thought to herself.

Then Damaris Hopkins came to the door on that frosty December morning and brought the painful news; Stephen Hopkins was dead. The children had gone to check on him, when he did not rise at his usual time, and found him lying in his bed, with a peaceful expression on his face and no life left in his body.

"Giles is with him now," said Damaris. "You must come, Constance! *You are our family's strength!*"

Once again, Constance was called upon to uplift her siblings; to be the strong trunk to their family tree, holding them all up, as if they were as light as the spindly sucker branches on the pine trees. They all drew from her deep roots of strength and sturdiness, when all she wanted to do was break down and cry like a little girl*!* *Why?* she thought, *why now at Christmas*? She went to them, of course, because it was her station; the oldest of the Hopkins children had now become the reigning matriarch of the family.

And when the men returned with a fat white tail deer for their Christmas dinner, Nick left everything to go to his wife's side; he took her hand and led her outside, down the road and toward the woods. He held her in his arms and let her weep onto his broad shoulders. She had always been his strength, encouraging him in their darkest times, never failing in her love and commitment to him. He let her cry until she had no more tears to shed, and they sat down on a patch of dry grass under the autumn sun. From the east, there was a slight breeze and it played with the strands that had escaped the braid in her red hair and he whisked them back with his fingers, pausing to touch the softness of her cheeks. She still looked as beautiful to him now, after eighteen years of marriage, as she had the first day he had seen her, cooking supper in the Hopkins house and sparring with her younger brother. She was not as young perhaps by the calendar's calculations, but she was certainly not *old*. Her beauty had blossomed over the years like a slow blooming rose, revealing its smooth petals one by one, unto perfection.

They sat there for a long time until she was able to smile again. He had something he had been wanting to say to her and now, with her father's passing, seemed to be the moment he had been waiting for; words that might cheer her on a day that had begun with sadness.

"How would you like to have a bigger house?" he asked.

Constance cocked her head and stared at him. After weeks of planning for a family holiday and the difficulties of keeping everyone all together, it was a bit late to think of building a bigger house. "What do you mean?" she asked. She could see the gleam in Nick's eyes that she saw every time he had a surprise for her.

"Well," he began. "I have been thinking of building us a bigger house, so that the children will have more space and you will have more room when we have company."

"Of course, that would be lovely," she replied. "But where would you build such a house? *In the middle of your cornfield*? Plymouth has become quite crowded, I am afraid."

"There is still a lot of good land out on the cape," he said. "We could build out there and be closer to Giles. We could start another *Plymouth* and our brothers and sisters could all join us."

It sounded like an outrageous plan, moving all the way to the cape and starting from scratch all over again. Plymouth had become their home; ironic as it seemed, she had begun to love the little town she had once hated. But they had definitely outgrown their little house on Leiden Street; she couldn't argue with that.

"We would be close to the Wampanoags, so we would have plenty of help working the land," Nick said, his voice taking on a tone of excitement.

"Have you spoken to anyone else about this? Would the governor approve?" Constance asked.

"The council has given approval to many already to start new settlements. Duxbury and Marshfield! Barnstable and Sandwich! I am sure they would grant us a charter as well!"

Constance could tell the subject had been on her husband's mind for a while; she could tell by the expression in his voice that it was something he really wanted to do.

"I know you would never have wanted to leave your father," said Nick. "But now…"

She nodded sadly. *"Now I needn't worry about him."*

Part Two "Eastham"

Chapter Fifty-Two "A Simple Staircase"

They named the town *Nauset*, after the tribe of Indians who had lived there, and the general council of Plymouth granted them *all the land between sea and sea,* referring to the strip of land with the Plymouth Bay on the west and the Atlantic Ocean on the east. Not only did Governor Prence give the plan his stamp of approval, but he also decided to go along with them and build a new home for himself there as well. The Snows, taking the three youngest Hopkins girls Damaris, Ruth and Elizabeth along with them, were also joined by the families of John Doane, Edward Bangs, John Jenkins, Josiah Cooke, Samuel Hicks, John Smalley, Joseph Rogers and Richard Higginson. Saying goodbye to his brother was difficult but Anthony had decided he was needed at the church in Plymouth to help the new minister there. Will came to bid the family farewell, but he declined Nick's offer to join them. They all agreed to keep in touch; after all they were not moving so far away; *Nauset was just across the bay from Plymouth*!

They set out together that early April morning, leaving Plymouth for the cape; ten families turned their milk cows into beasts of burden to pull makeshift carts which were piled high with all their earthly belongings. Everyone, including the children, was expected to carry *something,* whether it be bags of clothing and bedding or farming tools, on the long walk east around Plymouth Harbor. Giles and their Indian friends came along to help as the caravan trudged along the road and it was quite a long procession that took two full days. When they finally arrived, bedraggled and blistered, weary and worn, in the darkness after the second day of their journey, they built a huge fire with dried driftwood and spread their blankets out on the coarse sand around it to sleep.

When morning came, it announced itself with a brilliant purple sunrise from the east and they could, for the first time, view their new surroundings in the daylight, looking out on a far different scene than they had from their homes in Plymouth. To the west, there were meadows of fertile brown soil and great freshwater *kettle* ponds, filling in the massive holes left behind by glaciers of another age. Beyond them, was a forest of tall, whispering pines. To the east, beyond fields of tall reeds and salt spray roses, were long, meandering briny marshes that spread out like fingers pointing toward the Atlantic. After looking around, the men decided to settle on a spot that sat low and sheltered from the ocean winds on which to build. They wasted no time in getting to work, building pens to hold the livestock, while the women and children, knowing they would be there for a good while, made their open-air camp as comfortable as possible.

By the end of the week, the men had the bare framework of their meeting hall raised that would serve as a temporary shelter. Just as it had been back in Plymouth, all the older children were assigned duties; they went out in groups, so none would get lost in the wilds of the cape, to collect fallen branches for firewood, dig for clams in the marshes and tote buckets of water for drinking and cooking. To their delight, the youngsters found that the *kettle* ponds were home to colonies of green frogs and snapping turtles and that the banks of honey-colored clay along the east- facing beaches were ideal for sliding. It made their tasks a bit more fun, but their mothers had to forgive them for dawdling in the performance of their duties and coming home with clay-stained breeches and petticoats!

They had brought with them all their stored food, which would see them through while they cleared the land. They had learned from the fatal errors they had made in Plymouth, and, for the time being at least, they agreed to pool their resources and talents, just as they had done in the earlier years. Lobster and crab seemed to be abundant on the rocky shores a little further north and they soon had barrels of salted sunfish caught off the bay as well. In anticipation of future corn harvests, as soon as the meeting house was complete, the men began work on a grist mill; a tall cone-shaped clapboard structure on the bank of one of the *kettle* ponds. Once that was completed, they began to build their own individual houses.

Living in the common house with nine other families for the first few months reminded Constance of the hard days of Plymouth and she longed secretly for her own house again. Sleeping on the floor with her own nine children and her three younger sisters, while all their comfortable furniture sat outside covered with canvas, hardly *seemed* like progress. *It's only temporary. It's only temporary*, she kept telling herself, but she missed her feather bed, she longed for her precious intimate moments with her husband and the security of her own walls around her.

Every night, after she had counted heads to be sure she had her whole brood of little ones safely tucked into their beds, she would lie next to Nick in the darkness of the meeting house and dream of the future. Just like she had done when she was a little girl in the Hopkins house, now it was her children's futures she dreamt about. The wonder of who and what they would become, who they would marry, and who would be the first to give her grandchildren, lulled her to sleep each night. Sixteen-year-old Mark, their oldest son, seemed to shadow his father in everything, from working in the fields to building the roads that led into their new town of Nauset. He was becoming an expert marksman and had a knack for fishing too; much like his father there just didn't seem to be anything young Mark couldn't do. Mary loved to cook and seemed to have a natural talent for it, delighting her sweets-loving father with her pies and cakes. Twelve-year-old Sarah was clever with a needle like her mother and took over all the family's mending while ten-year-old Joseph liked to *build* things. As she looked out over their sleeping heads, she couldn't help but marvel at how *different* they all were; even though they all had red or yellow hair, the Snow offspring seemed to be different in every other way!

Governor Prence's house was built first, with an adjoining office on one side for him to conduct the business affairs of the colony, and a stockade to house their weapons and ammunition on the other. As the town was staked out into lots, the women started work on their gardens. Constance enlisted the older children to start turning the over the soil and the boys lugged rocks to border their yard, setting aside the larger ones for the hearth. Still imprisoned in the meeting house, it seemed like an eternity before Nick could finally break ground on their *own* house, but it was well worth the wait. When it finally began to take shape and she could see the framework of its lovely second story rising high above her, Constance's excitement was such that she left the babies in the care of the older children to assist the men. Picking up a hammer and a bag of nails, she helped attach the clapboard shingles to the outer walls and lugged rocks back from the stony shore in her apron. She inspired the other women to such a degree, that when it came turn for their *own* houses to be built, they too joined the construction crews. It seemed as if the little town of Nauset had a backbone of *very strong, industrious women!*

When they had been sleeping on the floor of the meeting house for nearly two months, finally Nick and Constance were able to unpack their furniture and belongings and move into their new home. The children loved the second story, which they could claim as their own, with windows looking out over the bay. Nick had, up until moving day, kept one secret from them all; a wonderful staircase instead of the rickety ladder they were all so used to! Indeed, all the Snow children felt like they were moving into a rich man's mansion that day and they ran up and down the stairs and slid happily down the banister! Long gone were the days of a one room cottage; it was a most proper house, with a dry sink, a built-in cutting board and lots of cupboards and trestle boards on the wall for dishes and cooking utensils. It had a great hearth, with a wide rock ledge, and an ample fire box for wood. That first night the Snow family had much to be thankful for!

Chapter Fifty-Three "A Near Tragedy"

And the little town of Nauset grew, as ships began to arrive every few weeks with new settlers. Nick was elected their first Town Clerk and he appointed his son, Mark, as his assistant. Governor Prence formed his grand jury and the men built him a proper courthouse.

Although they did not have a harvest that first year, they had acres of meadowland turned under and ready for the next spring, with fresh vegetables from their backyard gardens and ample supplies in the storehouse, promising to keep them fed through the first year.

In Nauset, every season was new to them and different in many ways from Plymouth. Spring brought broad-breasted gulls nesting under the newly thatched eaves of the common house and frogs croaking their mating calls in a continual drone from the ponds. On summer days, it was the barking of dozens of harbor seals, as they sunned themselves on the rocks and when darkness fell, the flapping of the wings of the owls, who hunted at night, soon became familiar sounds. In the fall, just when the foliage was changing color, Nick and Mark built a small *cat box* to fish on the kettle ponds for plump freshwater bass until the cape finally came under winter's harsh hand. And, when it came, the first snow fell silently and softly to the ground; the ponds froze over and there were icicles hanging down from the fences and eaves and

Constance, for the first time, gave birth in the dead of winter.

She worried at first; the bigger house was drafty and harder to keep warm than their little cottage on Leiden Street, so she kept their new daughter they named Hannah close to her in the same sling she had used for little Elizabeth.

"You are spoiling her, you know," Nick warned. "Remember how hard it was to get Elizabeth to sleep in the cradle, after you had carried her around for months?"

"I know that," Constance replied. "It's just so *cold* this year, I don't want her to get chilled."

And Nick would smile, knowing once his wife made her mind up, there was no changing it.

They kept the fire burning around the clock in the hearth and Nick sealed all the windows tight with wooden shutters to keep out the cold drafts. One thing was for certain; winter on the cape was harsher than back in Plymouth. Whether it was because they were surrounded by water on both sides or simply not as sheltered, as their old home had been, they didn't know, but the family stayed inside for much of the winter and Constance had to come up with projects to keep ten restless children busy. She showed the girls how to make corn husk dolls and wampum belts, like Hobbamock had taught her. Nick took the older boys ice- fishing but they soon rushed back to the warmth of the house after only a few hours on the freezing ice. They huddled together, as did all the families in Nauset, counting the days until spring.

When warmer weather finally came, Nick and the older boys were anxious to get out in the fields and, after being cooped up inside all winter, they went at it with ferocity, planting rows of barley, peas and corn. Constance went to work airing the stuffiness from the house, opening the windows wide and giving the floors a good spring scrubbing. Life was good, so far, in this strange, new place; Constance loved their new house, the children were happy and healthy, and Nick seemed content that he was finally providing properly for his large family. But their life could not remain perfect for long.

 It began with the onset of summer, when the girls, with baskets on their arms, had gone to gather cranberries. With the oldest of Constance's sisters, Damaris, in charge of watching out for the five younger girls, they all left Constance at home with the babies and started out, giggling and skipping down the road through the meadow. They passed the fields, where Nick and the boys were working and waved to them as they passed them by.

"Don't get lost in the woods!" shouted Nick, after them. "And watch out for black bears! They'll be looking for berries too!"

The sun was hot that day and they had labored for many hours under its unrelenting glare before the idea came upon them.

"Father," said Mark, the oldest. "Might we dive into the pond to cool off?"

Nick agreed with the boys that a dip into the deep cold water sounded like a good idea and the five of them ran to the pond and dove in clothes and all.

"This was a good idea you had, Mark!" Nick said as he swam to the shore. "Now we can go back to work feeling refreshed and more energetic!"

The boys wanted to linger but they begrudgingly went back to their furrows.

By the time the girls returned from the woods, with their baskets full of ripe berries, Nick and the boys had worked their way to the other end of the field and were out of sight. It was mid-day and the girls were all perspiring under their bonnets and long sleeved dresses, when the idea of cooling off in the pond came upon young Ruth Hopkins.

"Let's go for a swim!" she said excitedly.

Her older sister shook her head in disapproval. "I don't think Constance would appreciate us all coming home with wet dresses," Damaris said, "We have enough laundry to do as it is!"

"Oh, please!" Ruth begged, and the other girls chimed in. "There is no one around and we can slip out of our dresses! Our smocks and petticoats will dry if we walk home very slowly! Constance won't have to know!"

"What if someone comes along?" Damaris asked.

Ruth looked all around the pond and saw no one. "There is no one nearby! Oh please, Sister, can we?"

The other girls joined in the begging and Damaris, knowing she was outnumbered, finally gave in. Immediately the girls were removing their shoes and socks and dresses, jumping happily into the pond in their under drawers. Damaris sat on the shore, feeling too serious for such nonsense and wanting to please her older sister, while the younger girls frolicked in the water. *It does look enticing*, she thought to herself, as she watched her sisters and her nieces enjoying themselves. But she was in charge; Constance would expect her to be the *mature* one and not give in to the whims of children, so Damaris lay back in the soft grass, shielding her eyes under the brim of her bonnet.

While the splashing and squealing continued and the warmth of the sun shined down on her body, she began to feel drowsy and soon fell asleep.

When she awoke, it was to someone shaking her violently.

"Damaris! It's little Elizabeth! We can't find her!" Ruth was screaming in her ear.

Damaris jumped into an upright position and blinked her eyes, looking over the water and at the girls who had gathered around her. *"What do you mean you can't find her?"* she cried, jumping to her feet. "Where did you last see her?"

She quickly counted the heads around her; her two sisters, Ruth and Elizabeth, her two nieces Mary and Sarah. Her youngest niece, little five-year-old Elizabeth was not among them!

"I think she may have gone under the water," said Ruth. "It's *ever* so deep!"

"Why were you not watching her?" screamed Damaris, running down to the shore and leaping herself into the cold pond, dress and all, diving under the surface.

The girls on the shore watched in horror until Damaris resurfaced and took a deep breath before she dove under again. It seemed like an eternity, waiting helplessly for Damaris to come back. When she appeared finally, she had little Elizabeth in her arms, limp and unconscious, swimming toward the shore where she laid her down on the grass and began pushing on her chest.

"Breathe Elizabeth!" she shouted, opening her mouth and blowing her own breath into the little girl's mouth.

She went back to pushing on Elizabeth's little chest, harder, harder, with more intensity until she was practically *pounding* on her so hard, she was afraid her little ribs would crack. Little Elizabeth did not move, remaining as limp as a rag doll. More breathing, more pounding. The other girls began to cry hysterically around her.

Finally, Damaris stood up and pulled Elizabeth up, holding on to her tiny waist and slumping her over, squeezing tightly around her stomach. The little girl's light, red hair was dangling lifelessly, almost touching the ground. With one great squeeze, Elizabeth finally spat out the water and began to cough.

"Oh, thank God!" shouted Ruth and they all gathered around little Elizabeth, as she awoke and looked around her.

"What happened?" she muttered.

"You almost drowned, you little ninny!" said Ruth. *"You nearly scared us half to death!"*

Damaris sat down beside Elizabeth on the grass, exhausted and relieved that her niece was alive but feeling terribly guilty about falling asleep. "Perhaps we should not tell Constance about this," she said flatly.

"We won't!" promised Ruth and the others agreed to keep their secret.

The irony of it all was that now the *older and more mature aunt* would be the only one going home in a *wet dress*!

They started their journey home, all walking as solemnly as a funeral procession, giving Damaris' dress time to dry in the sunshine and very thankful that their folly had not ended in tragedy.

Chapter Fifty-Four "The Tie Breaker"

Captain Pierce came to visit with the Snow family every time he had business in Plymouth. He was very favored by Constance and the girls, for each time he would arrive with bolts of dress material, the latest trinkets and toiletries from London and seed packets for Constance's garden. This visit was no exception. As the women examined their gifts, the captain pulled out tobacco for Nick and several hunting knives from a bag for the boys as well.

"How many children do you have now?" he asked the same question each time he came to visit. "Sometimes, I lose count!"

"Ten of our own," answered Nick, "And three of Constance's little sisters. I am afraid the Snow men are losing their majority!"

"Well, you can't complain, as long as they are all good cooks, eh Nick?" asked the captain with a wink.

The playful *gender* contest between Nick and Constance was now locked in a tie, at five girls and five boys, but with their three aunts from the Hopkins family living with them, the Snow house was undoubtedly a preponderance of females. Nick stayed true to his words: *no wife of Nick Snow would ever lack for dresses*! And the same held true for his daughters and nieces; he kept a standing order with the captain for dry goods; *in all the latest fabrics and colors.*

"And where are you off to this time?" Nick wanted to know, always eager to hear the captain's itinerary.

"I hope to get at least two trips to the Indies in before I get back to Jamestown for the winter," said Pierce. "There has been a lot of trouble from the Spaniards, and I am trying to avoid getting in the middle of it."

"What is going on down there?" asked Nick.

The captain shook his head. "Our forces took control of Jamaica earlier this year, but the workers there refused to surrender. They took to the hills and have turned into a band of pirates. So, now we have them to contend with, as well as the Spanish fleet."

Constance laughed. "My husband is just worried that you will be cut off from the supply of sugar cane and tobacco, Captain!" she said smiling.

"Don't you worry about that, Constance!" replied the captain. "I know how to maneuver in and out of those ports very quickly! Unless they build a fleet of ships, they will have a hard time catching me!"

They laughed and enjoyed each other's company until quite late, when the captain finally went back to where his men were waiting with his longboat. It had been a pleasant evening, as always. Captain Pierce was a good, honest man and the Snows thought very highly of him.

"Take care, my Friend," said Nick.

"And you as well, Snow," replied the captain. "I will return soon!"

After they had gone to bed, Constance looked up at her handsome husband. "Did you want to go with him?" she asked.

Nick cocked his head and gave his wife a look of surprise. "To Jamaica?" he asked. "Certainly not! What on earth would make you think that?"

"I could see the excitement in your eyes when he spoke of *pirates* and the *Spanish fleet*!" she replied. "I know your life here is an endless amount of work. I worry that sometimes you wish you hadn't such a large family depending on you."

Nick sat up in the big feather bed and turned toward Constance, taking her firmly by the shoulders. "I never want to hear you say such a thing again!" he said adamantly. "You and the children are all I want and need for my happiness. Surely you know that by now!"

He leaned down and kissed her tenderly.

"It's just nice to hear you say it every so often," she whispered, putting her arms around him, eager for another of his kisses.

A few months after the captain's visit, the tie in the Snow family was finally broken, when Constance delivered another girl in the fall; Nick insisted on naming her Constance after his beloved wife and companion, and the family nicknamed her *Connie* to avoid confusion in the household.

And news came shortly thereafter, from a ship that had come from the south; *Captain Pierce had been killed by the Spaniards.*

Chapter Fifty-Five "Parting Ways"

The affairs of the town of Plymouth seemed, at times, remote to the Snow family now, even though their former home lay just across the bay. This was not so for Governor Prence, who was still a very integral part of the government there. When he received a message from Myles Standish on that cold October night, he left his office and went directly to the home of Nick Snow.

He knocked on the door and was received warmly by Constance. "Come in Tom!" she said and led the governor to Nick, who was sitting by the fire.

The two long-time friends shook hands and Constance offered the governor a tankard of warm ale to stave off the chill of the freezing temperatures outside.

"Nick," the governor began, "I have received some bad news from Plymouth today. It concerns your cousin, Will."

Nick rolled his eyes and sighed deeply. "What has he done now?" he asked. "I thought he had finally mended his ways."

"Well, *not quite,*" replied Prence. "Myles has arrested him for *vain and lascivious carriage* and there is to be a trial two days from now. I thought you might want to come with me."

Constance hurried the children upstairs and sat down to listen to the conversation.

"What exactly does that mean?" asked Nick. "He is drinking again?"

"Aye," said Prence. "And, making a general nuisance of himself, according to Myles."

"And what can *I* do to help the situation?" asked Nick.

"I thought perhaps he would listen to you," said Prence. "I don't want to banish him from Plymouth altogether but, if he doesn't change his behavior, I will have no other choice!"

Nick looked across the room at Constance. She knew it pained him greatly, for she knew how fond Nick was of his cousin.

"I would like to leave early tomorrow," said Prence. "Myles has sent the little boat over for us and we should not be away too long. Can you accompany me?"

"Yes, Tom," he replied. "I am not sure what good I will be, but I will go with you."

The next morning, Nick kissed Constance and the children and joined the governor on the shore, where they boarded the small shallop sent over from Plymouth.

"How nice of them to scuttle us across the bay!" he remarked.

"I am getting too old for the long walk," said Prence.

"Aye," replied Nick. "As am I!"

When they arrived at the dock in Plymouth, Myles Standish was waiting there to escort them to the stockade where Will was being held.

"What are the facts of the case?" asked the governor.

Standish explained the charges in detail; how Will had taken to drinking in excess and had been thrown out of Cole's Inn several times ending in a brawl. "This time, he was throwing bar stools out into the street!" remarked Standish. "It has taken him two days to sleep it off!"

When they had reached the top of the stairs above the meeting hall, Nick spied Will sitting in his cell, with his head in his hands, looking very contrite. Will had a sheepish look on his face when he saw Nick and the governor entering the room.

"I'm sorry, Nick," Will said. "I should never drink that Jamaican rum! It makes me go plumb crazy!"

"Aye," replied Nick. "But *why,* Will? Why *now,* when your life seemed to be going so well?"

Will had no answer. He just shrugged and shook his head. "I don't know why," was all he said.

They marched him downstairs to the meeting house, where a few interested parties had congregated. James

Cole was there, of course, to seek reimbursement for his losses and Will's friend and partner, Ed Doty, attended also. Tom Prence took his seat at the head of the table and recited the list of offenses, to which Will pled guilty.

"I want him to pay for my broken furniture!" said Cole, shaking his finger angrily.

"Very well, then," said Prence. "You will serve thirty days in confinement in the stockade, after which you will pay Mister Cole for the damages you inflicted on his establishment. You will hereafter be banned from Cole's Inn and any other public place where there is drinking."

"Yes, Sir," Will mumbled, with his head sunk low.

When they disbanded and the prisoner was taken back upstairs, Nick followed him and pulled up a chair beside the cell. "Will," he said. "Are you truly happy in this life you are living?"

"No," said Will.

"I can't help you," said Nick. "Anthony and I have done all we can for you to have a chance here in Plymouth. You have chosen to throw that chance away, drinking and gambling and running away from your problems."

Will nodded. "I'm sorry," he said quietly.

Nick reached through the iron bars and squeezed his cousin's shoulder affectionately. "We love you, Cousin!

But you need to take care of *this* one on your own. There is nothing else I can do for you!"

Nick rose and turned toward the governor. "Will you be leaving for Nauset right away?" he asked. "I thought I would pay a visit to my brother before we leave."

"Of course, of course!" replied Prence. "I have some other matters to attend to with Myles that will take an hour or so. Go on and have your visit. Tell Anthony I said hello."

He left the stockade and walked out onto Leiden Street, looking around at the town of Plymouth. Not much had changed since they had left; the houses were a little greyer from the weather and the gardens were all brown now that winter was coming. Anthony's house looked in good repair and the yard well-tended; his brother had always been the fastidious one. He knocked on the door.

"Nick!" exclaimed his brother when he saw him. "What brings you to Plymouth?"

Nick explained the situation with their cousin.

"I have heard of his behavior," said Anthony. "Please come in out of the cold!"

Abigail came forward, holding a baby in her arms. "Welcome to our home, Nick," she said.

Anthony introduced Nick to his four children: seven-year-old Alice, five-year-old Josias, three-year-old Lydia and the baby Sarah. "Will you be staying in Plymouth long Brother?" he asked. "Can you stay and have supper with us tonight?"

Nick shook his head. "No," he said. "I'm afraid I have to catch the boat back to Nauset, as soon as the governor is ready to leave."

"That's too bad," said Abigail. "We would love to have a good long visit with you!"

Anthony wanted to know everything about his brother's life in Nauset. "How many children do you have by now?" he asked.

"Two more girls since we left Plymouth," replied Nick, smiling.

"My!" remarked Abigail. "Does that make eleven now? Where *ever* do you put them all? Anthony and I feel cramped with only four under our roof!"

"We just hang them up from the rafters by their feet," joked Nick. "If bats can do it, why not the Snow children?"

Nick told them about their new house with the second floor and about the good farming land in the meadow.

"And your crops have been successful?"

"Yes," said Nick. "The land in the meadow is very rich. The winters are a little colder there but it's a good place to live."

Anthony paused and then said quietly, "We are moving north to Marshfield in the spring."

"Is that so?" asked Nick. "What draws you to the north?"

"I have been offered a position there in the felt business," replied Anthony. "I think I will take it."

"*A felt maker*?" There was surprise in Nick's eyes. "What happened to your dream of becoming a minister?"

"Well," Anthony said sadly. "Since Elder Brewster died, we have had three ministers, and none have stayed on. I am not fond of constantly changing ways of doing things."

"You could come to Nauset," Nick said. "We have plenty of room and we don't have a minister yet. We could build you your own church!"

Anthony shook his head. "No," he replied. "I just don't think I'm cut out to be a minister. I will never have the passion that Elder Brewster had."

Nick could see that the loss of his mentor still greatly saddened his brother. "Well, if you change your mind, let me know," he said. "You would be most welcome on the cape!"

They visited for an hour and Nick was unable to convince Anthony to come to Nauset. Then the brothers parted with a tearful hug, *not knowing if they would ever see each other again.*

Chapter Fifty-Six "Happenings"

Sometimes life runs in peculiar parallels. The following summer, Constance gave birth to their twelfth child, another girl they named Rebecca. Nick took the playful teasing from their friends about finally *having an even dozen,* while Constance somehow instinctively knew Rebecca would be her last. She remembered her stepmother's words concerning *the change* and the different way a woman feels and she had indeed been feeling different; moody and sad, sometimes bursting into tears for no reason. Nick always tried to comfort her, but she assured him it was just her body changing and there was nothing either of them could do about it. As was her nature, she went about caring for her family even when she had tears in her eyes, refusing to give in to feminine weakness if she could at all help it!

 Shortly thereafter, Thomas Paine, a young man who had recently moved to Nauset and had been paying a lot of attention to their oldest daughter, Mary, came to Nick one evening to formerly ask for her hand. He was a decent lad and Nick gave his approval and the couple was soon wed in the meeting house, with Governor Prence presiding. Nine months later when Mary gave birth to Nick and Constance's first grandchild, little Samuel Paine, it was just like it had been when Constance was raising her own babies alongside her stepmother, Elizabeth. It hardly seemed odd; women in the seventeenth century continued having babies until their change came upon them, sometimes when they were well into their forties and fifties, so it was not at all uncommon for mothers and daughters to raise their children together. Constance was now forty-five and Nick was almost fifty-one, but, still, the little cradle made of pine in the Snow house continued to rock new babies to sleep every night.

Much was happening in Nauset in the year that followed. The population continued to grow, with new families arriving from England every month. The town council decided that year to give Nauset a new name; they decided to call it *Eastham*. Some believed that calling the town *Nauset*, after the tribe of Indians who had formerly lived on the cape, was an insult to Massasoit and the Wampanoags, who continued to support and protect them.

Nick received word that their old friend, Samoset, from the north had died and they were greatly saddened by the news. Making the trip to Pemaquid for his funeral was out of the question, however, with winter setting in. He was remembered in prayer the following Sabbath, in a show of respect for the Indian who had helped them to build Plymouth. The Snow family knew that, without the friendly Indians, their survival in America would have been doubtful. Little did they suspect that the friendly relationship between the Wampanoags and the settlers was about to change.

Another message came from Will back in Plymouth; their cousin had finally married a woman named Rebeccah

Brown and it was most welcome news. Nick hoped she would be able to turn his cousin's life around. The note also mentioned that they were moving up north, to the new settlement in Bridgewater, which Nick was sure pleased Captain Standish and the town of Plymouth greatly. Nick sat down that night and penned a note to both Anthony and Will, sending them off with the next messenger going to Plymouth.

They had built a proper church that fall, hoping it would be an incentive to lure a good man of God to come to their little town if they could offer more than the shared use of their meeting house. They sent out advertisements to all the other settlements in their search and waited for an answer. Just when it seemed no one was interested in coming all the way to the wilds of the cape, a young man by the name of John Mayo arrived with his wife and child and to the young minister's delight was hired on the spot. Governor Prence and the others gave him a warm welcome and did not let on that he was the *only* applicant who had applied for the job, and they probably would have hired him *if he'd had two heads!*

After Mary's wedding, it seemed as if someone had opened the matrimonial floodgates and, one by one, the Snow children began to leave the family and go out on their own. Their eldest son, Mark, announced he had proposed to Anna Cooke, daughter of Josiah Cooke and they were married the following week. Anna was a small, frail thing. Whenever Constance looked at her new daughter- in- law she reminded her of a delicate, porcelain doll, as if hugging her would surely cause her to break into little pieces. But Mark was very much in love with her. Sadly, one month after they had recited their wedding vows, the fragile girl came down with the pox and her weak little body could not fight it. After only one month of marriage, poor Mark was left with the empty house he had just built. He came home for a while, not wanting to sleep alone, and spent the rest of the winter there. But, by spring, he had eyes for another, Jane Prence, the governor's daughter. They were quickly wed, and Mark's empty house was again full of life.

Their little blonde, blued eyed *daddy's girl,* Sarah, married a man named William Walker, a recent arrival from England. Joseph married Mary Higgins, the daughter of one of the original men from Plymouth. Young Stephen, their third son, who had been travelling back and forth to Plymouth taking care of Nick's business there, met young Susannah Deane, daughter of the late Stephen Deane, who had once been in love with Constance. He proposed and they too were married, and Stephen brought his young bride to Eastham. Constance was particularly fond of young Susannah; in some ways, she still harbored guilt over breaking her father's heart.

One by one, the Snow fledglings left the family nest to feather their own.

Chapter Fifty-Seven "Death of the Peacemaker"

On the day that he died, the sun did not shine, blotted out by the dark clouds that had moved in and lingered over the cape. The air was brittle and cold, like the hold of a ship in the dead of winter, like the chill of hearthstones, many days after the fire has gone out. The water on the bay was calm, without any sign of life, the birds remained huddled in their nests and the animals remained hidden in their dens. It was as if all of the Wampanoag gods were mourning. *Massasoit was dead!!*

His people grieved from the cape to the inland valleys, from the northern tip of Maine to the southern settlement of Jamestown, for Massasoit's great arms had reached out far and wide. The settlers worried; without the protection of the Wampanoags what would happen? No one knew the answer but every settler in the colonies realized that, without Massasoit, the relationship between the white men and the Indians would never again be the same.

The funeral was like none they had ever seen, attended by all the Wampanoag and lower tribes from all over Massachusetts and Maine and some from the west too. Those who were far away claimed the clouds that hovered over the land were gray from the smoke of the great pyre on which the *sachem*'s body was burning. The

Snow family sat on blankets that were spread on the ground, with Giles and Catone and their children, in the mass that had gathered at the gravesite, to listen to the sorrowful songs and prayers. Governor Prence wore an expression of more than sadness on his face. He was not well acquainted with Wamsutta, the eldest son of the great sachem, who would now be in power. He relied much on Nick's friendship with the Indians. On the long walk back to Eastham, the two men discussed what the future might hold without Massasoit.

"Wamsutta is a decent fellow," Nick assured him. "I trust that he will live up to his father's reputation."

"I don't know, Nick," replied Prence. "I don't get the same feeling with these Indians as I did with Hobbamock and Samoset."

"Well," said Nick. "There will never be another like Hobbamock. But I assure you, Wamsutta wants peace with us. My brother-in- law lives among them! If there was any need to worry, I am sure Giles would tell us!"

The three sons of Massasoit were very different in many ways. Wamsutta was indeed a good man, who wanted nothing more than to trade with and live in friendship with the white men, and he assured Governor Prence that he would continue to honor the treaties his father had signed many years before. His second son, Metacomet, was distrustful of the English and resented sharing their land with them, especially now that English settlements were encroaching from all sides. And there was Sonkanuchoo, the youngest son, who was seldom seen in public; some said it was because *he had bad spirits in his head*. Of the three, only Wamsutta, the new *sachem*, seemed to have inherited his father's fondness of the white men with whom they had lived in peace for many decades. Although he did not know Wamsutta as intimately as he had known Massasoit, Nick believed him to be a man of honor.

But unfortunately, Wamsutta fell ill and died shortly after, and the power immediately passed to Metacomet. The news came to Eastham on an otherwise joyous day; Stephen and Susannah had just presented Nick and Constance with a new grandchild they named Micajah, and the entire family had gathered to celebrate in the Snow's big empty house when Governor Prence came knocking at the door. The sounds of little voices in the house were always a happy sound to their grandparents' ears, running happily up and down the stairs with boundless energy and spirit. Constance was sitting in her chair, holding little Micajah, while Nick sat down with Tom Prence to discuss the situation.

"I think we should take measures now, in the event there is trouble, don't you?" Prence asked.

Nick lit his pipe and appeared deep in thought. "I don't think creating panic is a good idea," he said finally. "Metacomet has not done anything yet to arouse our suspicions, has he?"

"No," said Prence.

"We can do improvements on our stockade and purchase extra weapons, without too much attention," said Nick. "I am hoping for the best."

What Nick and the governor did not know at that very moment, was that, back in the Wampanoag camp, Metacomet was also having a discussion. He had called all the sachems from the many tribes who were loyal to the Wampanoags and even some from other rival tribes as well, hoping their common interests would bring them together to reach one goal: driving the English from their native land!

The English were growing in numbers, spreading out so far and wide, so that now the Wampanoag tribe was hemmed in on all sides. The Narragansetts, who had long been enemies of the Wampanoag, now came to sit at the fire with Metacomet, as, they too, were being squeezed between the Massachusetts, Connecticut and Rhode Island colonies and their enemies, the Mohawks. Across the Connecticut River, another former enemy of the Wampanoag, the Nipmucks, were being pushed toward the river by the Bay Colony. What was most agitating to all the tribes was that, once they had sold land to the colonists, they were no longer allowed to *cross* the lands and were welcomed only if they were hired to work in the fields. It forced the Indians to go miles out of their way, to travel over land and they were being treated as if they carried the plague, shunned and feared by the very people who had they had allowed to live in peace among them! *No*, Metacomet told his people, *his father had been far too gullible in selling so much land to the white men and far too lenient* when the English settlements began to multiply. Now, it seemed, the Indians had no place left to go!

The English and the Indians were definitely on a *collision course*!

Chapter Fifty-Eight "King Phillip's War"

The period of unrest began just after the death of the governor, Tom Prence. A new governor, Josias Winslow, who lived in faraway Marshfield, was appointed and the little town of Eastham, now far from their chief source of information, seemed to have lost touch with the *mainland* colonies. Despite the lack of communication from across the bay, the little town of Eastham found out trouble was imminent the day Giles arrived on Nick and Constance's doorstep with his half-Indian wife and his youngest daughter, all toting their belongings.

"Giles!" Constance said happily. "I didn't know you were coming for a visit!"

She opened the door wide and embraced her sister- in-law and her niece warmly.

Then, she saw the expression on her brother's face and realized there was something wrong.

"I need to speak to Nick," said Giles.

"You might as well tell me what the matter is, dear Brother," she said. "I am bound to find out anyway."

Giles began to explain. "I was hoping we could stay with you for a while, until this all blows over," he said.

"Don't be so mysterious, Giles!" said Constance hotly. "Until *what* blows over?"

"Metacomet has declared war on the colonies," he said flatly.

Constance could not believe her ears. "War?" she said. "But, *why?*"

"I am afraid he doesn't like our new governor," said Giles. "Winslow has been causing trouble ever since he took office. First, he had Wamsutta arrested for selling a parcel of land to a man in Plymouth. After he detained him, the *sachem* died on his way back to camp. Metacomet believes Winslow had his brother poisoned!"

Constance was shocked. "I cannot believe our governor would do such a thing!" she said.

"He is not *Tom Prence,* Constance," replied Giles. "He considers the Indians no better than slaves! He calls the *sachem Phillip* because he says Wampanoag names are too hard to pronounce and Metacomet *hates* it."

"And, because of this, he is declaring war on *all* of us?"

"It's not only that," said Giles. "They have been hanging Indians for minor infractions, without so much as notifying the tribal leaders. Now, the tribes are not allowed to set foot on the white man's land, unless they are sold as slaves to work the fields. There is nowhere left for the Indians to go."

"And you are fleeing from the Wampanoag camp because you are in danger as well?" asked Constance. "Catone is one of their own, Metacomet's own niece! *Surely he would not harm his own family!*"

"That is why I am here, Constance," said Giles. "Metacomet knows we have come to Eastham until the war is over. They will not harm the town, as long as we are here. The other settlements will not fare so well, I am afraid."

Constance shook her head in disbelief. Suddenly, she thought of Caleb and Deborah and their families back in Plymouth! "We must send for our brother and sister, Giles! We need to bring them here before the trouble starts."

"I was hoping Nick could get a message through to them," he said. "I don't trust sending a message with anyone else. It may fall into the wrong hands."

"Well, Nick will not be happy to hear this news," she said. "You are, of course, most welcome to stay with us. The upstairs is empty now that all the children are gone."

She looked down at her little dark-haired niece, nine-year-old Elizabeth. "But, what of your other children, Giles?"

"The others have made the decision to stay within the Wampanoag camp. They are all adults and quite able to make up their own minds," said Giles.

"They know we love them, and we will see them again, after all of this is over," said Catone quietly. "They will be safe with my people."

Constance prepared a big supper, with little Elizabeth and Catone at her side, while Giles waited nervously for Nick to return.

When Nick finally arrived and he heard what was happening, he and Giles immediately made plans to take the little cat box boat and travel to Plymouth to warn them.

"We should go tonight," said Giles emphatically. "It will not be safe to go in the daylight."

Constance insisted Nick sit down and eat a proper supper and then he gave Constance a quick kiss and the two men were out the door, travelling half the night in the little boat, to warn their friends and family in Plymouth.

And so it began. Once Nick and Giles returned just before the dawn, Constance could finally relax. "What did Caleb and Deborah say? Will they come to stay with us until the war is over?"

"They have done more fortifications in Plymouth since we left," Nick told her. "They feel quite safe where they are. You mustn't forget, Plymouth has six cannons to defend itself."

It did not comfort Constance. Cannons or not, she would rather have her siblings with her, where she could be sure they would not be harmed. Now, all they could do was watch and wait for news from the Wampanoag camp.

They could not hear the first shots of the war that were fired many miles away in the little town of Swansea. Prompted by a rare eclipse of the moon that night, the Indians considered it a good omen to begin their attack and they laid siege to the town, burning the houses to the ground and killing as many of the settlers as they could capture. Retaliation came quickly and swiftly from the Plymouth and Bay Colony forces; their soldiers descended upon Metacomet's camp in Mt. Hope and destroyed it completely. After that, the war spread like wildfire across Massachusetts and beyond. Neutral settlers and Indians were drawn into the conflict, being forced to choose one side or the other. The settlers who managed to escape the Indian raids, flocked to the larger, fortified towns for protection. The Wampanoags and the Narragansetts, who had once been bitter enemies, joined forces and moved all their women and children to outlying camps. But Metacomet remained true to his word and the little town of Eastham remained unharmed.

Their only news came to them from an Indian friend of Giles, who brought messages to him in the night. Many small towns had been sacked, he told him, and the

Indians showed no mercy, inflicting horrible atrocities on the settlers; scalping, beheading and dismembering every white man, woman and child in their path. But the white settlers were no less vicious. Nick and the other men in Eastham, kept their wives and children inside and went to the fields, armed with their muskets, and, for months, everyone felt the constant fear of attack.

When Metacomet was finally killed by the Plymouth militia, they had him beheaded first and then drawn and quartered, as well. His head was displayed in Plymouth for twenty years after the war had ended. It proved to be a costly war in both economic ways and in the loss of lives. Over six hundred colonists died and over three thousand Indians were killed, on the very ground that they had once shared peacefully.

It has been said that the great *sachem*, Massasoit, must have wept with the gods, not only for his brown- skinned sons and brothers, but for his white friends as well.

Chapter Fifty-Nine "Tears in the Fall"

Finally, there was peace again. With the death of Metacomet and the great loss of Indian lives, the fighting was finally over. Many Indians that were taken prisoner during the war were shipped off to the Indies to be bought and sold as slaves and the English went to work rebuilding the houses that the Indians had burned to the ground. Whether it stemmed from sheer battle fatigue or a sincere desire for harmony between the Englishmen and Indians, the men finally put down their arms and rested, gathering what was left of their families around them. It had been a hardship for the settlers. For the Wampanoag, it was almost *annihilation.*

The Snow house was eerily quiet, as Constance went about her chores that November morning. After Giles and Catone had returned to the Wampanoag camp to reunite with their children, she and Nick rarely, if ever, ventured up the stairs. Now, the aging couple warmed themselves by the hearth, ate their supper huddled together at one end of the long empty table and kept each other warm in their big feather bed at night, looking forward to every Sabbath, when the children and grandchildren would come to visit. But, most nights, it was just Nick and Constance getting to know what it was like to be alone together again after so many years in the constant company of children.

Earlier in the spring, the Snow family had mourned again and gathered around their son, Stephen, when his wife Susannah died in childbirth. Her tiny baby boy died two days later, and they buried him beside his mother in the little graveyard near the cove. Stephen came home to stay with his parents with his little ones and for a while the sound of children echoed again from the empty floor above. At Susannah's grave, where they all gathered, Constance found herself scanning the little cemetery at the cove, mentally picking out the spot where she wanted to be buried when *her* time came. She never thought about Nick dying first; her Nick, who was so strong and virile. She just assumed *she* would be the first one to go.

She always planned her garden in the winter, as if somehow it would bring on the spring a little sooner. Constance pulled out the little basket that held her collection of seed packets. She began to go through them, hollyhock, violets, rosemary, sage, and dill weed, wondering how much she should plant; she would need much less this year than last, now that all the children had moved away. It was the last seed packet that caught her attention then. Captain Pierce had brought it to her on his last visit. *Licorice.* The captain had explained to her that it was only the root of the plant that was edible; it was used as a sweetener like sugar cane. She had planned to plant it years before, before war had broken out with the Indians and it got shoved to the back of the drawer, forgotten.

Suddenly, the front door of the house burst open, and Mark and Stephen rushed inside, carrying Nick in their arms. Constance dropped the basket of seed packets on the floor and ran to them. "What happened?" she screamed.

"I don't know, Mother," replied Mark. "He was fine one minute and then he just fell to his knees, clutching at his heart."

They laid him gently down on the bed and Constance followed, taking his hand in hers tightly.

"Nick?" she said gently. "Nick?"

She leaned over and put her ear to his chest. She could hear his heart beating very slowly. "Nick?" she said again, stroking his forehead. "Can you hear me, Love?"

For a brief moment he opened his eyes and Constance could feel a slight squeeze on her hand. Then his eyes closed again, and his hand went limp in hers.

Mark was the first to burst into tears. "*He can't be dead*! *He just can't*!" he screamed and fell to his knees sobbing.

Stephen put his arm around Constance and hugged her tightly.

"I am afraid your father is gone," she said.

Then Mark and Stephen watched, as their mother did a very strange thing. Without a word, she climbed up onto the bed and lay down next to Nick, putting her arm over his chest and laying her head upon his shoulder, with her eyes closed.

"Mother?" Mark said. "Are you all right?"

"Shhhh," said Stephen. "Let her be. She wants to be alone with him. Let us give her that."

The boys left Constance and went to take the sad news to the rest of the family.

She remained there with him for several hours, in a sort of half-dream state, reliving the beautiful memories they shared over the years behind her closed eyelids, as if opening her eyes would bring back the harsh reality. She breathed in the scent of him and held it deep in her lungs; a mixture of sweat and sawdust and lye soap. She caressed the little hairs on his chest with the tips of her fingers. Constance wanted to stay right there with him forever; the mere thought of putting him in the ground where she could never see his face again brought sudden tears to her eyes and she wept, her tears running in rivulets down his shoulder and onto his chest. "My sweet Nick," she whispered. *"Whatever shall I do without you?"*

Chapter Sixty "The Licorice Tree"

Constance fastened her bonnet and threw her shawl over her shoulders. With her seed packets in one hand and her spade in the other, she went outside in the spring sunshine. Her daughter Mary had come to help her, by pulling the weeds that had sprouted and by reading the tiny words written on her seed packets, now that her mother's eyes were failing.

"What are you going to plant this year, Mother?" she asked.

"Well, let's plant the rosemary and thyme first," said Constance. "And some onions and garlic." She stopped and pulled the little packet of licorice seeds from the basket.

"Which one is that?" asked Mary.

"Licorice," replied Constance. "I was going to grow it for your father."

Mary smiled sadly remembering her father's fondness for anything sweet.

"It's the *root* you see," her mother explained. "You dry it and grind it and use it just like sugar."

"Well," replied Mary. "Where do you want to plant it?"

Constance was silent for a moment and then she turned and gazed down the road. "Come and I will show you," she said and briskly walked out of the gate.

With Mary following along, Constance walked down the road. They waved to their friends along the way, but Constance did not stop for conversation. She had her mind set, and, as Stephen Hopkins used to say about his stubborn daughter, *she could not be swayed when her mind was set!* Following close behind, Mary was, at first, befuddled by her mother's unusual behavior but by the time they reached the burying ground, she was beginning to understand.

Nick's grave was grown over with new, spring grass; the mound of earth was now slightly sunken in over the top of where his coffin lay, as if he was "just settling in" for his long sleep. At the top of the gravesite, next to the small, unmarked stone placed there, Mary watched as her mother began to dig a small hole. Then, opening the small seed packet, she emptied the contents into the hole, smiling through tears, and covered them up again with earth.

She sat down on the grass then beside her husband's grave, whispering to him and placing her hand on the ground just about where she thought his heart would be.

"I have brought you sweets, my Love," she said. "I meant to bake them in a cake for you for a while now and I almost forgot I had them. In a few weeks, the roots will take hold and you will forever have them to nibble on."

Mary could not hold back her tears at witnessing such a tender moment between her parents. She almost felt like she was intruding in some way. "Come, Mother," she said gently, helping Constance to her feet and they returned to the Snow garden, where they spent the rest of the morning sowing the contents of the rest of the little seed packets.

Six months later, on a clear October morning, Constance did not wake from her sleep. Mary had come to check on her and found her peaceful and prone in her bed, and the family gathered together to bury her next to Nick.

Mark and Stephen had gone ahead to prepare a place for her and by the time her sons lowered her pine box down beneath the earth, the little burying ground was full of people; her twelve children, their husbands and wives and all her grandchildren as well as almost all of Eastham came that day. Eastham's new minister, Samuel Treat, who had only been with them a short while, stood in front of the large crowd of mourners and began to speak.

"I sat down last night in the rectory, wondering where to start to compose a suitable eulogy for our beloved Constance Hopkins Snow," he began. "And, although I had only known her a short time, from the stories many of you have shared with me, I know she was a most remarkable woman."

The reverend paused and continued. "As I searched the scriptures for inspiration for her eulogy, I discovered that the Lord had already written what I think are the perfect words and I would not presume to improve upon them."

Opening his Bible to the book of Proverbs, he read:

Who can find a virtuous woman? For her price is far above rubies. The heart of her husband doth safely trust in her so that he shall have no need of spoil. She will do him good and not evil all the days of her life. She seeketh wool and flax and worketh willingly with her hands. She is like the merchants' ships; she bringeth her food from afar. She riseth up also while it is yet night and giveth meat to her household and a portion to her maidens. She considereth a field and buyeth it; with the fruit of her hands, she planteth a vineyard. She girdeth her loins with strength and strengtheneth her arms. She is perceived that her merchandise is good; her candle goeth not out by night. She layeth her hands to the spindle and her hands hold the distaff. She stretcheth out her hand to the poor; yea she reacheth forth her hands to the needy. She is not afraid of the snow, for her all her household are clothed with scarlet. She maketh herself coverings of tapestry; her clothing is silk and purple. Her husband is known in the gates; when he sitteth among the elders of the land. She maketh fine linen and selleth it and delivereth girdles unto the merchant. Strength and honor are her clothing, and she shall rejoice in time to come. She openeth her mouth with wisdom and in her tongue is the law of kindness. She looketh well to the ways of her household and eateth not the bread of idleness. Her children arise up and call her blessed, her husband also and he praiseth her. Many daughters have done virtuously but thou excellest them all. Favor is deceitful and beauty is vain but a woman that feareth the Lord she shall be praised. Give the fruit of her hands and let her own works praise her in the gates. Amen.

He paused again and looked out over the crowd. Tears were flowing from every eye.

"What more can I say? It was as if the Lord's words were written especially for her."

The minister closed his Bible, and the crowd began to disburse, everyone making their way sadly back to the little town, knowing that, without Constance, Eastham would never be the same again.

♥

It wasn't until the following spring that they noticed it, while the family was making their weekly vigil to their parents' graves after church on Sunday, something so subtle that it is doubtful that anyone but the Snow children would have realized its significance.

There, at the head of Nick's grave, the little licorice plant, nourished by the melted snow and the rich soil of the meadow, had finally grown into a little tree with blue, feathery leaves and dozens of tiny lavender-white blooms.

"Look!" said Mark with a sad smile. "Father finally has his sweets!"

Mary looked over toward her mother's grave.

"Indeed, he does!" she said. *"Both of them!"*

Author's Note:

It is with tears in this author's eyes that I end this book. Constance has become a part of me as I hope she has to my readers as well. She was a very special woman, strong and yet full of love for her family and friends with a bravery and strength that I will always admire. But the family saga must go on. Volume Four of the AN AMERICAN FAMILY series will continue next year with the stories of her children, most specifically Stephen Snow and his son Micajah, who were my grandfathers, and on down the generations as they expand and improve the little town of Eastham and slowly begin their migration west with the rest of the pioneers. We will learn what happens to Anthony and Cousin Will. We will check in with Giles and Catone and what is left of the defeated Wampanoag tribe. What lies ahead for all of them will be an exciting journey. Even though they had English roots, the Snow family will now have been in America for over a hundred years, and they are now *Americans.* We will follow them through the nation's Revolutionary War and a bit beyond. For those of you who might someday visit Eastham, Massachusetts, Constance and Nick still lay side by side in the little graveyard just south of town. Many years later a group wanting to honor Mayflower passengers gave Constance a proper headstone. There is nothing left to mark Nick's grave now; the groundskeepers say it was *gophers* that feasted on the roots of the little licorice tree that finally killed it, but the Snow family *was not so sure.*

J A Snow

Made in the USA
Coppell, TX
13 October 2021